# BEHIND
# HER
# LIVES

## Also by Briana Cole

The Wives We Play

The Vows We Break

The Hearts We Burn

The Marriage Pass

Couples Wanted

And

"Pseudo" from Justified

# BEHIND HER LIVES

## BRIANA COLE

www.kensingtonbooks.com

DAFINA BOOKS are published by

Kensington Publishing Corp.
119 West 40th Street
New York, NY 10018

All Kensington titles, imprints, and distributed lines are available at special quantity discounts for bulk purchases for sales promotion, premiums, fund-raising, and educational or institutional use.

Special book excerpts or customized printings can also be created to fit specific needs. For details, write or phone the office of the Kensington Sales Manager: Kensington Publishing Corp., 119 West 40th Street, New York, NY 10018. Attn. Sales Department. Phone: 1-800-221-2647.

The Dafina logo is a trademark of Kensington Publishing Corp.

ISBN: 978-1-4967-3875-2
First Trade Paperback Printing: November 2022

ISBN: 978-1-4967-3877-6 (e-book)
First Electronic Edition: November 2022

10 9 8 7 6 5 4 3 2 1

Printed in the United States of America

As always, to my girl, my sister, and my inspiration. I miss you more than you'll ever know. This is for you.
#Forever28

# Acknowledgments

Okay, so here I am again finishing yet another book. I'm sure everyone is tired of me thanking the same people, but oh well, I'm thanking them all again anyway. You know why? Because I have people in my life that I couldn't have done this without. And though no amount of 'Acknowledgments Pages' can suffice to show my appreciation, the least I can do is try. Because let's be honest, they know who they are, but everyone likes a little spotlight every now and then. Plus, they deserve it. So here we go!

First and foremost, I have to praise my Heavenly Father for pouring into me, nurturing my talent, and giving me the strength to get through when all I wanted to do was curl up and cry. I hope people see You, in me.

Of course, I have to thank my parents, Tequila and Anthony (I'm going to retire y'all one way or another, lol). But seriously, you two are my biggest champions and for that, I am eternally grateful. Thank you for putting up with all of my shenanigans. To my bonus family, Lindsey and Courtney, I love and appreciate your support. My monsters, Sean, Eli, and baby BJ. Mommy loves y'all, and I hope me pushing to my goals inspires you to achieve yours. To my man, Ben, you keep me going, baby, I swear. How do you deal with my crazy? Especially during deadline time. I'm so blessed to have you in my life.

To my Auntie Temieka, and my wonderful grandparents, Granny, Papa, and Grandma Sallie, thank you for constantly supporting me, even if my books were a bit much. Y'all still bought them from me and cheered me on every step of the way. (This one is not raunchy, I promise). To my Heavenly grandparents, Mr. Len-wood and Grandma Ann, love and miss you bunches. I hope I'm making you proud. To my aunts, uncles, cousins, I love all one million and seventy-three of y'all.

To my girl, my forever Angel, and sister in Heaven, Paige Christina, as always, everything I do, it's in your honor, Sis. Remember when you used to tease me about never finishing my novels? Lol. I wish you were here just so I could gloat a li'l bit. I push myself for you, my girl. Always.

To my baby sister River and my brother Malachi, y'all are too young for this but I hope one day you can look back and smile knowing that big sister has written a book or two. To my nephews Gavin and Gabriel, TiTi Bri loves you more than you'll ever know. God has you. Please remember that. Your mom is watching over you, and so are we. And to my in-laws, thank you for welcoming me into your wonderful family with open arms and hearts. Our like-minded creativity and entrepreneurial spirits brought us together way before Ben knew I belonged with you. Sorry, Ben. They're my family now.

To the illustrious Delta Sigma Theta Sorority, Inc., with special attention to the Henry County Alumnae Chapter and extra, extra special attention to the 56 D.D.C.C. I love you, Sawrahs.

To my super-agent, N'Tyse, we are working, girl! Four years ago, you said we were about to make magic. Now look at us. Thank you for bringing me on and giving me the wings to soar. To my phenomenal Kensington Family, especially my editor, Esi, thank you so much for believing in me and giving me the creative freedom to thrive in my craft. You all continue to amaze me with your publishing efforts to bring my books to life and I am honored to be part of the team. To my publicity team at BookSparks, y'all have shown out with expanding my brand and elevating my readership. I cannot thank you enough!

And of course, to my bomb ass Brigade! All my readers and

supporters who have rocked with me in any way over my career. Whether it's buying a book, sharing my post, or telling someone about me, thank you, thank you, THANK YOU!! I'm passionate about my work because you're passionate about me. I promise to keep bringing my all with every endeavor. I owe that to you. Let's ride this thing until the wheels fall off!

"The eye is always caught in the light, but shadows have more to say."
—Gregory Maguire

# Prologue

**Excerpt from the diary of Kennedy (Age 11)**

*Sometimes I wonder how it feels to die. I'm not saying I would kill myself. I don't think I would ever have that kind of courage. But I guess I wonder how my death would happen. Would it hurt? Would it happen fast or slow? Would I regret it? Probably my biggest question is, would my family be happy to see me go? My mom probably would. Is that wrong to say? Because it's true. I don't think she likes me very much. The thing is, I don't think I'm a bad daughter. I go to school, and I get good grades (well, except Social Studies because that's a boring subject). But it doesn't matter what I do, it's like none of it makes my mom happy. I'm a little pretty, but maybe she would like me if I looked better. I told Deven once that I couldn't wait to grow up so I could look like the pretty girls on TV. She laughed and told me I was overreacting. Easy for her to say, since she is Mommy's favorite. I'm not jealous or anything because I love my sister* *and she's really cool. We argue sometimes because I know I can be a little sensitive, but still, she looks out for me. So, it's easy to see why Mommy loves her the best. I just wish she had a little room for me too. It just makes me sad because I just want to make her happy. And I think it will make her happy if I'm not even here. :-(*

# Chapter One

Something was off about today. Deven could sense it.

Her sister called it a *devenstinct*, her therapist called it anxiety. And her boyfriend "joked" it was borderline crazy (though she'd been particularly repulsed by his comment). A Navy friend of hers once called it a *lull*—that calm before the storm. Either way, the moment her eyes flipped open, only seconds before her alarm pierced the eerie silence, she felt disturbed.

Reaching for the clock on her nightstand, Deven fumbled blindly with the buttons, pushing on each until one of them abruptly suppressed the noise. She sat up straight in the bed, shrouded in darkness, her eyes scanning the shadows of her bedroom as if the source of her trepidation would be evident. Deven could make out the silhouettes of her furniture, her mounted big screen TV, the full-length mirror positioned in the corner to catch the perfect angle of the less-than-spacious master suite. Nothing out of the ordinary, it seemed.

As if to serve as a bitter reminder, the mattress shifted next to her. Deven glanced over as the stocky figure turned, the sheets doing little to shield his naked frame. Justin. The memory of last night came barreling back, the images calibrating in and out of focus like a camera lens.

His call had been out of the blue, like all his calls had been for the past six months since the two had begun this long distance "thing" (could she really call it a relationship at this point?). And since he'd been ignoring her calls for days, Deven had wanted to reciprocate the disrespect. But as pathetic as it was, loneliness eclipsed the stubbornness, and she had answered on the first ring, accepting the dinner proposal before he'd even finished asking.

Knowing his track record, Deven shouldn't have been surprised when he'd come over straight from the airport feigning jet-lag. Too tired to take her out but evidently not too tired for sex.

Deven was frustrated at his antics. Well, she needed to call it for what it was—downright *pissed.* One minute, Justin was the doting boyfriend with impromptu gifts and calls. His spontaneity had become a staple and Deven had begun to anticipate arriving home to find him waiting outside, ready to whisk her away to some fancy dinner or event. But then on a whim, Justin requested for his corporate job to transfer him to Baltimore because it was a "better opportunity." Suddenly, his impulsive nature wasn't quite as attractive anymore and his decision to leave created more distance between them than the three-hour plane ride. Still, it was clear Justin expected her to go with the flow. *His* flow. Whether it was loyalty or sheer stupidity, she always did.

Deven frowned as Justin slept on peacefully, completely oblivious to her growing agitation. It was her own damn fault for ignoring her common sense. Now here she was, dissatisfied in more ways than one. On a sigh, she tossed her legs over the side of the bed, suddenly restless and eager for light. As soon as she peeled back the curtains to allow the first strips of the New Jersey dawn to peek through, she immediately felt soothed. And just like that, that ominous feeling was gone, for now. Which was enough to calm her nerves. Thank God. Still, she couldn't help but chuckle to herself as she looked out at the courtyard of her apartment complex. She was too damn old to still be afraid of the dark.

The apartment was situated in a prime location for Deven's prying nature. The courtyard was below her second story view, a stone T-shape walkway with benches and picnic tables resting underneath a covered pergola. The walkway was flanked by neatly trimmed hedges opening to plots of gardens that did little to deter the dogs from fertilizing it, despite the sign that clearly read *No Dogs in the Courtyard.*

A few tenants began to dribble from their apartments, cutting through the courtyard to head to their daily regimens: the two women who worked out together every morning and always dressed in matching yoga pants and sports bras, the family of four that were headed to church in their Sunday best, and the college student who always wore those plaid pajama bottoms since he was usually making a quick run to the neighboring bodega for coffee. Deven should've been in her scrubs, rushing right alongside them on her way to work, but she couldn't bring herself to move from the window. Something was still nagging her. But just like she had deduced only moments before, everything appeared normal.

Deven glanced to the parking lot as a police car pulled in and stopped directly in front of the office. They were probably headed to the couple in apartment A121. It wouldn't be the first time their domestic violence disputes had gotten out of hand.

"You're up early."

She turned her back on the hum of morning activity and watched Justin groan and stretch, the muscles highlighted in his body with the movement. She had to stop herself from staring. Probably one reason why she was in the predicament in the first place. Plus, she had to remind herself that no matter how sexy the man was with his champagne complexion and chocolate brown eyes, that was where it ended. The sex was less than mediocre, or as Deven's sister once described unsatisfactory sex, "like that sneeze that wouldn't come out." Yeah, that was it.

Justin sat up then, the sheets pooling at his waist as he leaned against the headboard. "You working today?" he asked.

Deven sighed and nodded, already dreading the twelve-hour shift at the hospital. "Maybe we could go get some breakfast before I go in," she suggested. The decline in his eyes was prominent before he had a chance to open his mouth again. "You know what, never mind. Don't worry about it." Dismissing her own proposal, Deven turned back around, willing herself to ignore the sting of rejection.

"Aw sweetie, I'm sorry." Justin rose and crossed the room, closing the space between them. He caressed her shoulders while placing gentle kisses on the nape of her neck. Deven felt her skin warm under his touch. It was a shame he still had that kind of effect on her body. "It's not that I don't want to," he reasoned. "It's just that, I'm only in town for a few days and I got some running around to do before I head back. But . . ." His hands were now making their way under her t-shirt to cup her breasts. "You can do me for breakfast—"

The sudden doorbell startled them both as it echoed through the room. Relief had Deven quickly stepping from Justin's embrace, glancing towards the doorway as if she could see the visitor through the walls. Justin frowned and, sharing the curious sentiment, tossed a quick look to the digital clock on the nightstand. 7:23 a.m.

"You expecting somebody?" His question had more of an accusatory undertone than Deven would've liked and had her rolling her eyes. Did he really have the nerve to be jealous?

Rather than entertain him with a response, Deven shrugged into her robe and belted it at the waist, murmuring a quick, "Be right back," before stepping from the room. And just because she knew it would raise his suspicions, she closed the bedroom door behind her for more privacy. Pettiness aside, Deven was just as curious as he was about the unexpected house call, so she hurried to answer the front door, flicking on lights as she passed through the hallway. Not bothering with the peephole, Deven flipped the locks and pulled the door open.

She froze, eyeing the two police officers as the first swell of panic ballooned in her chest, tight and suffocating. Now she wished she had made Justin answer the door. Maybe then she could cower somewhere in the bathroom and pretend that these two weren't here for whatever reason that brought them to her doorstep.

The female officer spoke first, her cinnamon complexion blanched with what looked to be exhaustion or discomfort, both of which were plausible in her line of work. But still she attempted a smile. "Good morning. Are you Ms. Deven Reynolds?"

Deven felt numb but apparently, whatever head gesture she gave them was satisfactory because the woman continued, taking a tentative step in her direction. "I'm Officer McKinney and this is Officer Wise," she introduced, motioning to the plump man at her side. "Can we come in for a few minutes?"

Deven's gaze volleyed between the two, her breath suspended in her throat. The look the officers wore was all too familiar. Working as a Labor and Delivery Nurse, it was unfortunately common to identify when tragedy struck; a twin was stillborn, a wife hemorrhaged during her cesarean, that baby girl didn't make it out of NICU. Each time, the staff, herself included, carried that same haunted look, eyes pained but hollow with desensitization. It certainly didn't calm her spirit seeing these two mirror that same demeanor.

Now it made sense. That feeling—that *devenstinct*—she had been experiencing all morning; like a foreboding pendulum teasing her, taunting her. Deven held her breath and shuffled to the side to let them enter. So much for the calm before the storm. Apparently, the storm had arrived.

# Chapter Two

"We are here to deliver some bad news," Officer McKinney began, compassion etched on her pretty face. "Would you mind if we all sat down?"

Deven couldn't move if she tried so, she just stood in place engrossed in the visceral images of every worst-case scenario that played like a movie on loop in her mind. Had something happened to her mother? Had there been an accident? A robbery? She shut her eyes against the intrusive thoughts as she struggled to let loose the few staggering breaths strangled in her throat.

"Ms. Reynolds?"

It was the man that spoke this time, Officer Wise, his gentle voice floating through Deven's subconscious like a melody. Just that quick, the morbid thoughts dissipated, and she opened her eyes again. Both officers were watching with such concern that she felt like she may crumble right then and there. And still, she had no idea what the hell was going on.

"Sorry." Deven nodded her acknowledgement. "What is it?"

"Would you like to sit down?" Officer McKinney offered again.

Deven shook her head. Never mind the fact that her feet felt like cinder blocks. "No. What's the news? Is it my mother?"

"No ma'am." Officer McKinney paused, took a laborious breath, then, "Your sister, Kennedy, died of what appears to be an accidental drug overdose."

Shock was an understatement. More like numb. Deven hadn't realized she was clenching her jaw until the tension had her head throbbing. She swayed, immediately throwing up her hands to ward off the officer who reached in her direction.

"Don't touch me," she whispered. Something warm bled into her chest before seeping up to bubble out of her lips. Laughter. Was that her laughing? Deven tossed her head back, the movement causing even more pain to rupture her skull. Still, she couldn't stop laughing at the sick and twisted cops who had traveled all the way to Mt. Laurel just to tell a joke.

Neither officer seemed surprised by her reaction and the way they just waited and watched prompted Deven to purse her lips together; a weak attempt to stifle the last few remnants of her chuckle. "Sorry," she said again, a restrained smile toying at the corners of her lips. "It's just, that is crazy. Kennedy doesn't do drugs."

"A woman was picked up at 918 Parkwood Avenue." Officer Wise launched into his explanation like he hadn't heard Deven's words. "Apartment B2. Is that your sister's address?"

Deven's heart skipped a beat. Sure, that was her address, but . . .

"I just talked to Kennedy a few days ago," she assured them, desperately relieved at the memory. "She's out of town." It was a mistake. A huge mistake. She couldn't fault the police for their ignorance.

*"How is Puerto Plata?"*

*Kennedy's voice was light, the sound of waves harmonious with her merriment. "Beautiful, Sis. Next time you should come. I'm sure you could use a vacation."*

*"How long are you staying?"*

*"I'll be back in another week."*

Deven shook her head again, her voice strengthened with a renewed vigor. "She's out of town and won't be back until next week. She wouldn't have come home without telling me."

Officer Wise looked back to his partner, an obvious nonverbal cue for her to pick up the conversation. "Your sister was nonresponsive in her home this morning," Officer McKinney said then, her tone patient. "She was already gone by the time paramedics arrived."

"That's not true."

"Ms. Reynolds, I'm so sorry, but Kennedy has died."

Deven's body stilled before the first few involuntary convulsions caused her muscles to ache. Now it was something different she felt, consuming her body like flames. She blinked and shook her head again, willing those damned words out of her ears.

"What the hell is wrong with you people?" she said, trying her best to keep a leash on her temper even as angry tears touched her eyes. "How could you say something like that? Why would you say that?"

"We're going to need you to come with us to identify Kennedy's body." Officer McKinney's voice was calm, sickeningly so. A direct contradiction to her words. It felt like a vacuum sucking the air out of the room. Out of her lungs. Deven braced herself against the wall on legs that felt like putty. *They were wrong. So, so wrong.* The tears were coming now, hot and heavy acidic drops burning her cheeks crimson.

"Is this some kind of joke to you? My sister doesn't take drugs. Fuck you and get the hell out of my house."

"Ms. Reynolds—"

"Get out!" Deven was screaming now, and she didn't give a damn how deranged she sounded. That's what she got for being so curious. She should've let that damn doorbell ring until the batteries gave out. Officer Wise and Officer Too-Damn-Nice could've knocked and knocked until their knuckles bled. Then Deven could have put the covers over her head and avoided waking from a dream to a nightmare.

"Hey, what's going on?" Justin padded into the foyer; a pair of basketball shorts slung low on his hips. Sleep clouded his face, but his eyes immediately widened at the sight of the uniforms. His arm circled Deven's waist. She welcomed the support, however territorial, and leaned into him.

"I'm Officer Wise and this is Officer McKinney," the man introduced with a nod in his partner's direction. "Are you Ms. Reynolds's husband?"

"Friend." Justin's tone was clipped as if he took offense to the mistake. If Deven hadn't been so enthralled with the situation, she would have had an attitude about his shitty correction. "What's this about?" he asked.

"We just shared with Ms. Reynolds that her sister died of an accidental overdose. We need her to come down to the medical examiner's office to identify the body. And we would appreciate if you could join her. I'm sure she needs your support during this difficult time."

Justin's body tightened—or maybe that was hers. It wasn't any easier digesting the news the second time around.

"Damn. Yes, of course. Let us get dressed and we'll be right along."

Both officers were visibly appreciative, and they stepped into the living room to wait. Part of Deven felt compelled to curse them again for bringing such bullshit to her doorstep on this otherwise gorgeous Sunday morning. The other part of her was too gripped by fear to address them. That could seem like an admission, and she wasn't ready to admit she believed them. Not yet.

Justin propelled her back to the master bedroom and guided

her to down to the disheveled bed; a bed where only moments before, Deven had been blissfully ignorant that she was in a world where her sister wasn't. She shifted on the mattress, the springs more pronounced under her legs. Her robe had fallen open, and a slight chill wafted to sprinkle goosebumps on her skin. Everything just felt wrong and soiled.

". . . just can't believe it," Justin was saying, his voice nearly inaudible from inside the closet.

Deven tried to tune him out, not interested in the idle conversation he intended to pepper with platitudes. Instead, she reached for her cell phone. Her fingers fumbled over the screen in a dazed stupor, and it took three tries to finally get the sequence of digits in the right order. She just needed to hear her voice, then maybe . . .

"You have reached—" Deven hung up on the robotic voice that signaled Kennedy's voicemail box. Not even a ring. But the fact that her cell phone was off certainly didn't mean she was dead, did it?

Justin reappeared in front of her, his shorts replaced with jeans and a black sweatshirt. He held a tiny pile in his arms which Deven recognized as her own clothes. When she didn't move to take them, he sighed and sat down beside her. "Come on, babe, you got to get dressed so we can go."

Deven shook her head. She couldn't go. If she didn't, she could still pretend, couldn't she? Kennedy was on a beach in the Dominican Republic, probably on the balcony in her villa drinking a mimosa and watching the sun break over the ocean. The tropical weather would've bronzed her skin by now and knowing her, she'd be using that arresting smile of hers to woo whatever tourist, lifeguard, or bellhop to the cabana for some vacation sex after breakfast. A glimmer of hope had the image crystallizing even more and Deven could almost hear those waves again, could almost taste the salt in the air. It calmed her nerves for the briefest of moments, but it was enough. She reached for her shirt then, her movements labored and forced with resolve. She would go. If anything, just to prove to the police, Justin, and hopefully herself, how very wrong they were.

---

She felt deceived.

Deven watched the world blur past the passenger window, the sun warming the glass despite the 64-degree thermometer reading on Justin's dashboard. But more than the temperature, Justin's silver Tesla eased down I-295 with as much leisure as a morning ride for breakfast. No one, not even her, would suspect they were headed to the morgue to identify a body.

But here they were, Justin tailing the police car, the red and blue lights from the siren flickering colored filters across their faces like a prism. Justin's arm was thrown across the console to rest on her thigh. Every now and then, he would give it a little squeeze. Deven didn't know if the gesture was supposed to be comforting, but she didn't have the heart to tell him otherwise. It soothed her to sit in the discomfort rather than risk disturbing the stillness. Because right now, with the mound of confusion and unanswered questions suspended between them, Deven could imagine, if only for a few moments before, that she wasn't teetering on the edges of sanity since the news.

Deven watched the buildings blur by outside the window. Funny how everything looked different now; how the tragedy had the world slightly skewed; like a myriad of incoherency through a tempered glass. The air didn't feel the same nor smell the same. How could life go on so easily with one less person in it?

Deven wondered if knowing how things turned out, whether she would have done some things differently. Maybe one shift in the matrix could have adjusted that perfectly synchronized chain of events that ultimately led to Kennedy's demise. Or maybe, just maybe the dominoes were already falling into place long before she opened her eyes that morning or accepted Justin's dinner proposal. Even more nauseating, she had been so selfish as to be so preoccupied with sexing Justin while her poor sister lay dying. Deven bit her tongue to keep from sobbing out loud. She wouldn't believe shit until she saw Kennedy for herself. Until then, she would cling to hope. That was all she could do.

"I didn't know Kennedy did drugs." Justin's comment pierced the quiet. He probably hadn't intended to sound so damn insensitive. Or maybe she was just extra emotional right then.

Deven turned to him, sure his peripheral could see her frowning at his profile. "She didn't," she snapped. *She wouldn't.*

Justin didn't seem offended by the tone. Or if he was, he didn't let it show. "The officers said—"

"I know my sister." Deven interrupted, her tone firm with agitation. She needed to believe that as much as he did. "She would never do drugs."

Justin's sigh was heavy, further heightening the palpable tension between them. "I just want you to be prepared for whatever we're about to walk into, Dev. That's all."

And that's where the blissful ignorance came in again. No one could ever be fully prepared for death. In no way, shape, or form. Of course, Justin wouldn't know that. He was the youngest of three, both parents alive with all four grandparents either traveling or living comfortably in their million-dollar homes. As far as Deven knew, the closest Justin had come to experiencing death was his dog, a Rottweiler named Barlow that he had as a teenager.

Deven on the other hand, had to watch her father deteriorate from lung cancer, then her mother's downward spiral as dementia corroded the mind left behind after the grief. And now she couldn't bear the thought of losing her only sister.

Deven's thoughts settled on her mom. She had good days and bad days, but which side of the mental impairment she received was a coin toss. What made it even more concerning was how she would receive the news that her youngest daughter had died. Would her mother's mind be strong enough to even remember who Kennedy was? Sure, their relationship had been slightly estranged, but that didn't diminish the bond, nor the pain. Deven would have to tell her, which meant trying to verbalize, and probably choking on, the words she couldn't even bring herself to comprehend. That realization was pure torture.

The cop car escorted them into the parking lot of a contemporary, two-story building that looked entirely too luxurious to be a morgue. In huge white letters, the words *HARRIS COUNTY MEDICAL EXAMINER* glared menacingly from the brick, only adding to the melancholy.

Deven shuddered but remained silent as Justin parked and killed the engine. He paused and she felt his eyes studying her. Maybe he expected her to say something. But what could she say? Her fingers trembled as she reached for the handle. Outside of the window, Officer McKinney and Officer Wise stood waiting on the curb and she was tempted to avert her eyes to keep from meeting those sympathetic gazes. Better to get it over with.

The four moved in a hushed huddle towards the glass doors, each consumed with their own angst. Justin held Deven close as he steered her up the sidewalk. Officer McKinney led the way, while Officer Wise pulled up the rear, only breaking the line to rush forward and open doors for them before stepping to the side to let them enter first.

Deven trudged through a lobby, surprised at how clean and professional it looked. It reminded her of the waiting area to an expensive corporate company with its semicircle check-in desk and armchairs positioned against the large windows. Between two matching couches in the center of the room sat a single coffee table littered with books, pamphlets, and glossy magazines, though Deven couldn't understand how anyone could read in a place like this. Or why they would even want to.

The group continued through the lobby and headed down a

narrow hallway lined with closed doors that smelled of antiseptics and deodorizers. No dead bodies, Deven mused, and the fact prompted a sigh of both surprise and relief.

Officer McKinney opened a door on the left and she gestured for them to enter. The conference room was spacious with a boat-shaped table circled by eight leather chairs. A woman was seated on one of the end seats, her hair pulled back in a neat bun and glasses perched on a nose sprinkled with freckles. She was dressed simply in a blouse and slacks, and her smile was one of sympathy as she rose to greet them, stretching her arm across the table.

"Good morning Ms. Reynolds," she said. On a subsequent thought, her eyes quickly flicked to a clock on the wall. "I do appreciate you both for coming down so early. I'm Maria, the Chief Medical Examiner."

Deven accepted her outstretched hand, the grip much colder and firmer than she would've expected for a woman of her petite stature. Unsure of what to say next, Deven nodded and gestured absently towards Justin. "Um, this is my—"

"I'm Justin," he said formally, replacing Deven's handshake with his own. "Nice to meet you."

A polite smile touched the corners of Maria's lips. She smoothed out a few nonexistent wrinkles from her slacks and took a seat. "Nice to meet you both. I apologize it's under these circumstances."

At her beckoning, Deven lowered herself to the nearest chair, directly across the table. She dragged a nervous hand through her short pixie cut and slid her eyes to the officers, who merely stood quietly in the corner by the door.

"At this time, I'm going to show you a picture," Maria started, bringing the attention back to her. Even in the stark room, her voice was warm, which Deven could appreciate. "This picture will be of a woman, shoulders up. There is no blood, no wounds, nothing graphic whatsoever. However, the woman pictured is not alive. Do you understand?"

Deven's tongue felt like lead. She swallowed. "A picture?" she asked. Every criminal law show she'd seen danced in her head. She assumed she would be escorted to some kind of sterile, metal room with a covered gurney that would be dramatically unveiled to reveal a dead body. Looking at a picture instead wasn't what she had in mind, though she should've been relieved at the practicality. Actually, seeing a dead body in person, especially her sister's, would've been an image permanently seared on her brain and sure as hell worth increasing her therapy sessions.

"Yes, it's just going to be a picture," Maria said with a reassuring nod. Either she'd sensed Deven's surprise, or she'd had to dispel the cinematic myth one too many times. *Things are never like they show in the movies.* "Are you ready?"

Those damn tremors were back, and Deven tensed, struggling to keep herself positioned on the chair. She flung a desperate hand to Justin's and squeezed for dear life. Oh, dear God, was this really happening? Suddenly, everything stung all at once, her head, her throat, her body. She could only manage a brief nod and hold her breath as Maria produced a single clipboard which had evidently been resting on the chair next to her. Clipped to the board was the photo, face down.

Deven couldn't be sure, but she thought she heard the police officers quietly step from the room and it suddenly felt smaller, more suffocating; like the air had been sucked out to dry. Instinct had her brain kicking into protect-mode and Deven shut her eyes, hearing the scrape of wood against wood as she heard Maria slide the clipboard across the table.

"The picture is in front of you now, but it's face down," Maria assured in that comforting voice of hers. "Please take your time. There is absolutely no rush. When you're ready, turn the picture over."

Then it was quiet and the only sound that could be heard was Deven's own breathing, roaring hot and heavy in her ear. There was a rub on her back, soft and encouraging, but Justin didn't speak. In one quick burst of desperation, Deven lifted a trembling hand to slide the photograph from the clip and flip it over, forcing her eyes open with breathless sobs.

Tears blurred her vision but even still, Deven could make out the woman, her skin tinged slightly gray with death. The picture was taken from above her as it was clear she was lying down. Gravity pulled her skin tight, her black hair like a crown fanned out around her head.

Deven blinked once, then twice, leaning forward to make sure her eyes weren't deceiving her. The woman had high cheekbones and a mole next to thick lips, parted ever so slightly. The similarities were undeniable, but the more Deven scrutinized, the quicker the surge of exhilaration, then relief, and finally confusion swelled like indigestion in her chest. She shook her head and looked up to Maria with a hint of triumph just below her sorrowful grimace. "No," she whispered.

Maria's forehead creased in confusion. "No, what?"

Deven jabbed the picture with her finger to further affirm her discovery. "This is not my sister. That's not Kennedy."

# Chapter Three
# Three Months Before

She didn't know which was worse, the tedious process of helping her sister unpack or the tedious process of helping her sister unpack while pregnant.

Deven sighed, her breathing labored as she slid a scissor blade across the tape of a box marked *Kitchen*. The flaps popped open like a springboard revealing a set of bubble-wrapped plates and saucers she'd never seen Kennedy use. Come to think of it, her sister hadn't stepped foot in the kitchen to cook at all (well not since they were kids), so the expensive dinnerware seemed like a pure waste. Even more reason why her assigned task of putting up the kitchen items was futile. Still, Kennedy insisted she handle the light stuff, something physically appropriate for a pregnant woman of twelve weeks. So, though Deven figured the dishes would remain untouched until it was time to pack for the next move, she started arranging them neatly in the cabinets over the gas stove with care.

In methodical pairs, moving men lugged in boxes and furniture, too engrossed with the work for idle chitchat. Their shirts were stained wet with sweat at the two-story climb to the spacious condo, but Deven appreciated their efficiency. One look out the balcony window and she saw the moving truck was nearly empty. Kennedy stood in the middle of the parking lot delegating what went where. She was completely overdressed for moving day in her red-bottom heels and skinny jeans. But that was her sister. Every week was New York Fashion Week.

Deven had managed to empty two boxes before she decided it was time for a break. She reached for her water bottle and crossed into the living room, threading through boxes stacked like Jenga blocks across the gray hardwood floors. She liked this place a lot more than Kennedy's last condo. For comparable places in Mt. Laurel, New Jersey, it was certainly large, which just meant the rent was even larger. Kennedy didn't do much decorating, which made Deven all the more excited to really glamorize the place once the packing was complete. She could see it now, lots of teals (her sister's favorite color) and it would accent the cream in Kennedy's upholstery beautifully. Deven's feet started to throb, and she was tempted to sit down, but decided instead to mosey down the stretch of hall to the two bedrooms.

The first bedroom, the smaller of the two, Deven assumed would be turned into an office. Kennedy was a marketing consultant, a job that afforded her a cushy lifestyle, one of which was working from anywhere that had a strong Wi-Fi connection. So, working from home was a common luxury.

Deven pushed open the door and had to chuckle. She had assumed wrong. Piles and piles of clothes were strewn across the floor, tags dangling from the designer fabric. Some garments were still on hangers or in garment bags, other items in wrinkled bunches as if Kennedy, or maybe the moving men, hadn't cared about their value. More stacks of boxes in here with the word *Closet* hastily scribbled on the cardboard.

Deven touched the growing pudge of her tummy, decided she was feeling a little better, and set to work to organize the room.

She started with the clothes, re-draping items that had, apparently, lost their hangers during the move. She then made new piles, one for dresses, one for one for shirts, and one for pants. Deven was amused at her own obsession for cleanliness. With six months to go in her pregnancy, she was way too early for what expectant mothers called the 'nesting' period—that sudden desire to clean and organize spaces before baby's arrival. Still, she felt a renewed sense of excitement as she tidied, and she couldn't wait to start setting up the nursery for her baby girl—at least she hoped it was a girl.

When she was satisfied with how she'd organized the clothes, Deven moved on to the boxes. Two of them had already been opened and Deven began pulling high heels out of the first one and lining them up across the baseboard. The second box was full of shoe boxes and, assuming it was even more shoes, Deven lifted the lid on one, sucking in a shocked breath at its contents.

The gun was purple, but it didn't make it any less menacing. It almost looked like a toy as it lay resting on top of folded papers and pictures. Deven was frozen. If she looked away would that trigger something? Was it loaded? What the hell was Kennedy doing with a gun?

Deven's fingers quivered as she gingerly sat the lid back on top, only able to release a staggering breath when the weapon was out of view.

"Sis, what are you doing in here?" Kennedy entered, her eyes panning the room. "I thought I told you to take it easy since you're lugging around precious cargo."

Deven snatched her gaze from the box and looked to her sister. "Ken, why do you have a gun?" she asked. She saw something, she wasn't sure what, flicker in Kennedy's eyes before her sister glanced down to the box between them, the flaps still open to reveal the closed shoe box. As if remembering, Kennedy lifted the shoe box and carried it to the closet.

"It's just for protection," she assured her. "Don't worry, it's not loaded." Kennedy put the box on the shelf and slid it to the far corner, then she turned with an apologetic smile. "I didn't know you were going to be in here."

"I wasn't—I didn't mean—I was just . . ." Deven blew a breath, not sure why she still felt uneasy. It was perfectly normal for a young, beautiful woman in the city to have a gun. She was right. She could never be too careful. "Sorry." Deven's smile was colored with embarrassment at her overreaction. "I finished the kitchen so I thought I would help you with your office. But I see you have other plans for this room."

Kennedy laughed and did a little turn to eye the clothes again. "Yeah, I decided to make this room my walk-in closet."

"What's wrong with the closet in your room?"

"It's not big enough." Kennedy shrugged and stepped out of her red-bottom pumps. "I figured I could add some shelving and some built-ins"—she pointed against one of the walls—" probably some bench seating over here. What do you think?"

Deven nodded, picturing the finished product with maybe a little mood lighting to calm the space. "I like it."

"I have a contractor coming this weekend to take measurements. I want to get it done before I go out of town."

"Where you headed this time?"

"Puerto Plata," Kennedy said simply and made no move to elaborate.

Deven picked up on the dismissive tone, which she knew was indicative that the trip was probably for reasons other than work. And since Kennedy wasn't always transparent about her cosmetic surgery, Deven could only assume that was the rationale. Though she didn't see what else the woman could do to look even more gorgeous than she already did.

On the surface, it was hard to tell they were indeed sisters, with the exception of their russet-brown complexions. The elder, Deven, was taller with a thicker frame, a feature she would attribute to her genetic body style rather than stress, poor eating habits, and lack of physical activity. It made it that much easier to hide her pregnancy from Justin, for the time being. Makeup was reserved for weddings and funerals, and Deven loved the convenience of her boyish tapered cut with inch-long curls.

Kennedy, on the other hand, was slim and petite with the perfect breast-to-waist-to-ass ratio, thanks to her cosmetic surgeon ex-fiancé. Even her face had been nipped and tucked to a slim nose, full pouty lips, and high cheekbones that made contouring completely unnecessary. And Kennedy made sure to keep standing appointments with her stylist because Deven had seen her with those lengthy tresses for so long, she often forgot it was a sew-in.

Kennedy stooped to pick up a green maxi dress with ruffles crisscrossing from the low V-neck. She held it up to Deven's shoulders, craning her neck to see how the chiffon fell over her frame. Satisfied, Kennedy draped the dress over Deven's arm. "Here. You can have this," she said.

The $239 price tag had Deven's eyes rounding, even as her body itched to try on the garment. "Girl, I can't take this."

"Why not? I don't want it. Besides"—Kennedy wiggled her eyebrows with a knowing smirk—"you're going to need something to hide that belly if you don't plan on telling Justin about that baby anytime soon."

The comment hadn't meant to be malicious, but the words still stung. Deven's excitement waned, and she frowned down at the dress. If only it were that simple.

"He'll be in town this weekend," she said as she took a seat on a nearby box. The cardboard bent under her weight. "I was probably going to tell him then."

*"Probably?"*

"They say you should wait until after the first trimester before you share the news. Supposedly the risk of miscarriage is lower."

Kennedy was already picking up something else, a shirt this time, and laid it across Deven's lap. "You didn't wait to share it with me though."

"Come on now, you know I had to tell you." Deven spared a little grin before she cast her eyes down once more. "It's kind of complicated."

"What's complicated? You don't think he wants a kid?"

*Doesn't want a kid, doesn't want me . . .* Deven pursed her lips, remembering one of the conversations that was now looming like a black cloud over their entire relationship. Well, could it really be called a conversation? *Argument* was more like it. One minute they were enjoying a dinner she had prepared, and the next he was dropping a bomb that he was moving to Baltimore. It was bad enough that he was having to go, but he had been the one to initiate the request for a transfer with his job, which was just downright heartbreaking. So, it wasn't like Deven hadn't wanted to tell him. There were just too many other variables in the mix. That was three months ago. And considering this was the type of news to share in-person, the fact that he lived out of state was really just a convenient excuse.

"I'll tell him this weekend. He's supposed to be coming home for a few days." Deven winced, not entirely sure of the truth in her statement. To be honest, she hadn't talked to Justin in over a week. For all she knew, his plans had changed, as they did. Often.

"I'll tell you what." Kennedy interrupted her thoughts. "Why don't we go to the mall? I can get you something to eat"— Deven's pointed look prompted her laugh—"and I can pick up this new purse I saw at Kate Spade." Deven was sure Kennedy meant the Fashion District in Philly, a mere thirty-minute drive from their location. That seemed to be her preference. As if she needed to go shopping, Deven mused, side-eyeing the mound of clothes that nearly hid the floor from view. Her sister may have had a little spending problem. But it wasn't like Deven could, or had a right to, monitor anybody's funds but her own. Besides, a Philly cheesesteak did sound delicious right about then.

Kennedy had splurged and purchased a new Tesla not even a month prior. So, breaking in her new ride, Deven estimated they had shaved half off of the travel time to the next state over. One of the perks of living in South Jersey. Before they could get comfortable in the crisp, leather seats, Kennedy was steering the car into the parking lot of the Fashion District.

It was unusually crowded for a Tuesday which put a small damper on Deven's mood. She wasn't one to frequent the mall, especially in comparison to Kennedy, but when she did go, she preferred as few people as possible.

"You like this?"

Deven turned, not realizing Kennedy had stopped in front of a nearby window display. She was pointing at one particular mannequin, dressed in a navy blazer and high-waisted short set. If she wasn't mistaken, Deven could've sworn she'd seen a similar outfit in the slew of clothes back in Kennedy's bedroom-closet. But she shrugged anyway. Taking that as permission, Kennedy disappeared into the store, leaving Deven to wander to one of the nearby kiosks to waste some time.

For it to be nearing Valentine's Day, she wasn't at all feeling in a lover's mood. The atmosphere was more annoying than stimulating, with gift baskets and stuffed animals clutching oversized hearts bearing those cliche expressions that reeked of procrastination. Deven fingered the ribbon attached to a balloon bouquet that danced in clusters above the kiosk stand. It would've been cute if it hadn't been so damn cheesy. But she would've given anything for Justin to be this cheesy.

"What can I get for you?" A woman, obviously working the booth, shuffled over with an expectant smile.

Deven opened her mouth to respond, pausing for just a moment when she noticed a man staring. He was across the hall, not too close as to be suspicious but not far away enough to blend in with the other patrons. His skin was dark like lacquer, and he was tall and slender with a head full of locs braided into a single cord down the center of his back. He was dressed a little too elaborately for a leisurely stroll at the mall, Deven noticed, the sleeves and turtleneck of a cream sweater poking from underneath his tweed jacket. If Deven wasn't so apprehensive, she would've been initially attracted to him. But there was something about the way he looked at her, glanced away, then looked at her again that made her a little uneasy.

It wasn't until Mr. Mysterious bent the corner for the escalators that Deven redirected her attention back to the kiosk lady. "Sorry," she said, though she wasn't exactly sure what she was apologizing for. The man was long gone but she still felt like his eyes were on her. Deven turned just as Kennedy strolled up with two shopping bags swinging from the crook of her arm.

"Hey," she greeted, sliding her eyes to the stand at Deven's back. "What are you getting? Something for Justin?"

Deven dismissed the question with a wave of her hand. "No, I was just looking. Let's go."

They started walking, Deven navigating them in the direction of the food court. "So, what did you buy?"

"Just a few things," Kennedy said with a shrug. "You should've come in there. I saw some really cute things for you."

"Girl, I don't need no more clothes."

"You only live once." Kennedy laughed and held up the bags as if to affirm her statement.

Deven rolled her eyes. "Now you sound like Mom." The woman they knew before, not the shell of the woman who remained. The mom who was carefree, loving, and fulfilled.

Kennedy didn't comment, which had Deven glancing sideways to watch her profile. It was clear by the clenched jaw Kennedy was in no mood for a discussion related to their mother. She certainly knew how to hold a grudge.

They entered the food court and immediately, a blend of onions, peppers, and spices assaulted her nostrils. Deven took a seat at one of the bistro tables while Kennedy took off to order their lunch. She returned with a tray, piled with two drinks, two cartons of fries, and two Philly cheesesteaks rolled, burrito-style, in sandwich wrap paper.

Deven bit hungrily into her sandwich. The melted cheese was hot on her lips but still, she savored the delicious flavor. She took a sip of her lemonade to cool her mouth.

"Oh, I meant to tell you, I met someone." Kennedy's dimples winked with an amused smirk before she stuffed a fry into her mouth.

Deven nodded for her to divulge the details, but at the same time something—or *someone*, rather—caught her eye. She couldn't be sure, but she thought she saw the single braid of some locs bouncing off a tweed jacket. But just as quickly, he was gone.

# Chapter Four

She felt like she was drowning.

Deven sucked in a greedy breath as the splash of water felt like ice on her skin. She coughed, nearly choking, and her throat constricted with the brief lapse in oxygen.

Finally, she leaned up from the sink to eye her reflection in the mirror.

She looked like hell. A dingy mirror in a morgue bathroom didn't need to tell her that. Water droplets cascaded down her face in sheets as her mind fumbled through the series of events.

*"That's not my sister."*

*The room went still. So still, in fact that Deven had to wonder if the other occupants had snuck off while she'd been so consumed with the photo. A stranger's photo.*

*It was Justin's arm suddenly falling away from her shoulder that prompted Deven to tear her eyes from the glossy image. She glanced first at him, then to Maria. Both of them carried identical frowns of confusion. Why were they staring at her like that?*

*"Did you hear what I just said?" Deven spun the clipboard around*

*and nudged it across the table back in Maria's direction.* "That's not Kennedy. That's not my sister."

"Babe," *It was Justin that broke the awkward silence first, his tone irritatingly delicate.* "I know this is hard to digest, but denial won't make her death any less true."

*Deven shook her head and stabbed the picture once more. He couldn't possibly think that was Kennedy. He had met her sister a handful of times. Surely, he couldn't be that forgetful.*

"Look again Justin. Seriously look at this woman. Sure, they favor, but that's not her." *A brief swell of hope bloomed in her chest when Justin angled his head to get a better look, narrowing his eyes in consideration. Finally, he sat back with sympathy marring his face.*

Deven's grip tightened on the porcelain of the bathroom sink, her headache returning with a savage intensity. She had a hard time accepting death. Her father's death had taught her that about herself. Her mother had retreated into the protection of her own mind; Kennedy couldn't relate since they didn't share the same father, so Deven had been left to maneuver the grief alone. And man, was it a lonely journey. Her coworkers tried to placate her with condolences about the five stages of grief that did very little to comfort her—she straddled the fence between denial and depression, apparently, never acceptance. This was only heightened after what happened with the twins . . .

Instinct had Deven touching her stomach, as if by some miracle she could still feel their little movements. It was losing her father that had inserted the knife, pretty much losing her mother that had twisted it, and losing the twins that had torn the wound open at the seams to leave her raw and bleeding. She'd been in denial then too, still was on most days. Was it any wonder that she was denying Kennedy's death?

Something moved behind her. Deven blinked once, then twice, struggling to clear the rest of the water from her vision. Sure enough, there was the faintest of glows as a woman floated up behind her, the bathroom stalls visible through her translucent skin. It was the woman in the morgue—their Kennedy—not hers. But here, up close she looked so much like her it was scary. Perhaps like Kennedy used to look before all the cosmetic surgery. The Kennedy before life happened.

The woman's smile was sad, and her eyes looked as if she was pleading, though Deven didn't know for what. Then, as fleeting as a whisper, she was gone. Deven turned around, but of course, the restroom was completely empty, the only sound coming from the water still gushing from the faucet.

That's how Officer McKinney found her when she swung into the restroom, standing frozen and looking dazed into thin air. "Ms. Reynolds?" she called.

Deven turned, her expression unreadable.

Officer McKinney walked over and flipped down the faucet, abruptly halting the stream of water. "How are you holding up?"

She almost seemed genuine. Deven had to remember this was the cop's job. So, she nodded and reached for the paper towels to dry her face. "I'll be okay," she answered. No use entertaining anything other than professionalism. This woman was not her friend.

"I know this is hard for you," Officer McKinney was saying. "I've lost a few very dear friends of mine in the line of duty."

Did she really think that was comparable? *Friends* who chose their dangerous career path? People who knew the risks and repercussions? A badge was target practice, plain and simple. A death like this . . . well, Deven didn't even know how to formulate the words for this one. But the officer's sympathetic attempt failed to extinguish the tumor of misery festering in her stomach.

"I just don't think that's her," Deven mumbled, almost to herself. Similar yes, but not her.

Officer McKinney paused, clearly trying to find the "right" words. "Denial is the first stage of grief . . ."

And there it was again. It was like everyone was reading from the same 'things to say to someone who suffers a loss' handbook. Had Deven also sounded this formulaic?

"No, you don't understand." She shook her head to clear the jumble of thoughts. "I know you all say that's her, but I don't think that's my sister. At all. They look alike but . . ." It was so hard to explain. None of them *knew* Kennedy. They knew their records and data analyses and blood samples and crime scene reports. They didn't know Kennedy's most recent surgery was to permanently arch her eyebrows, or that her lips had a very distinct pout or that she would never be caught dead—literally—without her sew-in hair. Not to mention Kennedy was overseas and she most certainly didn't do drugs. That woman in the picture, whoever she was, was not her sister.

"We found her wallet with her in the home," Officer McKinney reasoned. "It had her driver's license with her picture. She was found in the residence that is in her name and you did confirm was hers—"

"Yes, I know that but . . ." Deven blew out a breath. It just didn't make sense.

Officer McKinney sighed. "The coroner is going to run some more tests, okay? Just so we can cross all t's and dot all i's."

Deven felt the flood of relief. Good. Now everyone could stop with this nonsense.

"In the meantime," Officer McKinney went on, her tone gentle. "I would advise you to start making those preparations."

"Not until I hear the results of the tests."

The officer nodded, though she was unable to hide the shadows of pessimism darkening her face. "I understand," she said. "But I just don't want you to get your hopes up."

———•◦•———

The ride back home was different. Before, Justin seemed more empathetic, more understanding. Now, Deven noticed he just had a disconnected attitude about himself. Like he was uncomfortable around her. She wished he would turn on the radio or something, if only to conceal the tension with arbitrary noise.

"Now what?" she said when the silence grew maddening.

Justin tapped his thumbs on the steering wheel, an outward display that he was just as oblivious, if not more so, than her. "I guess I can take you home," he offered. "And maybe you can do like Officer McKinney suggested. Call your mom first, then maybe start with the funeral arrangements."

Deven was already shaking her head to dispel her growing agitation. "Justin, no. I told you I wasn't going to do that. You know why."

Justin gave a half-assed shrug. "Okay, whatever you want to do, Deven." The fact that he used her name further solidified his apathy and that sweltering tension settled between them once more, this time heavier. Deven turned back to the window and struggled to ignore the loud silence.

As soon as they returned to the apartment, Justin retreated to the bathroom and immediately, the sound of the shower spray wafted from the closed door. Not knowing what else to do with herself, Deven began making the bed, smoothing the wrinkles from the sheets and stacking her numerous decorative pillows against the headboard. She just needed to keep moving. Maybe then she wouldn't have to slow down to think.

Perhaps she should cook something. She certainly didn't have an appetite—in fact the thought of food made her nauseous right then. But Justin was probably hungry, and she didn't want the morning's events to dampen the little time they had left together. Maybe a little breakfast would soften their strain and they could discuss, objectively, a *reasonable* next course of action, whatever that was.

By the time Justin entered the kitchen sometime later, Deven had the smell of greasy bacon permeating throughout the apartment. She used a spatula to rake the cheese eggs onto a plate, scrambled light just like he liked them, and a timer dinged signaling the bagels in the toaster oven had just the right amount of crisp.

"Oh, I didn't know you were making something to eat." Justin spoke from behind her.

"Yeah, I figured—" Deven turned with plates in hand, surprised to see he was completely dressed, with his duffle bag slung over his shoulder. "You're leaving? Now?"

"Yeah, I told you I had to do some things before my flight in the morning."

Deven sat the food on the table, the dishes clanking a little louder than she intended. "Yeah, but I thought we could . . . I don't know, talk. Because of what happened this morning."

Justin's cell phone vibrated in his hand and without looking, he shoved it into his back pocket. "Well, I didn't think you wanted to talk," he said. "I tried to tell you to do what the cops said but you didn't want to hear it, remember?"

His annoyance was palpable and Deven had to swallow her disappointment. "Okay, but I still need you right now Justin. My sister—I mean I don't know what's going on, and"—shame had her lowering her voice—"I don't have anybody right now." She couldn't cry. She wasn't weak, dammit. But the past few hours had been slowly chipping away at her psyche. Any more, and she was likely to crack.

Justin reached for her, and she fell into his hug, almost desperately. His beard was still damp from the shower, and he smelled of her soap; honey and cocoa butter mixed with that sexy woodsy scent of the cologne he always wore. Deven inhaled, welcoming the comfort. Justin's lips touched her forehead, and his hand massaged the little space between her shoulder blades.

"You're going to be okay," he soothed. "You got this, babe. I don't want this to destroy you. You have to be strong for you, for your mother, for Kennedy. She would want you to."

She nodded against his chest and shut her eyes to stop the impending tears. He gave her one more kiss and pulled back to readjust the strap of his bag. "You call me if you need me, okay?"

Deven blinked back her confusion. For a moment, she thought he was going to stay. But that probably would've been too much like the loving, compassionate boyfriend Justin used to be. The one she hadn't seen since before the big Baltimore move.

Rather than argue, Deven nodded again and watched him leave, the door making a resounding *click* at his back. She lowered herself to the table and looked at the breakfast, probably now cold. Sure enough, the nausea had returned full force. Without a second thought, she scraped both plates in the trash, made sure the stove was turned off, and headed back to her room. She would clean up later. If she felt like it. As far as she was concerned, everything could sit in there and rot, for all she cared.

The muffled vibration of her cell phone could be heard as Deven stepped into her bedroom. She was torn for a brief moment. Part of her didn't want to answer it. But then there was the slight panic because it could have been the cops or the medical examiner, preferably with a break in the case. They probably wouldn't have finished their tests on the body that fast, but it was wishful thinking that perhaps someone, maybe that woman's *real* sister, had come forward to identify her. Deven could hear it now. *I'm so sorry Ms. Reynolds, this was all a big mistake. We've spoken with your sister, Kennedy, and everything is fine now.* The thought was too absurd to be true, she knew, but that still would've been less absurd than the string of madness that had taken place since she'd gotten up that morning.

Deven rummaged through her purse and found her phone in the junk of old receipts and loose change. It was the caller ID reading that had added a little more urgency to her movements. They didn't call often, but when they did, it was usually something important. "Hello?" she answered.

"Yes, Deven Reynolds?"

"This is she. Is my mom okay?"

Betty, the kind receptionist from Blessed Haven Assisted Living, cleared her throat. "Yes, your mother is fine," she assured her. "I was just told by her nurse to give you a call. Today isn't really a good day."

Of course, it wasn't. Lately, her mother had been having more and more of those. Deven didn't want to be irritated. But this, compounded on an already stressful day, wasn't what she needed right now. "If you could come down and help us calm her down, Ms. Reynolds," Betty went on. "Plus, we have a few things to discuss with you regarding her long-term care."

Something about the way she said it let Deven know there was something else she should be concerned about. "Okay, I'll be on my way," she said.

She hadn't planned on facing her mother until she had an idea on how, or if, she was going to let her know about Kennedy. She sure as hell wasn't ready. But it looked like she had about a thirty-minute drive to get ready.

# Chapter Five

*Excerpt from the diary of Kennedy (Age 11)*

*I was a mistake. But not like a bad mistake. A good mistake. Like when I'm in Ms. Wilson's class and I don't know the answer so I just "eenie meenie mini mo." But the answer ends up being right. (I think that's how Deven meant it). I'm so glad she's my sister. She makes me feel better and she loves me for real. Most big sisters hate their little sisters, but I guess I got lucky.*

*This one time I wanted Mommy to come outside and see me because I learned how to skate backwards (my friend BeBe taught me). She wouldn't come because Deven said she was sleeping, and she didn't want me to wake her up. So, I was sad, but Deven said she would come outside and watch me, and she did! She was clapping for me and told me that even though I wasn't the best skater, she was still so happy for me because I had learned how to skate backwards. She even tried* to show me how to do a little trick while I was skating but then I messed up and I fell and scraped my elbow. I was crying but she took me in the house and got me a band aid. It wasn't a lot of blood, but it still hurt and Deven told me that her daddy told her that we can't be too sensitive and when we fall, we have to always get back up. Even if we have some cuts and blood. That made me feel better.

That's why I'm lucky. Deven always knows how to make things right. And her daddy is really nice to me too. For a while it was just me, mommy, and Deven. And Deven's daddy, Daddy Jamie, would come visit a lot because Deven said her parents were trying to get back together (I asked if Mommy would try to get back with my daddy and Deven said hell no, I was crazy if I thought that would ever happen. I can't believe she actually cussed). Anyway, she was right. Her parents got back together because Daddy Jamie moved in with us last summer. But I don't mind because he is fun, and he makes Mommy happy. Plus, my sister is so happy that they can be a family again.

# Chapter Six

Blessed Haven Assisted Living was reminiscent of an 1800s-style plantation. The property was located outside of the city limits, nestled on about ten acres of farmland with its own private lake. It was a picturesque estate with its antebellum architecture, ornamental pillars and wrap-around porches. A first impression made it easy to see the basis for that $5200 a month they charged. But after twenty-two months, Deven had to admit it was well worth every penny.

It had been a bittersweet decision to even consider moving her mother into the residence. But with her father's death had come a lot of changes, some she was not equipped to handle on her own. Her mother was still mentally okay, for the most part, but she was so riddled with grief that she didn't bother taking care of herself. Deven was having to call around the clock, sometimes making two and three trips to visit just to make sure she was eating and bathing. Kennedy wasn't as active with that responsibility as she would have liked so, as the eldest, Deven took it upon herself to handle it as best she could.

When the miles (and time) became too much, Deven decided it was better to sell the house and move Mom in with her. Big mistake. Mom's condition seemed to deteriorate overnight. Her doctors attributed it to a culture shock; first losing her husband and then, losing that last piece of him that was familiar, the house. It was becoming too demanding trying to handle caring for her mother while working the rotational shifts at the hospital. Then, Iris wandered off in the middle of the night and a neighbor found her walking aimlessly in the courtyard in forty-degree weather with only a nightgown. That solidified that she needed around-the-clock care.

And true to its name, Blessed Haven had been exactly that, a blessing. Thank God for the money from the sale of the house and her dad's lucrative savings and life insurance policies, because it was certainly more than Deven could afford on her nurse's salary.

Deven steered down the cobble-stoned drive towards the side of the house where there was designated visitor parking. With it being Sunday, the lot was packed with cars, indicative of the family members taking advantage of the beautiful day. A look around showed just that, sprinkles of people with their matriarchs or patriarchs taking strolls over the expanse of landscaped grounds. Down by the lake, two men sat in wheelchairs with a chessboard propped on a foldout table between them while their aides stood nearby, chatting and gossiping.

Deven lifted a hand in greeting to a few seniors who sat rocking on the porch. She would make sure to bring her mother outside if she was feeling up to it. It was something about the air here that induced the tranquility.

In stark contrast to the charming appeal of the building's exterior, the interior had been completely renovated with all the contemporary luxuries and amenities to further enhance quality of life for the residents. The doors opened to a huge concierge desk with natural stacked stone wall panels to accent the cream and gray color scheme. Vinyl tile floors were made to look like wood planks running throughout the lobby, and a wall fountain acted as ambient music to the atmosphere. And since Blessed Haven prided themselves on creating a quaint home-y feel by capping their occupancy at twenty residents, the facility was able to maintain the appeal and cleanliness of a five-star hotel.

Deven approached the desk and punched in her four-digit PIN on the iPad. All the staff knew her by face, but as customary, she fished her driver's license from her wallet. Betty, the older woman who'd called her earlier, was behind the desk and she immediately looked up through the glasses perched on her nose.

"Oh. you got down here fast," she said with a smile.

*Well, you did make it sound urgent.* Deven nodded politely. "It was an easy drive," she said instead, accepting the visitor badge. "How is she? Better?"

"A little bit. Jan told her you were on the way, so she perked up a bit."

Deven relaxed at the mention of her mother's primary nurse. If anyone could handle her mother's sporadic tantrums, it was definitely Jan.

"By the way, we've got some fun activities coming up next month. We already sent this by email." Betty passed a calendar across the desk, the dates marked and color-coded with a host of recreational events; an ice cream social, movie night on the lawn (weather permitting), a tailgate party, and a senior citizen dance were just some of the highlights. Like every other aspect of their premium care, Blessed Haven poured a lot into keeping them busy, for their *Elder Enrichment* as they called it. Deven had always made a point to be as involved as possible and she wanted to keep it that way.

"You also mentioned something about my mother's long-term care," Deven felt compelled to mention. "Is there some kind of a problem?"

Betty's smile fell a few degrees. "Not necessarily a problem," she said. "But as you know, we pride ourselves on providing the best quality care for our residents. And since your father was a long-time friend, advocate, and sponsor of our lovely establishment, we would like your mother to remain with us for as long as she needs to be here."

Deven nodded, still not following. "Okay . . ."

"However," Betty continued. "If we feel that we can no longer provide the care and attention that your mother requires, we will have to, unfortunately, ask her to leave."

Now it made sense. Her mom could be a lot to manage, and it was only thanks to her dad's esteemed reputation (and financial contributions) to the residence that they were even allowing her to stay. Deven nodded, easily reading the insinuation in Betty's generic smile: Get Iris under control or they were going to kick her ass out, relationship be dammed. Of course, they couldn't let one challenging resident potentially impair their superior ratings.

"I understand," Deven said, stepping away from the desk. "Thank you so much for letting me know."

"And make sure to tell that sister of yours about the Elder Enrichment activities so she can join us," Betty added with a much lighter spirit.

Just like that, her words hit Deven with such force she felt momentarily disoriented. It was like a temporary paralysis, a shocking and bitterly painful reminder of that morning. Her therapist had been correct. When someone dies, they don't die once. They die over and over again. And that cyclical anguish was crippling.

Betty must've sensed something was wrong because her face had creased in motherly concern. Deven didn't speak as she hurried off to the sweeping grand staircase. Taking the steps as opposed to the elevator would buy her a little more time anyway. Maybe then she could decide how to broach the subject about Kennedy. But to say it out loud meant Deven would have to acknowledge the tragedy and acknowledging it made it too real.

And her mother would need—no, *deserve* answers. Answers she didn't even have yet.

Deven paused at room 213 and took a breath. Then, with as much strength as she could muster, she lifted a fist and knocked.

There was shuffling inside before the door opened wide and Jan filled the doorway, donning her usual burgundy scrubs with the facility logo on the breast pocket. "Hey Deven," she greeted, stepping to the side to let her enter. "I didn't know you were visiting today."

"Well, they called and told me they needed a little reinforcement," Deven teased. "I figured you must've been off because I already knew it wasn't anything you couldn't handle."

Jan laughed but it was clear she was flattered at the compliment. "I was supposed to go out of town to visit my grandbaby, but we changed it to next week instead." She gestured to the room. "I'll let you sit with her for a little bit, and I can come back later."

Deven thanked the nurse and waited until she left before heading through the tiny kitchenette to the combined living and bedroom area. The TV was mounted over an electric fireplace, the LED flame adding a cozy flair. Applause echoed from one of her mother's favorite shows, *Family Feud*, as contestants spat out absurd answers to overzealous cheers.

Deven's eyes swept the room, her gaze landing on the framed 5×7 picture on the nightstand. It was a candid shot of her and Kennedy, her arm extended to catch the selfie against the illuminated backdrop of Times Square. Deven picked up the picture and narrowed her eyes at the smirk on Kennedy's face. "What is going on with you, Ken?" she whispered.

"Hey, sweetie."

Deven turned as her mother hobbled in from the bathroom. Even at fifty-two, Iris Reynolds was still just as stylish, dressed comfortable in a sweater and some leggings, her graying hair flipped up into huge pin curls that framed her smooth face. Deven had always admired how her mother aged so gracefully with very minimal wrinkles. She certainly didn't look like what she'd been through.

Deven propped the picture back in its place and crossed the room. Her trembling took her by surprise as she pulled her mom into a desperate hug, inhaling her signature floral jasmine and rose fragrance. Apparently, Iris didn't notice the tremors. Or maybe the dementia kept her from acknowledging it.

"I didn't know someone was coming to visit me today." Iris pulled back to smile at her daughter.

Deven's spirit plummeted seeing that familiar blank smile, void of recognition but polite, nonetheless. "Mommy, do you know who I am?" she asked, gently.

"Of course. You're my nurse." Iris padded to the bed and took a seat.

Deven picked up the picture frame again and held it out for her mother to see. "No Mommy, it's me. Deven, your daughter." She pointed at the picture as she spoke. "And that's your other daughter, Kennedy. Do you remember her?"

Iris shook her head. "No baby, I don't think I have any children. You must have the wrong room." She paused as if she were thinking. "You know what? I think I do remember having children. Two girls."

"Yes." Deven's voice lifted in excitement. "That's us. See? I'm your first-born."

Again, Iris shook her head, this time with a deep-set frown. "No . . ." She stretched the word out like a little song. "No, my girls ran away when they were little."

It would be too much to correct her. It was only Kennedy that had run away, well, almost. But her mother was destroyed by her daughter's absence just the same.

Deven sat the photo back on the stand for the second time and took a seat next to Iris, her face downcast. There was no use in telling her about Kennedy. It would be falling on deaf ears. She would have to wait and decide what to do.

Iris's hand moved to cover Deven's. "Have you seen my girls?" she asked, her tone hopeful.

Deven hadn't expected to cry, but she couldn't stop the tears that began to stream down her sunken cheeks. Iris wasn't satisfied with the lack of response, so she asked again. This time, Deven nodded. "When you see them," Iris said, "can you please tell them I love them?"

"Yes, ma'am, I'll tell them."

With a grateful smile, her mother shifted her attention to the TV screen, leaving Deven alone to collect her thoughts. *Now what?*

# Chapter Seven
# Three Months Before

Deven keeled over the toilet, the vomit rancid and venomous as it gushed from her throat. She gagged, coughed, and gagged some more, bracing against the lip of the ceramic like a lifeline. The nausea had been running rampant all day. Now here she was, well into the evening rotation and she'd regurgitated everything but her core memories. Not to mention her vision was hazy and her head felt like it was on a swivel. *Damn morning sickness.*

When she was sure she could stand without toppling face forward into the bowl, Deven dragged herself to her feet. Sweat peppered her forehead and a veil of perspiration or leftover throw up (she couldn't be sure which) hung like a bib from the front collar of her shirt. She would need to change and then make up a realistic excuse regarding her frequent trips to the restroom. Food poisoning, maybe? It wasn't like the cafeteria had the best reputation, so that part was believable. Really anything would work except for the truth, for now.

It was no secret that Justin had had his share of women, ironically including a number of the nurses Deven worked with. And after she had nearly come to blows with one of them, it was idyllic to keep her personal life separate from work. Even after the nurse had transferred to a hospital in another city, the rumors lingered, only recently dwindling to covert smirks behind her back. It was embarrassing enough and she sure as hell wasn't trying to ignite the catty gossip once more.

Deven entered the locker room, glad to find it empty. A hint of musk tickled her nose and she had to swallow a fresh bout of nausea. She sank to the wooden bench and leaned forward to put her head between her knees. Please don't throw up, please don't throw up, she pleaded with her bubbling tummy. Any more of this and she would have to go home, or worse, hop on one of the beds on her floor and request to be admitted.

The door to the locker room pushed open and Deven groaned inwardly at the intrusion. But dammit, she didn't have the energy to care at that point.

"Hey, lady." The voice was accompanied with a hand on her back and Deven sighed in relief. Now Leslie, she could tolerate, even in her weakened state. The girl was one of the newer nurses on the floor and still had the kind, sweet, zealous spirit, with a full-fledged Alabama accent to match her southern hospitality.

Leslie slid next to Deven on the bench, their legs bumping companionably. "Is there anything I can do? You want some water or some crackers or something?"

Deven managed a nod. "Some water please."

Leslie seemed eager to oblige and she popped up and headed for her locker. She returned with a bottled water and what was left of her peanut butter cracker sandwiches in a Ziploc bag. Deven accepted both, taking greedy sips of the lukewarm liquid.

Leslie clasped her hands together, probably wishing there was something else she could do, poor thing. "Do you want me to call the nurse director?"

"No, I'm good, thank you so much, Leslie." Deven held up the half-empty water bottle for emphasis. "I appreciate your help. Just a little food poisoning."

Leslie laughed and tossed her ponytail over her shoulder. "Oh, it's no problem. I just figured you were pregnant."

Funny. Working in Labor and Delivery, Deven should have expected everyone to make the correct assumption. She didn't know how long she was going to keep up the facade, or at least keep it up enough for people not to question her. Perhaps after she told Justin this weekend. They still hadn't had a real conversation, but he did send a text message saying he would be flying in late Friday night and might need to come over to crash. The message had been brief, but it had pacified her.

The sickness feeling was dissolving and Deven pulled herself to her feet. She knew she probably looked like death run over. Leslie's hand remained steady on her back, just in case. "Do you think you can cover for me a little bit?"

Leslie's nod was instant. "Of course. You sure you don't need anything else?"

"I'm good. Just need a few minutes to get myself together. Brush my teeth," Deven added with a chuckle. That part was true. And she would. Later. She needed to do something else first.

Deven knew she should've made her health a bigger priority. It wasn't like she didn't want the baby. She just wanted the marriage more. Justin was supposed to be that husband, which made it even more disheartening when he still had not proposed. And instead of an engagement, she'd received the positive pregnancy test. The shock had left her reeling.

Deven checked her cell phone as she hurried into one of the empty sonogram rooms. She had a little time before someone would need it and she wanted to get a few ultrasound pictures for her big announcement that weekend. Plus, Kennedy would need a few more pictures for the scrapbook she was making. Deven knew she would have to eventually make an appointment with a regular OBGYN instead of sneaking these little ultrasound checks between patients.

A few buttons and the machine whirred and hummed to life. Deven lifted her shirt to smear the cool gel on her belly. She replaced her fingers with the transducer. As expected, the baby's image materialized on the monitor, the distorted pockets of grey and black shifting as she moved the wand across her abdomen. The baby's heartbeat filled the room, like galloping in water. Deven frowned at the sound. It was fainter and slower than usual. The image on the screen didn't look to be moving as much either. She took a step closer to press more buttons on the computer. Maybe if she saw some of the measurements, she could—

A brisk knock on the door had Deven snatching the wand from her skin and letting her shirt fall into place. The remnants of the gel left her wet and chilled, her scrubs clinging to her as she quickly shut off the machine. "One second," she called. She would have to worry about the baby later when she had more time. Between her incessant bathroom trips and now this, it was a wonder someone hadn't been lapping the halls to look for her sooner. Leslie could only stall for so long.

Deven was surprised to see Paul Bryant waiting outside of the door. He looked equally surprised, but pleasantly so, dimples pleating both cheeks with that gorgeous smile of his. It was infectious and she couldn't help but blush.

Paul Bryant was most certainly an attractive package. Not only was he probably the sexiest white man on the planet (especially when he left his facial hair unkempt), but he was a gym rat, evident by the lab coat that did little to hide his toned physique; one she'd had to pretend often not to notice. But aesthetics aside (as hard as that was), Paul was such a beautiful person. She'd seen that compassion firsthand when her father had his cancer diagnosis. He'd become more than just her father's oncologist, but a very dear friend; sharing the journey, the empathy, and yes even the pain when Jamie had lost the battle.

It wasn't until well after a respectable time had passed and they all were out celebrating with coworkers, that Paul confessed his crush on her. Granted it could've been the atmosphere or the alcohol talking, Deven never knew. She was flattered, but—and she would never admit this to him—she couldn't see herself dating outside her race. Kennedy had once called her prejudiced. Deven didn't know if she agreed with that, but still, she did her best to keep their friendship just that, *friendly*. That decision hadn't stopped her curiosity though. Especially when he looked at her like he was doing right then.

Deven cleared her throat to dispel the rising sexual tension. The man hadn't even said anything, so why the hell was she aroused like she was in heat? With a whole baby in her stomach, at that. *Damn hormones.*

Paul finally spoke up first. "Hey you. I didn't expect to see you here."

Deven lifted an amused brow. "Really? Because you know I do work in this part of the hospital."

"No, I meant not here"—Paul motioned an arm down the hall—"I meant *here*, here." He clearly realized how foolish he sounded, and he threw up his hands on a laugh. "You know, what? Forget it. How are you, Deven? It's been a minute."

Deven nodded. He was right. Since her father had passed, she didn't see him nearly as often as she used to. "Pretty good. Can't complain."

"You look good."

Was he flirting with her? It certainly wouldn't be the first time.

Warmth rose in her face and Deven had to look away. So much for platonic. Lord, she needed to be hosed down with cold water.

"Uh, what are you doing here?" Then to mimic him, she added, "You know. Not here. But *here*, here."

Her imitation prompted another laugh. "I'm meeting someone. She had an appointment."

"Oh? Your sister?"

"Girlfriend."

Damn, there was the cold water she had asked for her. The puncture of the one word instantly doused all the flirtation like an extinguisher. "Oh," Deven blinked, then failed miserably to put that light inflection back in her tone. "Congratulations. I didn't know you had a—I mean I didn't know you were about to be a dad."

"Yeah, we're excited." And he looked genuinely happy.

As long as Deven had known Paul, she'd never so much as heard about him going on a date or even seen a woman's picture on his desk. Of course, the hospital rumors had been active, tossing around that he was gay, or a virgin, or both. Then he had made his confession and all speculation went out the window. Apparently, that crush of his had also died down.

"Well, congrats again to you and . . ."

"Amber."

Deven frowned, feeling another pierce of pain. Amber sounded like the perfect doctor's wife.

They stood there a moment or two longer in a film of awkwardness before Deven stepped to the side to dismiss herself. "Well, it was good seeing you, Paul. And good luck to you and Amber on the new baby." She stopped as her stomach muscles clenched. More pain, real this time. The ache had her groaning and staggering into the wall.

"Deven, what's wrong?" Paul's arms circled her waist to hold her upright, but Deven could only hiss as her stomach knotted again in what felt like a rapid succession of stab wounds. Something was terribly wrong.

Deven felt her legs give out and then she was on the floor, the linoleum like a brick of ice against her cheek. All she could hear was Paul's muffled yells ringing in her ear as he called for help.

# Chapter Eight

Deven was afraid to fall asleep. If she did, she would likely have nightmares; images of death and the morgue and the beautiful Kennedy-looking phantom girl she had seen in the mirror. The girl who looked like she was trying to tell her something.

Or even worse, Deven pictured she would have some of the same visions that had been plaguing her all day; her sister being held hostage, or raped, or lying on the side of a country road somewhere with her body beaten into an unidentifiable corpse. Because what was even more torturous than knowing what happened, was *not* knowing.

It wasn't until the upper rim of the sun began peeking over the horizon spilling an ombre of color onto the waking sky, that Deven realized she had stayed awake through the night. She expected to be exhausted, but more than physical, it was mental. Her mind was too active to sleep, instead coming up with every kind of twisted what-if scenario to keep her anxiety running over.

Deven unfolded herself from the couch and stretched her stiff muscles. Desperately needing a drink, she trudged into the kitchen. It was only seven-thirty in the morning but her tongue ached for liquor. However, everything that had taken place served as a prevalent reminder that she could easily slide back onto that downward trajectory. Deven eyed the bottle of Grey Goose in her refrigerator, shuddering at the flashbacks of depression. There had been a period in her life where she was in a continuously inebriated state, like a zombie. And the domino effect was paralyzing.

Deven reached past the alcohol and grabbed one of the water bottles instead. Then, on a second thought, she pulled out the Grey Goose and poured the rest down the sink. She had been able to push through the temptation all this time and so far, hadn't had to worry about a relapse. But then again, she hadn't had to question the death of her sister either.

A mixture of fear and confusion had Deven's mind hazy as she sipped the bland water. Officer McKinney had assured her they would conduct some additional tests, but she had given no indication of how long that could realistically take. And there was no guarantee if the results would answer their questions, or present more. It was as if Deven's life beforehand had dissolved into some lucid dream. Interesting how traumatic events could make that division; *before* and *after. Was that before your sister died, or after?* Like two distinct and separate lifetimes.

The sudden ringing pierced the air like a siren and had a gasp clogged in Deven's throat. She let out a staggered breath, her eyes flickering to the window to confirm the early-morning hour. Who in the world could that be? She couldn't bring herself to make the short journey back into the living room to retrieve her cell. It was highly doubtful Justin would call this early. Could Officer McKinney have found out something new so quickly? But what if it wasn't? What if it was the nursing home? Or Kennedy? The thought had Deven shuffling across the floor. Her anxiety was now bordering on panic, and she knew feigning ignorance would just prolong the inevitable. Like she said before, the *unknown* was the worst part of tragedy.

Deven looked at the caller ID and frowned at the unfamiliar number flashing across the screen. Moments later, the phone went silent in her hand and just as quickly, the envelope icon popped up indicating a new text message. *Call me.* That was it. No name, no pleasantries, no sign of the source or the reason for the correspondence. Her finger hovered over the 'call' button for a split second before she opened the message again and typed in a reply. *Who is this?* She watched the screen looking for an answer. Whoever he or she was had just accompanied a phone call with a text message—at seven-thirty in the morning no less—so it had to be pretty important. Instead of another message, her phone rang again, that same mystery number flashing like a warning. This time, she decided to pick up. "Hello?"

"Hey, ma."

Deven pulled the phone from her ear to look at the ID again. The man's voice was vaguely familiar, but not enough for the informality. "Who is this?" She was insulted and she didn't bother hiding it. She had enough to deal with without having to worry about some idiot with an entitled disposition and wrong number.

The man chuckled at her attitude and Deven pulled the phone off her face, prepared to hang up on him. Then he spoke again, "Still the same old Deven, huh?"

Deven paused. The rhetorical question was like a blast from the past and she was suddenly engulfed in nostalgia. For a moment, she was catapulted back to her senior year of jersey dresses, pep rallies, Homecoming, and ditching class. And she didn't have one memory that year that didn't include Kennedy, and Kennedy's best friend.

"Benji?" Deven sank to the couch.

"Yeah, ma. It's me."

A series of emotions hit her at once. Surprise, confusion, fear . . . He could only be calling for one thing. The two weren't more than associates, joined by their mutual relationship with her sister. So Deven hadn't stayed in touch with him after high school. But she knew he was still in the picture because Kennedy spoke of him often. Last she heard, he had moved to Atlanta. So, this impromptu phone call certainly wasn't without cause.

"Hey," she said. "This is a surprise. How have you been, Benji?"

"I've been good. Listen," he started, skipping through the pleasantries. "I know this sounds strange, but I wanted to see if you could meet me."

Deven licked her lips moist and struggled to ignore the slam of each agonizing heartbeat against her tightened chest. "Uh, sure. When?"

"This afternoon. My flight lands at one."

He was flying into town. Why? What did he know? "Okay," she agreed. Then, she felt compelled to ask, "Is this about Kennedy—"

"I'll call you when I get there and we can arrange to meet," Benji interrupted. His voice was drowned out by his background all of a sudden. "I'll see you in a bit." And he hung up.

Deven placed her phone on the glass coffee table and collapsed in the cushions. Five hours. Five hours until Benji's plane arrived, and they could meet to discuss something she knew had everything to do with her sister. So much for even attempting to sleep now.

———⟫•⟪———

Thanks to Kennedy, Deven knew she and Benji shared their thirst for luxury and the finer things in life. So, when he texted an address on the waterfront at exactly 1:27, she expected a fine dining restaurant with white, linen cloths and menus with gourmet dishes and no prices. The GPS navigating her to the pier with a row of food stands was certainly not what she would have thought him to suggest.

Her jacket had been sufficient when she left the house. Now, thanks to the moisture wafting from the water backdrop, the temperature had dropped, and Deven shivered in the flimsy material. Her face was nearly numb with the cold and her breath billowed out to disappear in the damp air. Why the hell had he wanted to meet outside anyway?

Benji was standing under an awning in jeans, a sweater, and a leather coat. He was nearly hidden in the folds of an oversized scarf and hat as he turned to her. As she approached, she noticed his neatly-trimmed beard outlining thick lips that he pursed to blow warmth into his cupped palms. "Damn, girl," he greeted, stomping his feet to knock off the chill. "It's cold as hell out here."

"Yeah, you're not in Georgia anymore," Deven said, shoving her hands into the pockets of her jacket. "And you're the one that wanted to meet on the waterfront."

Benji nodded towards a restaurant nearby, the patio enclosed with vinyl plastic panels to block out the elements. "Is that place any good?"

Deven shrugged. As much as she and Justin had visited this area, she'd never tried it. "I'm not really hungry," she announced.

"I am." And with that, he led the way, not turning, or apparently caring, to see if Deven followed suit.

It was an Italian spot, by the distinct aroma of garlic, tomatoes, and basil Deven caught as soon as they pushed through the door. The restaurant was dimly lit to set the intimate ambiance, accented by a symphony of background music that was nearly drowned out by kitchen noise. Since it was a seat-yourself establishment, Deven followed Benji to a table (inside, thankfully), near the back of the restaurant. She assumed it was more so needing privacy to discuss their business as opposed to romanticism. Even if the latter was the case, Benji certainly didn't seem like the romantic type.

They hadn't even taken off their jackets before a teenager flounced over and sat two, laminated menus on the plastic checkerboard tablecloth. "Can I get you two something to drink?"

Deven waved her away while Benji ordered a beer. "You know you can order something," he said, untying his scarf. "It's not like this is a date or nothing."

Deven wrinkled her nose, unsure whether he was serious or just joking to break the ice between them. "I'm not hungry," she repeated her earlier sentiments from outside. Her stomach was in knots. She didn't think she could eat anything if she tried.

"You should eat something," he said, and left it at that.

The waitress returned and Benji ordered a Chicken Parmesan lunch special. And because she knew it would appease him, Deven went ahead and ordered a water and a Caesar salad that she didn't plan on eating.

"I'm glad you responded," Benji started as soon as they were left alone again. "I wasn't even sure that was your number."

Deven nodded, absently fiddling with her straw. "I didn't know you had it."

"Ken gave it to me, just in case."

Deven lifted her gaze to meet his. "What do you mean?" She watched him grip the neck of the beer bottle and casually bring it to his lips to take a sip. Still, he didn't answer but it was evident in his face that he knew something. "Benji," Deven leaned forward and lowered her voice. "Where is my sister?"

The question had a frown flitting across his face. "That's why I called you. I thought *you* knew."

Her heart sank to the pit of her belly. "What do you mean? You haven't heard from her?"

"Not in a couple weeks," he admitted. "I knew she was going out of town, and I had some stuff to take care of. We were supposed to handle some business over the weekend, but she hasn't called me back. That's not like her."

"What kind of business?"

"Just . . . work stuff," Benji waved his hand to dismiss the question. "That's why I had to come in town. But Ken would've responded to me by now so that's why I reached out to you."

Deven sat back feeling defeated as the waitress returned and sat their meals on the table. For some reason, she didn't think Benji was being completely truthful with her. Well, the part about looking for her she believed, but this "work stuff" and whatever he and Kennedy were tied up in, was the part that seemed suspicious.

She picked at her lettuce, but food was the last thing on her mind. How much could she really trust Benji? She didn't know. Still, she debated revealing the police and alleged suicide information she had received. But by the look on his face now, he seemed increasingly concerned since it was obvious Deven was just as clueless as he was. And if anybody could possibly know what was going on with Kennedy, it would certainly be her best friend.

The food smelled delicious, the sauce still bubbling with the heat. Benji just sat and stared at his meal, apparently having lost his appetite as well.

"Yesterday, the police came to my door," Deven began, noting how his face grew even more troubled at the mention of law enforcement. "They found a woman in Kennedy's apartment that had died of a drug overdose."

Benji's eyebrows widened in confused shock. "Wait, what? Who was it?"

Deven shrugged. "They said it was Kennedy, but . . ." she trailed off, remembering the picture she saw.

"Well, was it her?"

His urgency had the suspicion blooming again and Deven looked up at him through narrowed eyes. "Do you sell drugs, Benji?" she asked.

"What?" Benji's head whipped around to make sure no one had heard the accusation. He leaned in closer, his voice a little above a whisper. "What the hell are you talking about, Deven?"

The reciprocal question, the defensiveness . . . Deven was taken back at how she had clearly hit the nail on the head. "Wait a minute, did you give Kennedy drugs? Is that what was going on between you two? You were her supplier?"

"Hell no." Anger had his nostrils flaring as his eyes tightened to dangerous slits. "And Deven, I know we don't know each other that well, but you need to watch what you say to me." The inflection of his threat would have, under normal circumstances, evoked fear. But today hadn't been normal circumstances. Deven was functioning on determination and no sleep. There was no room to be affected by his intimidation.

Benji released a sigh and unclenched his fist which had unconsciously balled up on the table. "Look," he said, his tone more conciliatory. "It's clear you don't trust me. I get it. I don't really know you either, except through Kennedy. But right now, something has happened, and we don't know what. Let's try to figure this out. Fair?"

A pregnant pause and then, Deven gave a slow nod. "Fair."

"Now, start over and tell me what happened after the cops came," Benji said.

So, she did. Deven relayed what happened from that tragic morning when her doorbell rang. She told him how they had escorted her to the morgue, and she had to identify Kennedy by a picture and all the facts she knew, surrounding this mystery woman. He listened intently, not speaking until he was sure she had finished.

"So, the body you saw, it wasn't her?" he asked, just to be sure.

Deven closed her eyes and struggled to remember the details of the photo. The woman's hair, her cheeks, her lips, the delicate features that had not been distorted by death. Her thoughts then wandered to the restroom when she'd seen the woman in the mirror, those sunken eyes sad and pleading. Finally . . .

"I don't know," she admitted, her voice cracking with the admission. "I mean, she looked like her. But I'm not 100%. And Kennedy has had so many surgeries . . ." She glanced up, almost worried that she had divulged something perhaps Benji wasn't privy to. But the understanding upturn of his lips affirmed that he and Kennedy were indeed close enough for those types of secrets. "Everybody thinks that maybe it's just my denial," Deven went on with a labored breath. She failed to mention that part of her was afraid they were right.

Benji sat back in the booth, massaging his beard. "Okay, what do we know?" he mumbled as if to himself. "We both know Kennedy told us she was going out of town—"

"Dominican Republic," Deven added.

"Yeah, she told me that. The woman was picked up at Kennedy's apartment on a day we both know Kennedy should have been out of town. And drugs?" He shook his head. "Nah, I don't believe that. Did they do the fingerprints on the woman? Or anything else to ID her other than you?"

"They found her wallet," Deven said, suddenly remembering. "They said the ID matched Kennedy with that woman's picture. But they're going to run some more tests. One of the officer's said the fingerprinting would only come back if it matched in the public database. They're going to do a toxicology and some other stuff, but I don't know how long it would take."

"Yeah, too damn long. We got to go." Benji was already getting up and fishing in his pocket. He pulled out three twenty-dollar bills and tossed them on the table between their untouched dishes.

Deven slid from the booth. "What do you mean? Where are we going? To the police?"

"Kennedy's apartment," he said. "I'm thinking there are some answers there."

# Chapter Nine

Deven was already prepared to drive away. She was sure Kennedy's apartment would be barricaded with crime scene tape or something (though she wasn't sure an actual crime had been committed). Or at the very least, cop cars or news trucks swarming the complex. She was surprised to find none of the above. It looked like a typical afternoon with no signs of any unusual activity. Deven didn't know whether to be relieved or disappointed. Then, she had to remind herself that Kennedy wasn't some kind of prominent figure, except in her eyes. So, there would be no manhunts, no press conferences, no news stories covering what had happened. To everyone else, Kennedy's life and death weren't important enough to warrant media coverage.

Deven pulled her car behind Benji's rental SUV and scanned the parking lot. Part of her almost expected to see Kennedy strolling up the sidewalk headed to her building. *Sorry to worry you guys*, she would say with a smile as she stood with her hand tenting her eyes from the sun. *That was all a big misunderstanding*. Deven knew it was just wistful thinking.

Benji was waiting at the door once she climbed the stairs to the second floor of building B. "You got the key?" he prompted.

She didn't say anything, only reached in her purse for the key Kennedy had given her after she'd moved in. As she put the key in the lock, she suddenly felt nervous. A dead woman had been found here. What would they find?

Benji noticed her hesitation. "You okay, ma?"

Deven forced a nod and turned the key, the lock popping open with a resounding *click*. The door eased open without so much as a squeak.

The police had left the heat off, perhaps to keep from running up the bill, so it was freezing in the apartment. Benji must've had the same idea because he quickly fingered the thermostat, the heating unit kicking on with a mellow hum only seconds later. Deven glanced around, first noting how uncharacteristically clean the room was. Even the fresh smell of lemon and bleach hung in the air. Had the police returned to clean up the place? Had the dead body left some kind of lingering odor?

The living room held the aura of a museum and looked hardly used. Deven remembered how, only months before, she was helping her sister move in with wall-to-wall stacks of boxes. Kennedy had since decorated the place to feel more like home. She didn't have a TV in here, but she'd hung canvas wall art and even painted an accent wall a beautiful shade of gray.

The kitchen looked a little more settled as opposed to the living room. Dishes in the dishwasher, a single wine glass turned upside down in the drainboard. The refrigerator was a little skimpy, with the exception of some essentials and a Styrofoam box of leftovers. Still, nothing out of the ordinary.

Deven opened cabinets and drawers, not exactly sure what she was looking for. She knew she would recognize *it* when she saw it. However, nothing stood out, unless the junk drawer of miscellaneous household items and empty trash could account for something.

Deven glanced up, for the first time noticing that Benji wasn't in the room with her. She started down the hallway, assuming he'd found something of interest in her bedroom.

She wouldn't have known Benji was in the spare bedroom if she hadn't heard the faint rustling of papers. Why was he in there? And he had pulled the door closed to a crack, which was even more puzzling. Deven angled her eye against the inch slit and peered inside.

She couldn't see him, but she could definitely hear him, even though it was clear he was trying to be as quiet as possible. More papers being shuffled, then the snapshot of a cell phone camera. Twice. Three times. What was he taking pictures of?

The black of Benji's jacket came into view for the briefest of moments and Deven saw him trifold, then half-fold a small stack of papers and jam them into his pocket. He disappeared for a second, then his figure breezed by once more, blurred with his speed but clearly carrying something (was it a shoe box?) in his hand. Deven had to curse herself for trusting this man. Without any further hesitation, she nudged the door open and stood over the threshold, her eyes glaring at him.

Benji's head snapped up and true indeed, she saw the guilt before he quickly neutralized his face. "Hey," he greeted way too casually. "Find anything?"

She took a step into the room. "Nope. You?"

"Nope."

Of course, he would say that. So, what had he put in his pocket? What was he searching for? And the snapshot sounds, she knew those were from taking pictures. She could be naive at times because she wanted to see the good in people. But stupid she was not. Rather than let him know she was on to him, Deven pursed her lips to remain silent, her gaze picking over the room. Friends close and enemies closer.

Kennedy had made good on her word and converted this bedroom into a huge closet. The entire space had been glamorized with pink walls and white, floor-to-ceiling built-in shelving, cabinets, and cubbies. It looked as if there had been organization about the chaos at one point, but clothes and shoes now overflowed the space, protruding from their hangers and scattered on the floor with a careless precision. A chaise—or what looked to be a chaise underneath the mountain of jeans—sat beside the only window. The showstopper piece of furniture was definitely the marble island right in the center of the room with its jewelry drawers, inserts and even more cabinet space.

Benji was at the island now, his movements calm and calculated as he sat a lid back on a shoe box. Deven recognized the box immediately from when she helped Deven move. The gun. Was that what he was looking for? She crossed the room in three strides and, not waiting for his permission, snatched the lid back off the box.

Old pictures, papers, and a few credit cards. But no gun. Where was it? Had the police taken it? Had Benji?

Deven grabbed the box and angled it to Benji, though she was sure he could clearly see inside. "Where is it?" she demanded.

"Where is what?"

"Don't play dumb with me. The gun. You knew it was here."

Benji just stared, not confirming nor denying the accusation. His silence was admission enough and she scoffed at the realization. "Oh wow, I see. Is that why you wanted to meet me? To bring me here because you knew I had a key, and you were trying to steal some stuff from my sister? Really, Benji?"

Benji's face crinkled in shock, then absurdity. "Wow, is that what you think?"

"So, you're telling me, I'm making stuff up?" Deven tossed back, pointedly. "You're not here to take anything?" Her eyes squinted, almost daring him to lie.

To her surprise, he didn't. He let out a breath and glanced away from her stare, his expression wary. "Look, it's not like that." His voice was earnest this time, but Deven kept her guard up.

She nodded to the open shoe box still in her hand. "You took her gun?"

"No." Benji lifted his hands, palms out. "I was looking for it, but I didn't take it. I swear. It wasn't here."

"Is that why you brought me to her place?"

The conflict flickering on his face was minimal, but clear. To tell, or not to tell. She waited and her gaze never faltered, another silent dare.

"Not exactly," he decided with a sigh. "Part of the reason was for the gun, yes. And some other stuff. But I am concerned about Kennedy. I swear. She's like my family too and I've always looked out for her, haven't I?"

He had a point. A small one, but a point, nonetheless. Still . . . "Why were you trying to get the gun?"

"It's not . . ." He paused, and she could tell he was choosing his words carefully. "It's not registered to Kennedy. I don't want her to get in any kind of trouble."

Deven's eyes rounded. "She stole a gun?"

"No, she didn't steal it." Benji's exasperation was becoming more and more evident. "I gave her the gun. It's not stolen. I just don't want the police to trace it back to me. That's all."

So, something illegal. Her assumptions about him had been right. "Is my sister dead?" she asked. Her voice was so calm, given the situation, it surprised herself.

The question seemed to extinguish his combativeness and Benji gave a helpless shrug. Under the tough exterior, he was visibly hurting. That part was transparent. "I really don't know," he said. "She could be and that's why I'm worried. Because I don't know."

His confession weakened her. In one sloppy motion, Deven knocked the jeans on the floor and dropped onto the chaise. This was too much. So, the woman, the picture, the drugs? It didn't make sense. It was like, all the pieces were there but they just didn't fit. She felt like she was looking at things through a very weird, very distorted kaleidoscope. There seemed to be a pattern, but the more she analyzed, the more it just gave her a headache.

Deven looked to Benji who just stood back, watching, waiting. *Debating.* "Benji, what is going on?" she pleaded. "Please tell me. Was she on drugs? Was it suicide?"

"Your sister . . ." A beat. "Kennedy may have made a few enemies in her lifetime."

"Enemies? Why? Doing what?"

"She had a stalker before." Benji sighed and now it was his turn to sit down. Deven scooted over to make room, still in shock about his revelation. "It was years ago," he went on. "An ex. He . . . killed somebody to get to Kennedy then he came after her."

"Wh—what happened to him?"

Another pause, this time longer. "The police got to him," he said simply and Deven couldn't tell if he was lying again. "He's not the issue though," Benji went on. "The issue is, because she's had a stalker before, she could have another one. She was saved last time, but what if . . ."

He left the scenario suspended between them and something clicked. Deven remembered the man with the locs, the one she thought was following them at the mall months prior. Fear, then guilt coursed through her like a bolt of lightning. Was the mystery man Kennedy's stalker? Oh God, she should've said something. She should've known.

Benji must have noticed how ashen she became because he touched her hand. "Deven, what is it?"

"The mall," she whispered. "Kennedy and I went to the Fashion District a few months ago and there was this guy. I didn't think he was following us, but I saw him a couple times while we were shopping."

"What did he look like? Can you describe him?"

"Um, he had locs," she said. "Black guy, kind of tall, I think handsome . . ." Deven closed her eyes, trying to picture that day. But she was met with scraps of memory and a vague image of a man with a face too blurry to pull details from. "Dammit. I don't remember. What does her ex look like?"

Benji shook his head. "No, it's not him. I promise you."

She started to ask how he could be so sure but decided she would rather not know. Nor could she trust he would be 100% honest, especially if he was doing something illegal. She thought for a moment, the next idea causing her to jump to her feet.

"Wait, what if it's not him, but another somebody," she said. "Kennedy told me she had started seeing someone. Maybe she's got some kind of proof of the new guy around here. You think?"

Benji's eyebrows drew together in consideration. "That's possible. Did she tell you if she was going out of town with someone, or by herself?"

"She didn't say."

"Okay, I'll keep looking around in here and see if I can find something, maybe even proof of her trip to the Dominican Republic. You check in the bedroom."

It was probably just her paranoia, but Deven got the feeling he was trying to steer her out of this room. But she was too focused to worry about it right then. The possibility of this being a step in the right direction was way too coincidental to ignore.

She nodded and made a beeline for the bedroom, leaving Benji to look, or hell, not look. She didn't care at that point. A friend of his or not, Kennedy was *her* sister. And she would figure out what the hell was going on. Even if she had to do it alone.

Kennedy's bedroom was supposed to be a little larger than her spare bedroom-closet, but with the elaborate furniture, Deven certainly couldn't tell. The canopy bed was way too big for the space, piled with covers and decorative pillows that made the arrangement too high as well as too wide. Despite the piece dominating the room, she had managed to squeeze in two nightstands punctuating the bed and an armoire, albeit empty, in the corner. A flat screen TV and soundbar was mounted on the wall, swiveled to the precise angle for perfect viewing from the leather headboard. A set of French doors opened to an adjoining bathroom. Deven started in there first.

The air suddenly felt different, colder. Almost haunted, Deven thought with a shudder. She scanned the tile floor, the walk-in shower and jacuzzi with various bath bombs and shower gels, and other smell-goods collected around the lip of the tub. Hanging on the door of the shower were two towels and two washcloths, used but clearly placed there to dry. She wondered if the woman, the Kennedy in question, was in here when she was discovered. It was eerie to think about and Deven's gaze lowered to the floor as if a body would be lying right at her feet. Of course, there was nothing.

Deven took to the sink next, flipping open the cabinet door to push past toiletries, pads, and shampoo. She leaned up and, noticing the protrusion of the mirror, pulled it open. There were a few empty pill bottles turned on their sides on the shelf. Bottles for medicine she had never heard of. One-by-one, Deven shoved a few of them into the pocket of her jacket. She would have to do some internet searches on these when she returned home later.

Back in the bedroom, Deven went for the nightstands next. One was completely empty, except for some lipstick tubes and a couple pairs of earrings. The other one contained what looked like receipts and credit card statements. Discouragement was beginning to settle as Deven absently pushed past the paperwork. Then, something caught her eye, and she pulled the photos into view. The first was a sonogram. Kennedy's? And to her trained eye, the baby was about twelve weeks gestation, or roughly three months. Deven fingered the top of the picture, noting that it had been severed where the mother's name and doctor would be printed. Had Kennedy been pregnant? And she'd hidden it?

Deven's eyes shifted to the second picture and her confusion only intensified, overshadowing her previous discovery. What the hell was Kennedy doing with a picture of Paul?

# Chapter Ten

*Excerpt from the diary of Kennedy (Age 11)*

*Every other weekend I go to visit my daddy. My mom meets him at this gas station because she says she doesn't want him to know where we stay. Deven goes with us, and she gets to sit in the front because she's almost thirteen. I'll be twelve next month and maybe then I can sit in the front. So I have to sit in the back by myself and I don't say much because I know I talk a lot sometimes and it gets on everybody's nerves. But Deven and Mommy sing together and I just listen to them.*

*My daddy says I'm his baby girl and he is nice, but he can never really do much because he's always working. So, when I go over to see him, I have to stay in the bedroom a lot because he has company. Or sometimes he leaves me at home by myself and I get really bored and really lonely because I don't have anyone to play with over there. A few times he has stayed out all night and I got scared but he tells me not to tell my mom because she would be really mad at both of us. So that's our little secret. But he lives in an apartment, so he tells me I don't have anything to worry about because he has really nice neighbors and they look out for me while he's away. The only bad thing about my daddy's house is that it always smells like smoke and it stinks but I don't tell him because I don't want to hurt his feelings. And he says he's trying to stop smoking and he never smokes in front of me. Just on the steps outside with some men from the other apartments.*

*I love my daddy a lot. When he's not working, we do fun things together and he buys me stuff sometimes. Like my dolls. I want to make clothes when I grow up and my daddy buys me all these doll clothes so I can dress them up. Now that is fun. I wish it was like that all the time.*

*I'm going over to spend the weekend with him, and he says he has a surprise for me. I can't wait to see what it is!*

# Chapter Eleven
# Before

The headache woke her first. The shards of pain like nails grating across the length of her brain to the point tears stole from her lids and dribbled down her cheeks. Deven moaned and winced at the sting of raw tissue coating the inside of her throat. A chorus of beeps and buzzes echoed, and she blinked away the fog clouding her vision. A hospital room. She should've known by the stench of antiseptic permeating the air between the pale blue walls. The realization of her whereabouts had her eyes shutting as a tumble of memories came barreling back full force.

*They were dead.*

Despite the dull ache throbbing in her abdomen, Deven turned on her side and pulled her knees to her chest. The fetal position was somewhat comforting because it reminded her of her baby. No, babies. Plural. *It* had become *they* and *they* had become *dead*, all in a matter of hours. There was no preparation, no explanation. And poor Leslie had tried her best to offer her support. *Miscarriages happen all the time. You did nothing wrong.* Deven had quoted the same speech herself on many occasions.

Except this time, she wasn't the nurse, she was the patient. And these just weren't some random babies. They were hers. So, the comfort had felt more mocking than genuinely sympathetic.

But Leslie was more tolerable than the rest of her coworkers. The news of Deven's miscarriage was a hot topic and nurses revolved through her door for two days straight offering their disingenuous condolences and disguising their nosiness with concern. Deven hated being the subject of ridicule, yet again, but after a while, she was too heartbroken to care.

She toyed with a little piece of fabric from her sheet, not bothering to turn over or hell even respond for that matter, when there was a knock at the door. Whoever it was would just come on in. They always did, with or without her permission.

"Hey, Sis." Kennedy's voice floated across the room as she entered, closing the door behind her. Her sister had called damn near every hour on the hour through the duration of her stay, but this was her first time visiting.

She rounded the hospital bed, a rose and lilies bouquet in her arms. If it had been anyone else, Deven would have continued to ignore the person. But since this was her sister, she managed an appreciative smile.

"How are you feeling?" Kennedy asked.

"I've been better."

"I know, Sis." She placed the vase on the bedside table and glanced around the quaint hospital room for a chair she could pull close. Seeing none, she resorted to the pullout sofa near the window. A Nike duffle bag was slung over her shoulder which she sat beside her. "I stopped by your place and packed some stuff." She gestured to the bag. "Change of clothes, toothbrush, snacks . . . I didn't know how long they would keep you."

Deven nodded her appreciation and watched Kennedy smooth her hair back into place. It was freshly done, she noticed. And she was dressed especially nice for a weekday. Skinny leg jeans, white leather Gucci boots, and a matching leather jacket with fur on the collar and cuffs that fell to her knees. She shrugged out of her outerwear now, revealing one of those white oversized turtleneck sweaters.

Deven suddenly felt embarrassed because she knew she looked like hell. She shifted on her back to keep the IV needle in her arm from pinching. "Date night?" she guessed with only the slightest hint of envy.

Kennedy's subsequent smirk let her know the assumption was accurate. "Something like that," she said. "But I wanted to stop in first and make sure you were okay and bring your overnight bag. You need anything?"

"No, they're just watching to make sure my bleeding gets regulated."

"When do you think they'll release you?"

Deven shrugged. Whenever they decided couldn't be quick enough.

"Well, you know you can come stay with me," Kennedy offered. "I can look after you."

Even in the midst of her angst, Deven had to chuckle at the irony. "Little sister taking care of the big sister," she mused. "Mom would be so proud."

The air chilled, as it often did whenever she mentioned their mother. But Kennedy quickly recovered to lighten the mood once more. "Hey, you would do the same for me," she said with a half shrug. "That's what we've always done, right? Look out for each other."

"Yeah, I appreciate you. I think I'll be okay though." Wishful thinking, but it helped to say it out loud. "I have to get back into some kind of normalcy. Miscarriages happen. That's life."

"Yeah, that's life." Kennedy's murmur was heavy, and she gazed off as if reflecting on something long ago. Something not entirely present. Because Deven kept staring, she gave a brief nod, silent admission of what she knew they both were thinking.

Deven's heart immediately cracked open and not only her pain but the pain she now shared with her sister. "Oh my God," she whispered. "You've had a miscarriage? When was this? Why didn't you tell me?"

Kennedy swiped at a tear that had escaped her eye. Her smile was forced, but courageous. "Because that was something I didn't want to burden you with."

"Burden? Kennedy come on, nothing dealing with you is a burden."

"You're a fixer, Deven," she said. "You always try to fix stuff. That's why you picked the perfect profession. The miscarriage was just something I didn't want you trying to fix for me. It's just my own damn karma."

Deven frowned at her choice of words. "I hardly think that's karma. Come on now."

Kennedy gave a look in return. It wasn't exactly readable, but she quickly shifted gears with a shake of her head. "All I know is"—she rose and stepped up to the side of the bed—"you need to stop worrying about other people's problems and focus on trying to get better."

"Yeah, some fixer, huh? I'm so worried about everyone else and look where that has gotten me." Deven was starting to sound like the poster child for depression. She hadn't meant to appear so operatic. And certainly not when she had company that had genuinely come to lift her spirits.

Kennedy leaned over and planted a peck on Deven's forehead. "Nope, you're not going to do that," she chided. "You can be hurt but you're not going to feel guilty for things you can't control."

She was right. And Deven would pick herself up. Later. Right now, she just needed to wallow. Her hand went to her belly. It was still somewhat firm, but it definitely felt hollow now, only further amplified by the compounding guilt. Maybe if she had wanted them more, had taken better care of herself, had made the babies a priority. She had even withheld their presence from their father. She had never felt so low. And selfish. "You think it's still worth me telling Justin about them?" she asked.

Kennedy's mouth thinned into a disapproving line. "You think he's going to make you feel better?" The question was rhetorical, so Deven didn't bother answering the obvious. He certainly couldn't, especially with him being in Baltimore.

"He's coming in town tomorrow," Deven said with an exhausted sigh. "He's going to want to know why I don't want to see him right now."

"There you go worrying about other people again," Kennedy said with a playful pop on her shoulder. "So what if you hurt his feelings? For once, Deven needs to take care of Deven. Okay? Promise me."

Deven nodded. She couldn't bring herself to agree, no matter how right her sister was. "Anyway," she said, tugging at the sleeve of Kennedy's sweater. "Enough about me. Tell me about this new man of yours."

"Oh girl!" Kennedy turned then, as if remembering her plans. "I meant to ask you. Is your car still here?"

"Yeah, it's in the employee parking lot. Why?"

"You'll let me borrow it? Just for today," she added quickly. "We had to take my car to the shop earlier, so I had Benji drop me off."

Deven was already reaching for her purse to sift for her keys. "Sure, but you know you don't have to explain. You know you can use my car anytime. Only thing is, you'll have to pick me up to take me home when they discharge me." She held out the keys for Kennedy who accepted them with a nod.

"Of course."

"So, Benji, huh?" A knowing grin spread on her face as Deven watched her sister.

Kennedy quickly dismissed the budding insinuation. "Girl please, it is not like that," she said. "You know Benji is my friend. He's in town on some business and we're just catching up a little. That's all."

Something seemed to glint in Kennedy's eyes, and it was clear she wasn't bothering to hide her blush. The girl looked smitten, and it was sickeningly cute.

"So, is this little date thing with Benji?"

"No, not Benji. Someone else." Typical Kennedy. How did she keep up with them all?

"Who is he?" Deven pressed.

Kennedy tossed her jacket over the crook of her arm. "Nobody important," she said with a wink. "Just having a little fun. But I better go before he starts looking for me."

"Okay well be careful, Sis. Remember I told you, boyfriends are smart—"

"Husbands are dumb," she quoted. "Yeah, I know. Trust me though. I'm not even thinking about marriage right now. But if I do, you'll be the first to know."

Deven watched her sashay from the room. If she didn't know any better, she could've sworn her *devenstinct* was signaling a looming sense of trepidation about Kennedy's brief visit. But after everything that had just happened with the loss of her babies, she figured it was probably just hormones. Those, like everything else in the past few days, had been completely nonsensical.

———◆———

"The voicemail box is full."

Restrained frustration had Deven jabbing the button on her cell to hang up, for the fifth time. *Where was she?*

Deven held her abdomen as she eased back down onto the

hospital bed. She was fully dressed in the clothes Kennedy had brought the day before, and she was armed with pain meds and pads for her at-home aftercare. The nurse would be in any moment with discharge papers, so she was ready to leave. Had *been* ready to leave. Being poked and prodded for four days in the hospital under the scrutiny of her coworkers had left her restless, exhausted, and irritable. She wanted nothing more than to get back home, scrub off her misery, and lay in the comfort of her own bed. But it didn't seem like that would be happening as quickly as she would have liked.

Deven frowned as she dialed Kennedy's number again. And again, she was met with the same operator tone, indicating Kennedy's phone was off or she just wasn't answering. Both scenarios were equally strange. She should've been on her way. Actually, she should've been there hours ago, if Deven was tracking the minutes.

They had spoken earlier that morning while Deven was nibbling her way through an insipid breakfast of oatmeal, eggs, and fruit. Kennedy had said she would be leaving within the hour to pick her up and she would take her to a brunch spot for something more appetizing. Kennedy had texted a quick *on my way* message at around eight-thirty. Deven's eyes lifted to the wall clock, the hands nearing noon. She was upset, rightfully so, but concern was beginning to weigh in.

The knock at the door dispelled all worry and Deven sighed in relief. "About time," she called rising as the door open. Not Kennedy, but Janice, the nurse director and Deven's supervisor. Janice hadn't bothered to come by at all so her visit now was a little bit of a surprise. Not that Deven should've expected niceties from her.

Janice had the 'short-woman-complex;' her direct demeanor often misconstrued as callous, no thanks to her military background. But she seemed to wear her bitch-badge with honor. Deven had never seen Janice so much as crack a smile, which was sometimes off-putting given their line of work. But as she stood just inside the doorway, Deven noticed she seemed softer, somewhat pleasant.

"Hey, how are you doing this morning?" She continued to stand by the door, as if waiting on permission to approach.

"I'm okay. A little sore, of course."

"Of course." Janice folded her hands in front of her, but still, she didn't budge from her position. "Listen, I wanted to talk with you about your leave options."

And there it was, the bitch-badge was back on display. Deven should've known it was more to her visit than just compassion. "Okay, what about it?"

"Do you need some time off?"

The question seemed insensitive given the circumstances. But if it was left up to Janice, she probably would have Deven clock in at that moment and help with patient intake. Deven counted to five to keep her temper in check. She didn't want to lose her job for cussing out her boss. "Yes, I was going to take some time."

"How much?"

*One. Two. Three.* "I hadn't thought about it honestly, Janice."

"Okay, well you don't have much PTO. Maybe only a few hours, so . . ." She trailed off for Deven to comment. She didn't. They both knew Janice could approve sick leave at her discretion. Now whether she would or not, was a different story. Some of the nurses had already said Janice could go rampant on her power-trip sometimes, throwing around her authority as she saw fit. So now, Deven didn't know if the conversation was meant for her to ask, grovel, beg, or all of the above.

Like a reprieve, Deven's phone vibrated in her hand, and she silently thanked the high Heavens for the interruption. "Okay, let me get discharged and get home to rest for a bit," she said. "And

I'll let you know. I have to take this, excuse me." Then in an effort to dismiss her, Deven answered her phone right in her face, praying it was her sister. "Hello, Kennedy?" Janice rolled her eyes, but she took a hint and backed out of the room.

"Hey Deven." Not Kennedy. Paul.

Deven struggled to keep the exasperation out of her voice as she slid her eyes to the clock. "Hey, Paul. How are you?"

"I'm good. Just checking on you. How are you?"

*Sore, and pissed, thanks to Kennedy and now Janice. Exhausted. Ready to go home. Grieving.* But admitting all that was probably not what he wanted to hear. So instead, she just said, "I'm hanging in there."

"That's good. I know I haven't called because I wanted to give you time to rest, but I have been talking to the nurses to make sure you were okay." He was such a sweetheart. If only . . .

"Thank you, by the way," Deven said, her eyes growing misty at the memory of when she first collapsed. Paul had jumped right into action with making sure she got the medical attention she needed. It had happened so fast, and she knew she'd been nothing but a screaming, crying, bleeding, blubbering mess. And he was right there when she needed someone most.

"No need to thank me," he said, the smile in his voice. "I'm sorry it happened, but glad I was there to help. How long are you staying?"

"I'm actually supposed to be leaving." Deven started to add the bit about Kennedy's no-show, but she figured Paul had already done enough to help. On top of helping with her miscarriage, listening to her complain was probably a little excessive.

"Okay good. Well do you need anything?"

Deven started to decline, but her eyes slid back to the clock once more. "Actually, yes. Do you mind picking me up?"

Of course, he didn't mind. Paul was pulling up within the hour, pushing her out to his Jaguar in one of the hospital wheelchairs. Deven still hadn't heard from Kennedy, but at that point, she would deal with her later.

They rode in comfortable silence, the windows down a crack to let a little of the February air seep through. Deven's head bopped on the leather seat, the quiet purr of the engine threatening to lull her to sleep. She couldn't tell if it was the car, the company, or the fast-food burger he'd brought and insisted she eat, but Deven was completely satiated. And for a brief moment, she had completely forgotten about her pain. She had Paul to thank for that.

Just as quickly as the thought came, Deven felt a surge of guilt. This should've been Justin, comforting and nursing her back to health. And she hadn't even told him what was going on. She had wondered what, if anything, she would say to him once he called. He hadn't, but Deven didn't know if that was a good or bad thing. And it did nothing to calm her nerves.

"I did want to give you something," Paul spoke up as he pulled a business card from the middle console. He held it out and Deven accepted it with an inquisitive frown.

"What's this?"

"A therapist," he said. "Dr. Felicia Bradshaw. She's really good with grief counseling and . . . well I didn't know if it would help considering those feelings because of the loss of Jamie. Just everything." He seemed flustered but his benevolence had Deven's spirits lifting. He was truly a sweetheart.

"Thank you," she said and tucked the card in her purse. Maybe she would get up enough nerve to use the reference. Either way, it was so extremely thoughtful of him that she couldn't even be offended.

Paul pressed a button on his touch-screen radio and immediately, an instrumental ballad of a jazz song flooded the car. Deven recognized the saxophone belting out the chords to Michael Jackson's "You Are Not Alone."

"You like jazz?" he asked, turning up the dial to raise the volume.

"I do, but I don't think this really counts as jazz."

Paul feigned offense. "This definitely counts. Just listen to the notes." He hummed along to the music, wiggling his fingers in the air as if he were playing an imaginary piano. Deven relaxed in amusement.

"Okay, it's not classical jazz. More so contemporary," she said. "I'll let it slide because it's the King."

"You know I'm just teasing with you. I'm not a big jazz fan. Not like Amber."

Deven turned to watch the city zip by outside of the window. He didn't realize his absent comment had ruined the mood, though she knew it was innocent enough. A friend talking about his girlfriend. That's what normal, platonic friends did. So, why did she feel so damn insulted? She wanted to inquire more about Amber, but it didn't feel like her place. Where did they meet? What did she look like? Why *her*? Things were different now. Paul may not have realized it, but Deven certainly did. She would never admit it to him, but his attraction to her was part of that alluring chemistry between them. Now, Deven just felt awkward in his presence.

The tension had shifted, thick and suffocating. Paul obviously sensed it too. Deven felt him looking at her profile, but she just swallowed and kept her eyes trained on the road.

"Hey, I'm sorry about that," he voiced to break the stilted silence. "That was inconsiderate of me."

She glanced at him in confusion. What was he apologizing for? That's when she read the pained look in his eyes, and she wanted to do nothing but reach out and console him. She had forgotten all about Amber being pregnant. No wonder he felt bad for bringing her up during her bereavement. Truth of the matter was, that wasn't what bothered her at all. But rather than correct him,

Deven was just satisfied he wouldn't feel obligated to bring her up again.

Paul pulled up to the curb in front of Deven's apartment building and got out to open her door. She didn't necessarily need his assistance, but it felt nice when he circled his arm around her waist and held her close, bracing against her weight. Her stomach muscles ached and stretched under the pressure of gravity, indicative of the pain medicine wearing off. If she could just get to her apartment, she could take her medicine with a shower, and—

"Uh, hey Deven."

Deven's head whipped up at the familiar voice and she suddenly felt lightheaded.

Justin stood on the sidewalk, a scowl etched on his face, his glare bouncing between the couple. If Paul hadn't been gripping her so tight, reflexes would've had her snatching out of his arms. Even if it did make her look as guilty as she felt.

Paul either was trying to keep the mood light or pretend Justin wasn't shooting daggers his way. He shifted to get a better grip on Deven and extended his hand in the man's direction. "Hey. Paul," he introduced himself, not waning when Justin didn't accept it. "I'm Deven's doctor."

It wasn't entirely the truth, but it wasn't entirely a lie either. The title was easier than trying to rationalize the nuisances of their relationship. Justin merely lifted an eyebrow, clearly not convinced. "Doctors still make house calls these days?"

Paul chuckled to mask his discomfort. "And friend," he added. "Deven just needed a ride home from the hospital."

Deven inhaled sharply and began to squirm from his grasp. *Pleeease, shutup, shutup, Paul.* "Thanks for the ride," she said dismissively. As much it pained her (physically and emotionally), she stepped from his arms and stood next to her boyfriend. Justin was seething, that was more than obvious, and she prayed he would remain quiet until she could get him upstairs.

Paul's face wrinkled in confusion, but he took the hint. "Okay, well it was nice to meet you . . ." He waited for Justin to fill in the dead air with his name. But like a stubborn child, Justin remained silent.

"I'll talk to you later," Deven said, not really sure if that would happen. Paul nodded and escaped to the sanctuary of his car. She couldn't even be mad at his hasty retreat. Justin had made the interaction unnecessarily difficult and embarrassing as hell. She wouldn't be surprised if Paul didn't bother with her again.

The duffle bag and her purse were heavier now, and she switched them to her other shoulder, wincing under the weight. Justin didn't seem to notice, or care, for that matter. "So, who was that?"

She groaned and clutching her stomach, headed for up to her apartment. "My friend," she mumbled.

"Yeah, I heard. And doctor. What was he doing bringing you home?"

No mention of the obvious pain she was in, no mention of the fact Paul had relayed she was in the hospital, no mention of why she even needed a doctor. Deven should have felt relieved he was asking the wrong questions, as insecure and inconsiderate as it was.

In his rush, Justin had left the apartment door wide open. Deven shuffled through, nearly stumbling on the luggage he had left right in the middle of the floor. "You didn't tell me you were here," she said, making her way to the bathroom.

"And you didn't tell me you would be out with your *friend*." Justin's emphasis had Deven rolling her eyes.

"He brought me home. That's it."

"Where is your car?"

Good question, but that was none of his business. "Look, I've had a rough morning," she said, finally. "You've clearly had a rough morning—"

"No, I've had a rough night," he corrected. "Because I fly in to surprise my lady, and lo and behold she's spent the night elsewhere."

Deven whirled around at the insinuation. "If you were so worried about me, why didn't you call then?" He didn't have an answer and she didn't expect one. Sighing, she stepped into the bathroom and shut the door in his face. She couldn't be sure, but it sounded like he was packing up after he stomped from the door. Good, let him leave.

She eased down onto the toilet and at the same time, searched her purse for her cell phone. Where the hell was Kennedy? Now, she was for sure worried. Deven dialed her number again, already preparing to hear that stupid operator voice once more. To her surprise, Kennedy picked up. Sirens were blaring in the background nearly drowning out the sound of Kennedy's sobs. She was mumbling something and Deven held the phone tight to her ear, straining to hear better.

"Kennedy, what's going on?" she was all but yelling.

Kennedy sounded like she was on the verge of a nervous breakdown. She was hyperventilating, nearly making her words inaudible as she wailed through the phone. "Deven, somebody assaulted me!"

# Chapter Twelve

Surprise was an understatement.

Deven sank to Kennedy's bed, the mattress sagging under her weight. A myriad of emotions surged through her mind like a tsunami, but her eyes remained paralyzed on the picture in her hand.

It wasn't like the photo was risqué or anything. Paul was standing on the wooden balcony of some kind of cabin. Judging by the way his face was tinted pink, it was especially cold, despite how he was swaddled in an oversized coat, hat and scarf. A panoramic expanse of mountain terrain spanned behind him, serving as a picturesque backdrop comparable to a postcard. If Deven had to guess, she would assume he was in the Poconos. Which would seem like a completely normal picture to have exchanged among friends or lovers. So, why then, did Kennedy have it?

As far as Deven knew, her sister hadn't even met Paul. He was the acting oncologist for Deven's father, Jamie, so it was she who had to frequent his office during cancer treatments. Plus, before Paul moved his practice, he worked at the hospital with Deven, so they ran in the same circles among hospital staff. As close (or close enough) as Deven felt her friendship was with Paul, even *she* didn't have a casual picture of him. The thought was laced with a twinge of jealousy that felt foul and bitter, though she would never admit that to anyone but herself. Still, the questions lingered, murky with confusion that settled on her mind like smog. And the one woman who had the answers wasn't there.

"Hey, you good?" Benji's voice carried across the room, snatching Deven's attention from her daze. He flicked a questioning look between her and her hands.

Deven debated only briefly before holding the picture in his direction. "Do you recognize him?" She watched Benji's face for some sign of recognition. She wasn't surprised when he shrugged and passed the picture back.

"Nah. I've never seen Kennedy with him."

"Yeah, me neither. But I know him."

"He a friend of yours?"

*Good question.* Deven hesitated over her response, her thoughts flitting over one of her last phone calls with Paul. The dialogue had been very pedestrian, both of them still riding on embarrassment from the run-in with Justin after the miscarriage. In total, the call had lasted an excruciating five minutes. But what had been even more painful was hanging up, not knowing when (or if) she would even talk to him again. So far, she had been right to be concerned. Three months without so much as a word.

"He was my father's doctor," she said, finally, and left it at that.

Benji's nose curled with the news. "Your dad? Did Kennedy ever take him to the doctor or something?"

"Not that I'm aware of."

Deven knew they both were thinking the same things, though neither actually voiced their perplexity. How—better yet *why*—did Kennedy have a picture of Paul? It was too much of a coincidence to ignore; like a clue hidden in plain sight. To what, Deven had no idea. She sure as hell knew Paul had nothing to do with the situation surrounding her sister.

Benji must have read her mind. "I'll look into him."

"That's not necessary."

"Look, Deven. Even if you *think* you know this guy—"

"I *do* know him." *Didn't she?* Deven stood up and folding the picture in quarters, she shoved it in her back pocket. Since Benji was still watching her with that skeptic arch of his brow, she sighed. "Okay, I know this looks weird," she added. "It looks weird to me, too. As far as I know, Kennedy has never even heard of Paul. So . . . let me just talk to him."

"People lie."

She didn't like how his tone was infused with enough pessimism to have her nearly doubting her own notions. "I'll talk to him first," she reiterated. "And I'll let you know how it goes."

"And then?"

"Then we'll talk about it and see what we need to do."

It was clear Benji wasn't satisfied, but instead of another rebuttal, he just shrugged. "I think we're done in here." He didn't wait for a response and Deven didn't offer one. She was consumed with enough uncertainty, and it was making her head hurt. So much so, that it wasn't until she and Benji parted ways, that she realized she hadn't asked him whether he found anything in Kennedy's apartment. Nor had he willingly divulged that information either.

————◦•◦————

Deven didn't even realize she was headed to Paul's office until she saw his building come into view. Interesting that she hadn't been to his office in years, but her muscle memory steered her down the proper streets like it was second nature. Sure, the route was familiar, but everything else was different. Yet, all the torment she had experienced before came barreling back with enough intensity to leave her blinking back tears.

James "Jamie" Reynolds was certainly not one who liked to show weakness. Even when he was diagnosed with stage IV lung cancer, he still maintained that tough and determined exterior. It was never, *I have cancer,* but *they say I have cancer and I'll be glad when I prove them wrong.* Deven had always been close with her dad, but she felt they had grown especially close during those car talks when she was taking him to see Paul. He talked about her mother and how they'd always known they would be together, even when she cheated during an especially drunken night and had an affair. Sure, they had taken a little break to heal from the deception, and another one when they found out the affair had conceived Kennedy, but the two were like magnets, always finding their way back to each other.

One of the very last conversations they'd had in the car had been quieter than usual. Deven knew the entire process was taking a toll on her dad. But for the first time, he appeared completely broken.

"I tell you, karma is something," he had mumbled completely out of the blue.

"Karma? What karma, Daddy?"

"Mistakes you may have made in the past," he said with a shrug. "Things you've done that you wish you could've done better. People you wish you could've treated better."

The comment was random, but he hadn't bothered elaborating. For a moment it was quiet again as Deven drove and Jamie stared out the window, having retreated into the recesses of his own mind. Then, when the silence had stretched for another fifteen minutes, he said, "You'll promise me something?"

"Of course, Daddy."

"You'll promise to take care of your mom for me?"

Deven had hated hearing those words. It meant he had done what she'd tried to keep from doing for the entire year: give up.

"Daddy, don't talk like that."

"Promise me, Deven. I need to know you'll take care of her. And your sister," he added after a brief hesitation.

Deven remembered finding that last bit a little strange. Not unusually so because her dad had pretty much always been welcoming to Kennedy, despite the circumstances under how she was conceived. It was the fact that he'd never seemed to go out of his way to do so.

Instead of agreeing, Deven had begged him not to talk like that because he would always be around. Then she had cranked up the music so they could duet to "Ain't No Mountain High Enough" by Marvin Gaye and Tammi Terrell. And though they were horribly off key and transposed a few of the lyrics, it was a reprieve from the inevitable.

Paul's office was among many in a business park that locals had dubbed "Clinical Campus." Brick buildings were grouped in geometric fashion that spanned fifty acres, all containing various medical practices from wellness to dentistry and gynecology. Deven navigated through the maze of streets and signage to *Lenwood Hematology and Oncology Center*. It was nearing five o'clock, so the adjacent parking lot was nearly empty and Deven had to swallow her rising panic. Impulse had drawn her out here but now she was wishing she had called first. What if Paul wasn't even here? He could have been working on-location at the hospital or gone home for the day. Or worse, what if he was actually here? What would he say about Kennedy? Deven realized she was dreading that part even more.

Deven pulled out her phone and, instead of calling Paul's cell like she had been accustomed to doing many times prior, she dialed his office. Part of her expected no one to pick up since it was so late in the evening. No, not expected. Hoped.

"This is Lenwood Hematology and Oncology," the cheery receptionist piped. "How may I assist you?"

Deven hesitated, drumming her fingers on the steering wheel. She craned her neck to look at the building. Were her answers in there? "Hi, my name is Deven. I'm a . . ." Why did this part always stump her? ". . . friend of Paul's. Is he in, by any chance?"

"Yes, he is but he's finishing up with a patient right now. Would you like to make an appointment or leave a message?"

"I'll leave a message," she decided, though she wasn't sure at all what she was going to say. *Hey, I know we haven't spoken in some months, but my sister is either dead or missing and I'm guessing you know what happened to her.* She was sure she sounded as crazy as she felt.

The receptionist had already transferred the call, but Deven didn't give Paul's voicemail message box time to answer before she hung up. Maybe it was a bad idea to come. What could Paul possibly tell her about her sister that she didn't already know? *Everything.* The thought sent a shudder racing up Deven's spine. Kennedy's apartment had brought more questions than answers, and she wasn't sure if she was more scared not knowing or knowing what her sister had been up to. Speaking of questions . . .

The pill bottles were bulging from her pocket and Deven pulled them out to look closer at the labels. Were these the medications from the overdose? It was probably still too soon to hear back from the police for the toxicology, but now this seemed like some incriminating evidence to further solidify their suspicions about the woman in the morgue. Maybe it wasn't wise to mention the medicine to anyone, not even Benji. Not until she found out what the hell was going on.

Deven eyed the prescription labels. *Mirtazapine* was an antidepressant written out to Kennedy. So was the *Tramadol* which was for pain (though it didn't indicate where). Deven placed the bottles in her cup holder and fished in her pocket for the next two.

*Diazepam* she knew was for seizures and anxiety. She was about to put it down when something else on the label caught her eye. Erika Garrett, the label read. Not Kennedy. Deven picked up the other bottle and zeroed in on the name. This one was Yolanda Hyatt. Who were these women and why was their medicine in Kennedy's bathroom?

The sudden vibration startled a gasp from her lips. Deven released a breath and took a weary look at her phone, the unfamiliar number glaring against the translucent screen. She hesitated, only briefly, before deciding to answer. At this point, what else could surprise her?

"Hey Deven." Paul's voice floated through the receiver to greet her. An unexpected welcome. He seemed to have a knack for that.

"Uh, hey."

"I saw you called me," he explained at her prolonged silence. "I was wrapping up with a patient. You didn't leave a message." There was an awkward pause. "Is everything okay?"

The question was the needle to pop her restrained emotions, and Deven's tears erupted like a cannon. Paul's voice was inaudible through her sobs, but she detected the concern, which for some reason made her cry even harder.

"I'm on my way," Paul was saying. "Where are you? At home?"

"No." Deven felt a wave of embarrassment. "I'm . . . outside."

"Outside where?"

"Your office."

His shock was nearly tangible even through the phone. More silence inflated between them until Deven was sure he had hung up. Probably fed up with her bullshit. Then she glanced up through the windshield and saw him emerge from the building, his eyes scanning the parking lot, the phone still clutched to his face. "Where are you?" he asked. "Come inside. Please."

Obediently, Deven hung up and towed herself from the vehicle. The crying had exhausted her, not to mention the added humiliation once Paul looked her way. To her surprise, and appreciation, he looked anything but pitying at her weakened state. Only worried. They walked in silence into the building, Paul leading the way up the stairs to the second-floor suite.

Inside, the lobby was now empty, the receptionist having already left for the day. Deven wondered absently, if it was the same kind receptionist who had helped her on many a visit with her father. They passed down a long hallway with, what Deven recalled, were examination and testing rooms.

The office was comprised of three oncologists, Paul being the youngest and most recent addition to an already successful practice. Because of his short tenure, he had one of the smaller offices between them, but still just as grand with its oversized desk and two chevron chairs. Save for a few abstract paintings he'd placed on the walls, it looked exactly the same as she remembered. A creature of habit, she had teased him once.

Paul closed the door behind her and rounded the desk, taking a seat in the executive chair. Deven stood in place, not really sure what she should do. "You know, you can sit down," he invited, his voice filled with understanding at her discomfort. "Unless you would prefer to stand."

She would prefer to leave, but Deven kept that thought to herself. She sat down in one of the chairs and eyed his desk. File folders were neatly stacked, each labeled and tabbed with names that were written in the handwriting only he could read. A single frame sat on his desk, the picture angled in his direction, which only piqued her curiosity about the image. He worked from a laptop which was already closed, a sign she was keeping him from leaving. That made her feel even worse and again, she regretted coming.

"How have you been?" he started. The leather squeaked with his movements as he leaned back in the chair.

"I've had better days."

"What's wrong, Deven?" He paused, clearly unsure of how to broach the subject. "Is it the miscarriage?"

Interesting how she wished it was something as uncomplicated as that. "No. Not really."

A shadow fell over Paul's face, something dark and unreadable but it obviously had dampened his mood. "I know how you feel," he murmured. "We haven't spoken in a while, so you don't know. Amber and I lost the baby."

"Paul, I'm so sorry." And she was. That pain was all too recognizable, and she wouldn't wish it on her worst enemy.

He held up his hand to cease any further condolences. "I guess I didn't realize at the time how much it affects you."

Deven reached across the desk, her hand finding his. "Yes, you did. You were there when I needed you. You helped me."

"Did you see the therapist I recommended?" Paul shifted gears a little.

"Yeah."

"And? How has it been going?"

Deven shook her head to dispel further inquiry. "That's not why I'm here, Paul. I need to talk to you about my sister."

A frown creased his handsome face. "Your sister? I don't remember meeting her."

"Kennedy."

He shook his head to indicate the name didn't register at all and his eyes crinkled with his apparent confusion. Deven sighed and dipped into her pocket for the picture. She unfolded the paper and slid it across the desk.

Paul's frown deepened when he saw the image. "Where did you get this?"

"It was in my sister's bedroom."

"I don't get it." His eyes flickered between the picture and Deven as if she were the culprit. "Who is your sister again?

Kennedy? I don't remember you bringing her with you with your dad."

"I didn't. We don't share the same dad so she wouldn't have come. Does the name ring a bell at all? Maybe you met her at a bar or something?"

Again, Paul shook his head, this time slower. Deven could see the gears turning, clearly not making any type of correlation. "There's not many people I would've given a picture to," he said. "Hell, I don't even remember giving this picture to anyone."

"This is crazy." An overwhelming cloud of anxiety began to settle and Deven stood to pace. None of it made sense. "Who took the picture?"

"I don't remember who took this picture specifically. It was a couples' trip so a group of us went to the mountains. Everyone was just snapping pictures."

"And Kennedy wasn't one of the friends?"

"No, she wasn't. These were some friends from college. Just two other couples, me and Amber."

Deven stood looking at the window but not seeing anything. Her thoughts were in shambles and causing a headache to brew. "Maybe one of them is friends with Kennedy," she reasoned.

"Okay, that could explain the how. But why would they give a picture of me to her?"

"I don't know." Deven released a frustrated breath and massaged her temples. The budding ache in her head was now a full-blown hammering and it was causing her eyes to water. "Listen, something is not right. My sister is missing, or maybe dead, or—"

"Wait, your sister is dead?" Paul's eyes grew round like saucers. "Oh my God, Deven. I'm so sorry."

"No, listen Paul. I don't think she is. I mean—I don't know what's going on but I'm not sure if she's dead. There was a woman found who they say is her but . . ." Deven threw up her arms, completely spent of both energy and ideas. She felt like she was spinning in circles pleading for answers that weren't there. She didn't even realize Paul had crossed to stand with her until she felt his presence pepper goosebumps on her skin. Then his hands were on her shoulders, turning her body to face him. His smile was completely platonic, a direct contrast to the *fuck me* vibes Deven was savoring from his woodsy cologne that assaulted her nostrils. Lord, she was a complete mess.

"Okay, I'm not sure what's going on," he said. "But we'll figure this out, okay? Have you talked to your mom about your sister? Her friends?"

Deven didn't even have the strength to verbalize a response, so she merely shook her head. Truth was, what friends? Outside of Benji, who else did Kennedy have? The fact that she didn't know had her pursing her lips in shame. She already felt bad as it was, and she refused to give Paul another reason to color his perception of her failures.

Instead of pushing the issue, he merely patted her arms as if he understood. "Okay, I can ask my friends to see if they know her."

"What about Amber? Has she ever mentioned anything about Kennedy?"

"Nope." Paul's tone was clipped. Then, realizing his attitude was more abrasive than he intended, he offered a small smile. "We're not together anymore."

If there was a record for the number of times a person could feel like shit in one sitting, Deven sure as hell was reigning as the champion. Shame stung her face, and she cursed her insensitivity. "I'm so sorry," she said. "I didn't even think to—"

"No, don't worry about it." Paul shrugged as if he didn't care, though the lingering pain was more than evident. "But, to answer your question, no. She never mentioned a friend named Kennedy." To Deven's dismay, he looked to be telling the truth, not that he would have a reason to lie. Unless he was trying to cover up something. Deven had to roll her eyes at her own paranoia. This whole situation was clearly playing with her psyche. Her therapist would have a field day. "Where did your sister work?" Paul asked suddenly.

Deven frowned. "She was a marketing consultant, why?"

"No reason. I just thought maybe she had to watch me for some reason."

"A private investigator?"

Paul averted his eyes, but the motion was enough to indicate that wasn't what he meant. Deven's eyes widened at the realization. "A stalker?" she asked incredulously. "You think my sister was *stalking* you?"

He held up his hands, palms out, to signal his peaceable intentions. "Hey, I don't know," he said. "I'm searching for answers here, too. All of this has me baffled like you."

"Kennedy's not a stalker." *Was she?* She wished her tone could have held more conviction, even if she didn't entirely believe it.

"Okay, let's forget all that," Paul said, gentler this time. "I'll tell you what. You got a picture of her? I may have seen her around with Amber or one of my friends and maybe they called her a nickname or something. I'm better with faces anyway."

Good thinking. Deven began pushing buttons on her cell phone, scrolling and swiping until she had navigated to her gallery. She knew she didn't have many. Kennedy wasn't really one to take pictures, which was crazy given her boisterous personality and gorgeous looks. So, it took a moment for Deven to even find something. Finally, a picture filled her screen. Deven remembered trying to snap the candid while they were out at a restaurant for dinner one night. Kennedy had tried to throw her hand up to block her face, but she hadn't been quick enough, and the movement had caused a little bit of a blur. But still, her face was unmistakable, even with her pout and eye rolling at Deven's spontaneous photo shoot.

Deven angled the phone in Paul's direction, giving him a clear view of her screen. She watched his face for any signs of recognition. Sure enough, it was there. He knew the woman in the picture.

"What the hell?" He seemed angry for some reason as he pointed a finger at the phone. "Why do you have a picture of her?"

"What do you mean? This is Kennedy."

Paul lifted his head with eyes glazed over in shock. "I don't know Kennedy," he said, his words slow as if he were trying to convince himself. "But the woman in this picture is my ex-girlfriend, Amber."

# Chapter Thirteen
## Before

Kennedy wasn't one to show her vulnerability. She'd always been tough, putting on a brave face despite whatever inner turmoil she was going through. Deven had always loved that about her baby sister. She wasn't easily broken. Which made it that much more painful to see Kennedy in a state of distress. Even the strong ones had their breaking points. And clearly this assault had exceeded Kennedy's tolerance.

She sat on the couch with knees drawn to her chest and red-rimmed eyes, relaying the scenario to a stout police officer with lips tinted black from one too many cigarettes. He was nodding and listening, but Deven noticed he looked like his mind was everywhere but present, especially with the scowl on his face. Further evidenced by the way his pen hovered over his notepad but he'd yet to write anything down, she noticed. *The bastard.*

Deven remained perched at the dining room table as she watched, catching snatches of Kennedy's recount of the incident. Apparently, she'd been walking to her apartment building from the parking lot when someone in a navy hoodie had started following her. She'd taken off running and the person had chased her to her door. Deven hadn't even bothered asking where Kennedy had been all day with Deven's vehicle, or why she'd been a no-show at the hospital. She seemed shaken up enough by what happened.

Deven took an absent sip from the bottled water Kennedy had declined, the sweat from the plastic wetting her fingers as she drank. She had missed her medicine dosage and she knew she would be paying for it very soon. The other police officer, the one who had picked her up and brought her back to Kennedy's apartment, re-entered the living room, his thumbs tucked into the belt at his waist. His gait reminded Deven of a country western show where the cop brandishes a Colt and tips his hat saying, "This town ain't big enough for the both of us." He even had a little Texas drawl that did put her in the mind of Yosemite Sam. Deven had to stifle her chuckle with another sip of water, scolding herself to behave. That cop—what did he say his name was, again?—he was nice on the drive over. And honestly between the two of them, Officer "Wild West" was the one who seemed to care about what happened to Kennedy, more so than the other one. It was his idea to search the place, just in case. So Deven was appreciative of his efforts.

"Did you get a good look at him?" the scowling officer interviewing Kennedy asked. His eyes panned the room as if he would see someone there other than the four occupants.

"No." Kennedy's shoulders slumped with the admission. "Can you just have a patrol car or someone sit outside to watch my place?"

"No Ma'am, I'm sorry we can't." Officer Scowl's tone was dismissive. He flipped his blank notepad closed and shoved it in his back pocket. "But if you hear or see anything else, you be sure to call us back."

Officer Wild West tossed Deven, then Kennedy, an apologetic

look. "Everything looks clear, ladies," he reassured. "No signs of a break-in or anything like that. Do you feel comfortable staying here tonight or is there somewhere else you can go?"

"I'll stay here with her," Deven piped up, catching Kennedy's pointed glance in her direction. She looked like she wanted to object, but she didn't speak. "Or I'll take her back to my place," Deven added trying to read her sister's expression. "Either way. I got her." That must've been enough for Officer Scowl because he was nearly out of the door without so much as a farewell.

The other officer, clearly the "good cop" of their little partnership, hung back for a few extra minutes. "Are you going to be okay?"

Kennedy nodded.

Satisfied, he pulled a business card from his pocket. "You call me if you need anything," he said passing the card to her. "I know this can be a little scary, but this was probably just some neighborhood kid trying to terrorize you for shits and giggles. We get a lot of those around here."

Kennedy wasn't appeased, but she nodded again anyway and followed him to the door.

As soon as they were gone, she snapped her locks into place and took one last peek out of the window.

Deven joined her at the glass and watched the men stroll back to their police car. A few neighbors were sprinkled across the parking lot, obviously inquisitive about the cop's presence. One couple looked up to Kennedy's apartment and whispered to each other. But other than that, nothing else looked alarming. No hooded figure waiting in the shadows watching for the uniforms to leave.

Deven waited until they had driven off before she pulled the blinds down and drew the curtains closed. "Are you good, Sis?" she asked.

"Yeah." Kennedy sighed and headed for the kitchen. It was clearly a lie. She didn't look good. But it was something else.

Something Deven couldn't quite put her finger on. It was to be expected that Kennedy would be slightly on edge after the ordeal, but there seemed to be more simmering under the surface than just shock or fear. She was pissed.

Utensils clattered as Kennedy riffled through her drawers and then cabinets. Deven took a seat on the barstool overlooking the kitchen, realizing she was pulling out the makings for a sandwich. She remained quiet but her attitude was loud. *Probably because the police hadn't done much of anything*, Deven assumed. A waste. Seemed like officers weren't good for anything until AFTER something bad happened.

Kennedy placed turkey on white bread and spread mayonnaise on both sides. Then she cut her sandwich in half like she liked it. Deven decided to ignore the fact her sister hadn't asked if she wanted one. She wasn't really hungry anyway. "So, what do you think?" she said as Kennedy bit into her sandwich and chewed thoughtfully. "You want to stay here tonight, or do you want to go back to my place?"

"We can stay here."

"You sure?"

"Yeah." Her voice was curt and Deven couldn't help feeling like she was getting the backlash of Kennedy's anger.

"What's wrong?" she asked when Kennedy continued to eat in vexed silence. Her jaw was doing that clenching thing like it did when she was trying to restrain herself.

"Them bastards didn't even bother looking for—" she smacked her lips to stop her mumbling.

Deven frowned. *Did she know the person?* "What were you going to say? Do you know who it was?"

Kennedy blinked as if she were remembering Deven was even sitting there. "I said, they didn't even bother *looking*," she exaggerated, her forehead crinkling at the miscommunication. "No, I don't know who it was."

Deven nodded, confused at how she had misheard but resolved to let it go. "What about the way the person was built?" she suggested. To make her point, Deven lifted her hands and held her palms apart at varying distances. "Was he or she slimmer, or broader? Breasts? Muscles? Shaped more like a man or woman?"

Kennedy's sigh was laced with irritation. "I'm going to tell you like I told Officer What's-His-Face," she said rolling her eyes. "It was dark, the person had on a hoodie. I couldn't even see the face. And the sweatshirt looked a little baggy. I just don't get why they didn't even search the area," she added with a sulk. "Like they checked in here but why didn't they check outside? Isn't that what they do? Check the perimeter or something?"

Deven chuckled. "You watch too much *Law and Order*," she teased. "But maybe they're right. It was probably just some stupid kid."

"Yeah maybe." Kennedy was clearly not convinced.

Deven watched her sister. She looked as if something was weighing heavy on her mind. Did she know more than she was letting on? "Do you think it could be anyone else?" She studied Kennedy's expression as she spoke. "Someone you know? An ex perhaps?"

Kennedy looked as if she were turning over the idea. "There's this guy I dated once. He was a little . . . possessive. I ended up having to get a restraining order on him."

"What? Who was he? Did you tell the cops?"

She shook her head. "No, it's not like that," she said. "He was harmless, and the restraining order was really me just trying to be petty to prove a point. Besides, that was years ago."

Deven thought of the coincidence at the mall with the man she saw repeatedly. "Did he have locs?" she asked.

Kennedy frowned. "No, why?"

"No reason."

Mirroring an expression that Deven used all too often, Kennedy narrowed her eyes and pursed her lips, signaling her disbelief in the statement. Still, she said nothing and neither woman pushed the issue. *Guess we're both hiding something then,* Deven pondered. But instead of dwelling on it, she changed the subject. "Are you sure you don't want to just go back to my place?" she offered again. "You may be able to sleep a little better there."

"I'll be fine. But hey, you don't have to stay if you don't want to. I know it's late and you're probably tired."

"I'm staying." Deven took her time climbing down from the bar stool. "Just promise me that tomorrow, you'll go to the store and get some security cameras—" She winced as the shooting pain returned full force, throbbing in her lower abdomen like a cramp. Damn, maybe she did need to go home for her pain medicine. She'd been thoughtless to run out of the house without it. But then, she didn't think she was going to be gone too long either.

Kennedy rounded the bar and grabbed Deven's arm in concern. "Are you okay?"

Deven hissed through the ache as it slowly began to ebb. "Yeah. Just the last-minute effects of the miscarriage."

It was as if the word was like a light switch and Kennedy's entire face went ashen. "Oh shit, oh shit, I'm so sorry," she said, her fingers flying to her mouth. "Deven, oh my God, I completely forgot to pick you up!"

"It's cool."

"No, it's not. Damn, I'm an idiot. How are you feeling? What did the doctors say? And I got you out here late with this foolishness when you're the one that needs to be resting."

Deven waved away her sister's concern. Not that it was disingenuous. It just didn't matter anymore. Besides, there were more pressing matters at hand. "I'm fine," she insisted. "Just a lot of bleeding and cramping. It's like a really bad period. I've got some pain medicine but unfortunately I left it at home."

Kennedy was already rushing to the back of the apartment. She returned, moments later, popping the cap on a prescription bottle. "Here, I got some stuff," she said, shaking two white pills into her palm. "It's strong so it'll probably knock you out in less than an hour."

"Well, if that's the case I don't know how much help I'll be staying over," Deven teased.

"I don't need you to protect me, Sis," Kennedy said with a smirk, dumping the medicine into Deven's hand. "It'll be nice to have you over though. We haven't had a sleepover since . . . hell I don't remember when."

"Probably kids."

Kennedy retrieved Deven's bottled water from the table and passed that to her as well. Appreciative, Deven knocked back the pills and chased it with the warm liquid.

"Do you need anything else?" Kennedy asked. "Pads or panties or something for the bleeding?"

"I didn't know you wore panties."

"Oh, you got jokes." Kennedy led the way to her makeshift closet in her second bedroom and immediately began rummaging through a box she'd yet to unpack. Pulling out some sweats, a t-shirt, and sure enough an *unopened* pack of Victoria's Secret cotton bikini panties, she handed them over. "There's some products under the sink in the master bathroom," she said. Deven nodded her thanks and headed to change.

By the time she was ready for bed, Deven had begun to feel the meds kicking in. Thankfully the pain was gone but it had been replaced by the drowsiness that had her struggling to keep her eyes open.

Kennedy, too, had already changed into her pajamas, a satin short and tank top set, and she'd bundled her hair under a bonnet. Deven had figured she'd dozed off but to her surprise, she was sitting up in bed, on the phone when Deven emerged from the bathroom.

"Okay," Kennedy said casting a quick look in Deven's direction. "Love you, too. Bye." She hung up her cell as Deven eased into the bed beside her. *Who could that be?*

"Benji?" Deven guessed.

"No, not him," Kennedy said evasively, as she leaned against her headboard. "A friend of my dad's. I had called him earlier before I called the police, so I was letting him know what they said."

Deven didn't know why the comment sounded odd. Last she knew, Kennedy's dad, Keith, was dead, and before that, prison, for the fifth or sixth time (Deven had long ago lost count). It was one reason, among many, their mother hadn't wanted the man in her daughter's life. Either way, Keith had been into so much criminal activity that any "friends" of his were sure enough, birds of a feather. Why would her sister still be maintaining an active relationship with that crowd?

Deven snuggled against the pillows, the cool material caressing her face and lulling her to relax. "What did he say?"

"Not much," Kennedy said. "He just wanted to make sure I had locked up. I told him you were staying with me, so I was good for the night. I did call Benji too and he'll be here this weekend to install my cameras for me."

"Good."

"Hey, Sis," Kennedy added as Deven began to drift in that gray area between consciousness and unconsciousness. "I'm sorry again about earlier."

Deven couldn't even muster the energy to respond. If she wasn't so sleepy, she would have acknowledged that Kennedy had merely offered an apology. Not once did she mention a reasoning for her mysterious disappearance.

# Chapter Fourteen

*Excerpt from the diary of Kennedy (Age 11)*

My dad's new girlfriend is the B-word. I know I'm not supposed to say it, so I don't want to write it either, but you know what I mean. She doesn't really talk much to me but she's always looking at me and frowning like I've been bad even though I don't do anything. I met her for the first time this weekend. Daddy said he had a surprise for me, and it wasn't a toy or book or doll like I thought. It was his new girlfriend. Daddy invited her over and she brought a lot of groceries and cooked spaghetti and bread and salad. It wasn't as good as my mom's spaghetti because my mom's spaghetti is homemade, and this was just out of a can. But it was okay, I guess. She told me to call her Ms. Erika with a k. (She stressed the k part). The cool thing is she did bring her daughter with her and she is kind of nice but really quiet. My friends at school would call her a nerd. So we didn't really talk much.

*My dad kept telling me to be nice to Ms. Erika with a k so I did. I smiled and asked her questions about what she liked to do and if she liked to skate. But I heard her tell my Daddy I talk too much. I guess she doesn't really like me either. I want to tell my Daddy this, but I think it would hurt his feelings because he seems to really, really like Ms. Erika with a k. I think he loves her like mommy loves Daddy Jamie. I asked Daddy if he wanted to ever get back with Mommy and he said no with the F-word. Then he told me to go to my room. I was sad until he came in later and brought me a cookie and told me that my mom wasn't really a good woman so he couldn't love her anymore. I didn't know what that meant so I asked Deven, and she said that I must've heard wrong because my dad was a jerk and he wanted mommy, but she didn't want him. So he was bitter. Deven then told me that mommy and her daddy were getting back together and I didn't need to ruin that because they were a family. And she was right.*

*When they did get back together, my daddy was really mad about that. But he seemed sad too. That's why I'm kind of okay with him being with Ms. Erika with a k. He needs someone to make him smile again and I guess she does that. He said it's like we're a big, happy family. That's like what Deven brags about. So that part is kind of nice to hear.*

# Chapter Fifteen

She'd lost all sense of reality. That had to be it. Somewhere between leaving Kennedy's apartment and arriving at Paul's office, Deven must have slipped into some Twilight-Zone portal where nonsense made sense and the lines of truth had been blurred into some kind of mirage where it was hard to tell where fact ended and fantasy began.

A cell phone was vibrating, maybe it was hers, maybe it was his. Deven couldn't be sure. But Paul's comment had siphoned all her mobility and she couldn't move if she wanted to. Surely, he was joking. Why, she didn't know. But that would be the only rationale for such absurdity.

Paul grabbed her phone, pinching and spreading his fingers on the screen to zoom in closer on the picture. His eyes narrowed, then widened, a silent confirmation of his earlier analysis. "Oh my God," he whispered. "You know Amber?"

"Did you hear what I said? That's Kennedy."

He shook his head. "I don't get it. How is this Kennedy? Is that her middle name? She never told me you were her sister."

Deven retrieved her phone to look at the picture again, though she was already very familiar with it. It had been a last-minute thing to celebrate Kennedy's promotion. They'd met at a Mexican spot in the city and Deven had mentioned sending the picture to mom. Of course, Kennedy had been opposed but Deven hadn't cared. So, she'd caught what she could, a frowning Kennedy amidst a table of empty margarita glasses and chips and queso dip. Kennedy had never mentioned dating, much less *knowing*, Paul. And where the hell did the Amber-name come from?

Deven's phone vibrated in her hand, an unknown number popping up to temporarily replace the picture. She swiped the screen to ignore the mystery caller and walked back to the chair to have a seat.

"Okay, I need details," she coaxed gesturing for Paul to sit down as well. "Start from the beginning. Where did you meet Kennedy, what happened? Where is she?"

"Wait, is she dead or not?"

"That's what I'm telling you." Deven threw up her hands. "I don't know. That's what they say but I don't know if I believe it."

"Did you see her? The body?"

The memory of her visit to the morgue had a chill running down Deven's spine. She wished she could *un*see it. "They said that it was Kennedy. I mean, the woman favors her . . . but it's not adding up, Paul. The woman she's not—I don't . . ." Deven shook her head to dispel her own apprehension. "Listen, just tell me where Kennedy is. Do you know?"

Paul sighed. "I told you, Amber broke up with me. I haven't talked to her in months."

"Do you have a number for her? An address?"

"She moved," he said with a trace of bitterness. "And blocked me. She was pretty upset about the breakup."

The little sliver of hope Deven had was beginning to dwindle. She sat back in the chair on a dejected breath. "Okay what happened?"

"The breakup?"

"Yeah, that but everything else too," she clarified with a little more urgency in her tone.

"Maybe you know something, and it could help me figure this shit out." Deven was not going to go into one of her underlying reasons for asking about the details of their relationship. She swallowed the hint of jealousy like a potent flavor on her tongue and steeled herself for Paul's revelation.

"We met at the hospital," he said with an absent shrug. "I think she was visiting her mom or brother or someone and we ran into each other—literally—in the elevator."

"She told you her name was Amber?"

He nodded. "Yep, Amber Wright."

"Why would she lie about that?" Deven could only shake her head again as she mumbled more to herself.

"Hell, I didn't know she was lying. I didn't think to ask for her driver's license and birth certificate." It was a weak attempt at humor that neither found funny.

"What else did she say?"

"She was from Charlotte," he continued. "She had a brother. Said she was up here in Jersey on a temporary detail for a year with her job. She was considering relocating but she hated being so far away from family." *Lies, lies. All lies.* "We clicked, started dating . . ." he shrugged. "I'm sure you can fill in the blanks."

Deven grimaced and nodded as she tried not to picture the abundantly kinky sex she figured they had. "Then, she got pregnant?" she prompted.

"Yeah. I thought it was kind of crazy since she told me she was on birth control. But it was what it was."

"Then what?"

"We started planning for the baby. Doctor's appointments and ultrasounds. She would send me pictures—"

Deven's head snapped up. "Pictures? You weren't there?"

"I tried to get off when I could," he said. "But the appointments were at the most inconvenient times. Or she'd have to reschedule.

Like remember when I was at the hospital with your . . ." he trailed off and Deven nodded, knowing he was tiptoeing around her miscarriage tragedy. "She had an ultrasound scheduled," he explained. "I was meeting her at her doctor's office when she said they had sent her to the hospital for blood work and more testing. Something about a low heartbeat. I was meeting her over there and that's when I ran into you and all that happened."

"Did you end up meeting her?"

"No, she had left by the time we got you situated," Paul's comment had Deven offering an apologetic smile. "But she texted me a picture of the ultrasound afterwards and said everything was fine. So, I really didn't expect anything to go wrong."

Paul snatched his cell phone from the desk and scrolled for a second before slanting the phone in Deven's direction. Sure enough, a picture of a sonogram stretched across the screen. The baby looked like a little bean. It reminded Deven of her own sonograms. She noticed it didn't have any details regarding the OBGYN or mother's name, just like the sonogram she'd found in Kennedy's apartment earlier. What would it say? Kennedy? Amber? It was clever to crop that part out to keep down confusion. But now it did leave Deven wondering . . .

"So, then what happened?" she urged.

Her question had Paul's eyebrows drawing together as he took one last, longing look at the picture. Then he turned his phone face down on the desk as if to hide the baby, and the memory, from view. "Everything was fine," he mused with the faintest of smiles playing on his lips. "The baby was a surprise, but we were both happy. We had started buying things to prep the nursery, and even making plans to move in together. Amber had expressed things were moving a little fast and I had to agree, they were. But we were happy. I was happy. And I thought we both were committed to trying to make it work even though we threw a curveball at our relationship."

He sounded hurt as he spoke, like a piece of his heart was

aching. *He had fallen in love with her*, Deven realized, pursing her lips to keep from saying it out loud. He may not have wanted to admit it, even to himself, but she had picked up on the emotion emanating from his pores like a fragrance as he spoke so lovingly of her sister. Or Amber, rather. She couldn't be sure which woman had stolen his heart.

"Then, not too long after what happened with you," he went on, carefully, "she called me and said she had started bleeding. Because of what happened with you, I immediately started to panic and told her I would meet her at the hospital. But she said she had already called the doctor and there was really nothing they could do to stop the miscarriage. I told her I was coming over and she said she wasn't home, that she'd gone to a hotel to be alone. Then she hung up. She wouldn't answer my calls for the rest of the night but the next day I got a text saying we had lost the baby and she was in a really bad headspace because of it so she couldn't be with me anymore. She told me not to come look for her because her mind was made up."

Deven waited for more, but Paul merely held up his hands and made an absent gesture to signal he was done. "And you haven't heard from her since?"

"Nope."

"How long ago was that?"

Paul thought for a moment. "About a month and a half," he guessed. "I figured she had just gone back home to Charlotte because of what happened. Especially after I went to her townhouse and found it was for rent."

Deven sat back in a daze, her thoughts scrambling to process the new information. Kennedy had dated Paul and made up a completely new name and life. Gotten pregnant, lost the baby, and disappeared from Paul's life. For what? And why didn't she tell Deven? Why the secrets and lies? What the hell was her sister into?

Then a thought crossed her mind, something even more arresting. What if her sister was in danger? What if this Amber-alias was a way to duck into hiding because she was afraid of something—or someone? Deven thought again of the stalker they had encountered at the mall. No, she hadn't seen him since, but Kennedy had made mention of a restraining order for some mysterious ex-boyfriend. Could he, whoever he was, have something to do with what was going on? Maybe she should share this new insight with Benji. Or better yet, Officer McKinney. The police could launch some kind of investigation or something. There had to be protocol and procedures for this kind of thing, right? Because technically Kennedy wasn't dead, she was a missing person? Wasn't she?

An image of the mystery woman in the morgue billowed up like smoke once again and Deven shivered. Even more questions with no answers. A jigsaw puzzle to solve but the pieces still didn't fit.

Deven's phone buzzed again, probably for the fourth time. Maybe it was the fifth. She'd lost track. The air in the office was now stifling as it hummed with an ominous tension that had her climbing to her feet. She had just wanted answers. She didn't know those answers would come with a slew of skeletons and webs of deceit. But she couldn't close Pandora's Box just yet.

"I need that address to the townhome, if you don't mind," Deven said. She would have to go see this place. Even if it didn't yield any results, it was vital she researched it anyway.

Paul nodded. "I'll text it to you," he said. "So now what?"

"I don't know," Deven admitted. "But you've given me some new things to consider. I'll have to see what to do with that."

"Okay. Well, is there anything I can do to help?"

"You've done a lot." Deven started to hug him, decided against it, and instead backed away to the door. Something about knowing he was in love with her sister made the appreciative gesture extremely invasive. "If you could just get me that address. And maybe the phone number you had for her. Really anything you think would be helpful so I can figure this thing out. Thanks, Paul."

"No problem. And Deven," he added once she was at the door. His voice had softened, his next two words almost like a whisper. "I'm sorry."

She didn't know what he was apologizing for. Her tragic circumstances, his part in the chaos, falling in love with another woman . . . The comment was loaded, like he was telling her nothing and everything in the simplest of ways. All Deven could do was reply with a brisk nod before making her hasty exit. She wasn't strong enough to face him again after the weighted admission.

Deven raced back through the office, the parking lot, and expelled a jagged breath only when she'd made it back to the safety of her car. She'd managed to suppress as much as she could and now, she just felt completely depleted. And numb. The evening air had chilled a few degrees and Deven now shook in her seat. She cranked her car and a blast of air hit her face, first ice cold and then heating to warm her skin. This was enough for the day— hell the *year* if she was being honest. She would go home and regroup. Get some rest. And she needed nourishment. Deven couldn't even remember the last time she ate. Maybe then she could come up with a plan. But one thing for sure and two things for certain, this was definitely becoming way more than she could handle alone.

Deven pulled out her cell phone to see if Paul had texted the information she requested. He hadn't just yet. Probably still reeling from the shock of it all. She couldn't blame him. He'd just found out his girl was a liar and a fake. That was what they knew. Imagine what they *didn't* know.

Instead of a text message, however, Deven did see a notification for a voicemail, along with four missed calls. One was from a number she didn't recognize, three were from the County Police Department. Deven's heart quickened as she dialed into her voicemail box to listen to the message. Her finger trembled over the *Play* button of her voicemail prompts, Officer McKinney's voice echoing in the car with practiced cadence. Whether from fear or the cold, Deven's body began to convulse in a vicious quiver, and she hugged herself in a weak attempt to calm the anxiety. Now was not the time to hyperventilate.

"Ms. Reynolds, this is Officer McKinney. I have some additional information about your sister. Please give me a call." That was it. The message was minimal but clear. She was once again delivering some tragic news.

# Chapter Sixteen

Deven hadn't wanted to lie. It was just that when Benji called, he mentioned wanting to go back to Kennedy's apartment. Then he asked if she could meet him over there. So Deven had to lie. She couldn't very well tell him what she was about to do to get some additional information. Then, Benji would've wanted to come with her. She would've had to divulge some details she wasn't entirely sure she wanted to. Because, if she could be honest with herself, she still didn't trust him. Not yet anyway.

So as much as Deven wanted—no, *needed*—to go back to Kennedy's apartment, as much as she felt Benji had some ulterior motive for getting back there and she was curious to know why, she patched together a story about needing to go see her mom and she was unavailable. In actuality, she had already planned to go back to Kennedy's apartment herself. With or without Benji. Now that she had some extra details from Paul, Deven needed to do a more comprehensive search through her place through a new, critical lens. She was sure there may have been something there that she had originally overlooked.

In fact, Deven had spent all night scribbling in a notebook. She had drawn a line down the middle, dividing the page in half, with two headings across the top: *What I Know* and *What I Need To Do*. Under the *What I Know* column, she had bulleted the raw details she'd discovered since Sunday. Everything from the ghostly woman in the morgue, to the prescriptions she found at Kennedy's apartment with names of other women, the missing gun, and now Paul's revelation about the missing Amber.

On the other side of the page, Kennedy had made a checklist of sorts, leads that she had to do more research on and things she needed to look into. There were about five items on the list (so far, because Deven was hoping she would be able to add more). Going to the police station to talk to Officer McKinney was the first item on today's agenda. So, Benji would just have to wait. She was sure he understood. It wasn't like he had been immediately forthcoming with whatever the hell he was snooping around about either.

The drive downtown was quick, way too quick for Deven's liking. She'd come prepared with the 'Kennedy Notebook' she'd been filling up with notes, and she was armed with a few more questions for the police. It wasn't until she'd been jotting down her observations that Deven realized she hadn't asked any more details about the discovery of the body in Kennedy's apartment. At the time, the inquiry seemed trivial. But now, she was anxious to know more to help put the pieces together. Now whether she was going to relay her information to the police, well the jury was still out on that one. But Deven had to admit, she did feel better equipped with a little more knowledge in her arsenal.

The lot was peppered with police cars, uniformed officers decorating the sidewalks as they moseyed in and out of the brick building. Deven wheeled into one of the parking spaces in the back and grabbed her purse and notebook to get out. The muffled chime of her cell phone stopped her short. She released the sigh before she realized it and she dug in her purse for the device. She had already figured it was Justin before even confirming it with a distracted glance to the screen.

Of course, it was him. Deven had already ignored his call twice. Once last night when she was too engrossed regurgitating the details of Kennedy's case on paper. She'd sent him to voice-mail with a hasty, *in the middle of something, I'll call you back* text. But she hadn't. Then again this morning, she hadn't bothered clicking over while she was talking to Benji. Once was forgivable. Twice was pushing it. Three times and Deven knew she'd never hear the end of it. So even though she was anxious, Deven sat back against the leather interior and answered the phone.

"Hey baby," she greeted trying to keep the impatience out of her voice.

"Hey. I've been calling you," he said without a lick of concern. If anything, he seemed more suspicious. "What have you been up to?"

"Just tired. A lot of back and forth with my mom and stuff for Kennedy."

"Stuff for Kennedy?"

Deven chewed on her bottom lip trying to pick over exactly what to say without saying anything. "Yeah, just her affairs. Cleaning up her apartment, paperwork and stuff."

To her relief, Justin's tone softened with understanding. "Sweetie, I'm sorry. Is there anything I can do? Do you want me to come this weekend and help?"

"No, that's not necessary." Deven hadn't meant to answer so quickly so she tried again. "I mean, you don't have to come all this way for that. I'm getting it handled." She felt guilty for sending up a silent prayer that he took the hint. She didn't need him getting in the way. Besides, Justin was too busy with . . . well Justin, to care or even try to understand what Deven had to do.

"I'll let you know if I come in town," he said. "I've got some things to take care, but I was thinking we needed to talk about some things."

That had Deven lifting an eyebrow. "Things like what?"

"Just us. We just need to talk about it in person."

Deven didn't like the sound of that, but she really wasn't in the headspace to press the issue. So, she diverted. "Okay sure. We'll talk this weekend," she promised, though she had no idea if that would be the case. It was a weak stall, she knew, but a stall, nonetheless. And it worked. They ended the call and Deven flipped her phone to silent. She didn't need any more distractions.

The police station was buzzing with activity as Deven marched through the automatic doors. Ringing phones and static voices through walkie-talkies served as a background to the chaos as law enforcement officials milled about with less urgency than she would have expected. A fleeting scent of weed, leather, and cigarette smoke pervaded the air and had Deven's nose wrinkling at the pungent odor.

Eyes averted from the few folks being escorted in handcuffs, she crossed to the desk where a young-looking officer sat behind a glass partition. The woman cast Deven a polite smile as she approached. "Hi, may I help you?"

"Yes, I'd like to speak to Officer McKinney, please."

"Is she expecting you?"

*Good question.* Deven glanced around the busy lobby. She hadn't thought to return Officer McKinney's call yesterday. Now she was kicking herself for being so careless. "She left me a message that she needed to speak with me."

The officer nodded and picked up the desk phone to make the call. "What's your name?"

"Deven Reynolds."

"Hm, that is an interesting name."

Deven nodded but didn't comment. She knew what the officer meant since she'd heard it more times than she could remember.

Deven was an "interesting" name for a girl. Her father's homage to the baseball legend, Devon White. It had certainly been a conversation starter throughout middle and high school.

It wasn't long after the officer hung up the phone that Officer McKinney strolled from one of the back offices and headed their way. Like the woman behind the desk, she too, offered a polite smile before gesturing for Deven to follow her. That little smile thing must've been in their rule book. It did little to make Deven feel welcome or comfortable. Probably because they both knew her presence there was not on the most desirable of terms.

They passed a few cubicles before she was led into a cramped office towards the back of the precinct. Deven had to step in and behind the door just to afford Officer McKinney enough room to close it. Then she took a seat in one of the weathered guest chairs with upholstery dingy from use or age, or both.

The desk was in utter disarray with papers and folders littering the tabletop in skewed stacks. A half-eaten Caesar salad rested on top of the keyboard along with a Powerade and, wouldn't you know it, a box of Krispy Kreme doughnuts. McKinney quickly made a weak attempt to shuffle some of the clutter out of the way, though she decided to leave it be when it was clear there was nowhere else to put it.

"Sorry about the mess." She gestured sheepishly to her desk. "Lots of fires and not enough time."

Deven nodded though she didn't know how to feel about that. What would that mean for her sister's case? "Well, I appreciate you calling me so quickly."

"Yes, of course. Though I hate you had to waste a trip down here."

"Well, this is important, and I figured it was best discussed face-to-face."

A few wispy hairs had escaped the ponytail and now danced around McKinney's face. She used both hands to push them back. A nervous habit, Deven noted and struggled to remain patient as the officer plucked one of the folders from the top of a pile and flipped it open.

"I wish I had better news," she started. "But I called you because the toxicology report came back. As well as the fingerprints."

Deven held her breath. "Okay."

"Well, first the fingerprints confirm that is indeed your sister, Kennedy."

A week ago, the news would have sent Deven spiraling into a negating frenzy. But now with everything else she knew, well *thought* she knew about Kennedy, she couldn't be so sure. "What was in the other report?" she asked, her voice monotone.

McKinney flipped the folder around to reveal the page from a lab with charts and percentages that didn't provide any clarity. She went on to point out a few of the drugs found in the body. It didn't even appear like the doses were egregiously high, but it was the combination of the medicine that proved lethal. Deven recognized that the names she had found on the prescription bottles were listed, indicating some trace of them had been found in her system.

". . . that's why it was ruled accidental," McKinney was explaining with care. "She had also been drinking so it was like a fatal chain reaction. Unfortunately, she had liver damage, so the medicine just accumulated in her system. There is no other evidence pointing to an intentional suicide attempt." She paused for Deven to digest the recent information. "Again, Ms. Reynolds, I am truly sorry about this."

She seemed genuinely sympathetic. Deven could appreciate that. But still, the other nagging details plagued her thoughts. The stalker, Kennedy's previous assault, Amber Wright, the pregnancy. More importantly, Deven didn't care what fingerprints or clinical data, or DNA registered in their precious system. That woman, their Kennedy, was not the sister she knew. But hell, who *was* the sister she knew? Even her truth had been corrupted.

"Are you able to do some research for me?" Deven asked suddenly. She hadn't even been sure she wanted to introduce this new element to the police, but now it seemed like she had no choice.

"What's that?"

"I don't want to get anyone in trouble. But can you look into an Amber Wright for me?"

McKinney frowned as she picked up a pen and began scrawling on a nearby sticky note. "Who is Amber Wright?"

"I'm not sure, but I think she's got something to do with my sister."

McKinney's pen paused over the paper as she looked up. "You mean, she was possibly there at the apartment?"

Deven shook her head, her mind grating over scenarios that sounded imperative and believable, but not incriminating. She chose her words cautiously. "This woman, Amber Wright, I think she pretended to be my sister," she said. "I'm not sure, but I'm friends with someone who says he dated Amber Wright, but she was using my sister's information. It may not mean anything, but if it's something there I was hoping we could find out. Especially with the discrepancy."

McKinney's brow lifted, making it clear there was no discrepancy. Maybe the lie worked. Maybe she didn't want to see through Deven's bullshit. Or maybe she just felt sorry for the poor woman who was so far steeped in the denial stage of grief she couldn't even recognize her own sister, despite all of the hard facts. Either way, the cop sighed and brushed those billowing strands of hair from her face.

"I can't make any promises," she said, finally. "But let me see what I can do."

Deven pulled out her cell phone and pulled up the information Paul had texted her about Amber. She rattled off the name again, as well as a phone number and some other identifying information he had managed to collect. She made sure to skip over the address he had provided. No use sending the police when she planned to do a little investigation of her own.

# Chapter Seventeen
## Before

She dreamed of dead babies. Rows and rows of little lifeless bodies like cornfields, all with faces that looked the same; pallid, sunken, and eyes frozen in time. Deven stumbled through the maze of corpses, tiptoeing so as not to step on any of the scattered limbs. She could hardly see where she was going through the film of tears.

Somewhere in the distance, a baby's high-pitched cry echoed. "I'm coming, sweetie," Deven called though she couldn't figure out which direction the bawling was coming from. The baby sounded like it was in pain which only caused Deven's panic to soar. Too many babies. Stretching for miles. Which one was crying? Then another baby's cry lifted to harmonize in a somber duet. Her twins. Her babies.

Something cracked beneath her shoe and Deven looked down. A baby's arm had broken underneath her footstep, its limb now disjointed at a painful angle that had her swallowing a surge of bile. The cries echoed from somewhere and she collapsed, cradling the dead baby with the broken arm.

Deven woke up slightly disoriented, that overwhelming sense of disgust still seething in the pit of her belly. It took a moment for the room to stop spinning and she glanced around to get her bearings. Not her room. Kennedy's. Last night's horror materialized into focus. Rushing over to her sister's house after her assault was not planned, but she prayed her presence had at least elicited a good night's sleep for Kennedy. Lord knows she felt like a train wreck, having caught snatches of a turbulent slumber that had left her even more exhausted. Remnants of the nightmare hovered like a phantom in her head and Deven pressed her fingertips against her closed eyelids to clear that last little bit of sleep. She needed water. No, she needed air.

Deven tossed back the covers and threw her legs over the side of the bed. She steadied herself before pulling up on weakened limbs. The medicine Kennedy had given her last night was still doing the trick. No pain, thank God. She eased herself from the mattress and glanced backwards to Kennedy's side of the bed, surprised when she realized it was empty. Morning light spilled onto sheets disheveled with swift abandonment. The digital clock on the accompanying nightstand illuminated the time with a harsh, red glow. 9:42 a.m. She hadn't even felt Kennedy get up. But then again, she hadn't expected to sleep so late.

Deven found Kennedy curled up in a corner of the couch. She sat propped with her feet placed on the cushion and knees pulled up to her chest, balancing a notebook on the flat part of her thighs. The top of a pen fluttered with fervor as Kennedy wrote. On the coffee table, her cell phone rested next to a champagne flute, foggy with pulp residue of whatever she had been sipping on.

Kennedy's head whipped up as Deven padded into the living room. She seemed to visibly relax once she registered her sister's presence. "I was wondering if you were going to get up today. You feeling a little better?"

Deven nodded, deciding not to mention the lingering trepidation from her nightmare.

"You need some more pain medicine or anything?" Kennedy asked.

"I'm okay for now." Deven crossed the room to make herself comfortable next to her sister. A plush throw blanket was thrown across the back of the couch and she pulled it across her legs. "What are you writing?"

In response, a knowing smirk bloomed on Kennedy's face, and she lifted the book from her lap to reveal the cover. Deven recognized the lilac purple diary immediately. Butterflies and rainbows adorned its tattered cover, and a sleeve held the now broken heart-shaped lock. A gift for her eleventh birthday, Deven remembered. She'd received an identical diary, only hers had been a powder blue. Another difference? Deven had only used her once while Kennedy had actually been faithful with writing in hers, all the way up until she moved out.

"I didn't know you still had this," Deven said.

"Of course, I do. Lots of memories in here." For emphasis, Kennedy thumbed through the pages, the colored inks blurring together like a watercolor painting. "I like to go back and read stuff every now and then."

"What did you put in there about me?"

"What makes you think there's stuff in here about you?"

Deven rolled her eyes at the taunt. "Because we didn't get along, so I know you were cussing me out a few times."

Kennedy eyed the page, almost pensive. "Actually no, there's nothing in here about that. Just how much I looked up to you."

Deven felt the stab of guilt at Kennedy's admission. Thankfully, her baby sister hadn't been tainted by her little sibling jealousy from time to time. It certainly made up for it because of their close relationship now.

"You still have your diary?" Kennedy asked.

Deven pictured the book in her closet among her storage containers of childhood trifles. She didn't even know why she had bothered keeping it. "Yeah, it's at home somewhere," she said, vaguely.

Kennedy placed her pen in the crease between the open pages and leveled her eyes with Deven. "Let me ask you something. Why didn't we stay in touch when I left?"

Deven felt convicted. Kennedy's twelfth birthday party had been the catalyst for the change in their family dynamic. But hell, what could she do about that now? She'd only been fourteen, a child herself. Deven's shrug was cagey camouflaged as nonchalance. "I mean, we were kids," she reminded her. "It's not easy having different dads because you have your family and I had mine, you know?"

Something that looked like pity (or maybe it was disgust) crossed Kennedy's face before it was replaced with a grin. "Yeah, I guess that makes sense," she said.

The conversation had discomfort settling. Instead of dwelling on it, Deven pretended to reach for the diary. "So, what else did you write about me in there?"

"That you can be a bitch who doesn't know how to mind her business." Kennedy flipped up a playful middle finger before closing the diary and unfolding herself from her seated position. "So, what's going on today? You have any plans?"

"I was going to relax a little. Why?"

Kennedy's back was to Deven as she journeyed into the kitchen. "I was thinking we could go see Mom."

If Deven hadn't been sitting, the suggestion would have knocked her ass over. Kennedy and their mom hadn't been close in years, and it seemed like anytime Deven brought her up, her sister would change the subject or get agitated with the dialogue. Not that Deven didn't understand this little grudge and maybe she was partially to blame. But Kennedy trying to make amends was as bizarre as the dream she'd just woken up from.

Deven waited, half-expecting her sister to burst out laughing while yelling *sike* like she often did when they were little. Her stoic face reinforced her sincerity which shocked Deven even more. But whatever the reason for this little change of heart, however slight, Deven wasn't going to question it. It just made her happy to know Kennedy was capable of forgiving.

———————

"Hey Deven," Betty, the front desk attendant, greeted. "Good to see you again."

Deven smiled and, as customary, signed in on the iPad. "You too, Ms. Betty. How has everything been?"

"Oh, you know I can't complain." Betty flicked a curious gaze to Deven's companion and angled her head to peer over a set of oval-framed glasses. "Kennedy, baby, I'm so sorry. I didn't even recognize you. It's been so long, chile. How have you been?"

Kennedy grimaced, and it was clear she didn't know how best to acknowledge the greeting and petty insult. "I've been good," she responded.

Betty's smile bloomed. "That's so good to hear. Your mom will be happy to see you. Both of you," she added, accepting the IDs they held across the desk. "Today is a good day. One of the best she's had in a while."

Deven was relieved. Not that it should discourage Kennedy from returning, but she knew her mother's condition was fragile and required some patience. If a 'good day' could make the visit a more pleasant one, Deven was just going to count her blessings.

"Yes, I've been busy working," Kennedy lied through a bright smile. "How has it been around here?"

Betty chuckled, causing her body to tremble with the boisterous gesture. "What can I say. Sitting around with a bunch of us old folks definitely keeps the days entertaining." She handed them each their visitor badge. "I believe the residents are milling about right now," she said. "Your mom may be in the activity room."

Deven thanked her and led the way down the hall, past a gym, theater, and then an oversized dining area where nurses were already prepping the tables with plates and silverware. Looks like they were just in time for lunch. Some kind of chicken entrée, judging by the savory aroma coming from the kitchen.

Up ahead, French doors were propped open to reveal a converted sunroom with skylights. Floor-to-ceiling windows gave scenic views of the lake and fold-out tables had been strategically placed to accommodate the card and board games that now engaged the residents. On one wall, the crackle of a fire from the stone fireplace fused with the harmonies of a soulful ballad to create a comforting ambiance. Deven couldn't help but grin at the overwhelming sense of peace once she stepped into the room. It felt like home here. It reminded Deven of growing up, of Christmas mornings and lazy Saturdays with her parents. After Kennedy left, Deven felt a different kind of contentment, however serendipitous. She entertained that tiny ripple of nostalgia before scanning the room for Iris.

Her mother was seated with another woman at a table near the bay window. They were playing cards and by the looks of the grin plastered on Iris's face, it was definitely a good day. She looked alert and jubilant, slapping cards on the table with the expertise of a pro in her prime. She certainly didn't look like she had recurring days where she didn't even remember her name, much less how to play a card game. So, this was certainly a refreshing sight to see.

As they approached, Iris's companion brushed some scattered curls from her face and another wave of memories hit. Deven recognized the old lady, now laden in wrinkles, from years past. Her mom's neighbor and good friend, Debra, always had candy and kind words for the girls. Not to mention a few stern looks when she caught them getting into neighborhood shenanigans behind their mother's back.

It was she who spoke first when her eyes landed on Deven. "Well look a here, Iris," Debra said, using the support of the flimsy table to help herself to a standing position. "My goodness, you girls have gotten so grown."

"Hi, Ms. Debra." Deven allowed herself to be folded in a motherly hug, the fragrance of hair spray and Chanel No. 5 wafting from her pores.

"Good to see you little DeeDee." The pet name sounded funny rolling from the old lady's tongue after all these years. She turned then to Kennedy and paused. Her eyes flickered over Kennedy's face as if trying to place her. *Uh oh*. Deven cringed at the prolonged pause. She didn't know Ms. Debra was wrestling with dementia as well.

"Ms. Debra you remember Kennedy, don't you?" Deven prompted, touching her sister's arm.

"Of course, I do." Embarrassment colored her cheeks and a smile strained across her face.

Iris didn't give the awkwardness another moment to linger. She stood and pulled Kennedy into her arms, not knowing—or seeming to care—that her daughter didn't readily return the embrace. Deven could count, maybe on one hand, how often the two had spoken since Kennedy had come back into their lives. It was a shame that time hadn't healed all wounds.

"Hey, my baby girl," Iris said as she pulled back and placed her hands on either side of Kennedy's face.

Her smile was plastic when she spoke. "Hi Mommy."

"Hi Mama," Deven greeted pulling Iris's attention long enough for a hug of her own.

"Oh, both my girls have come to visit. Debra, do you see this?" She didn't wait for an answer as she ushered them both into nearby chairs. "Kennedy why didn't you tell me you were coming?"

"I thought I would surprise you."

"A surprise indeed." Iris clasped Kennedy's hand in hers and held it to her breast. "How have you been?"

"Pretty good."

"And your father?"

A pause. Deven had to frown at the odd question. Iris knew Keith had passed years ago. But even if she didn't remember that, why did she care?

Kennedy cleared her throat. She looked to Deven who gave a subtle shake of her head. It was a good day. They didn't want to ruin that. "Everything is good," she answered, evading the question.

"Good, good. That's good to hear."

"How long have you been here, Ms. Debra?" Kennedy asked.

Debra looked around at the room's commotion. Someone had put on the Electric Slide and now the staff were leading the residents in the line dance. "Just a week," she said. "I was glad to move in and see a familiar face. Iris and I have had a lot of fun times when she stayed over in the Villas."

She was speaking of the estate homes Deven had grown up in, Cambridge Villas. Luxury at its finest, thanks to her dad's long money. Deven had hated having to get rid of the home, and the memories in that house. It'd felt like part of her childhood had been sold to the highest bidder. Of course, some memories weren't as fond as others, but they were hers just the same.

"Kenny, baby," Debra went on. "I remember your mom used to come over every Thursday and pick up a fruit roll-up from my candy dish." She tossed her a wink. "You remember how much you liked those?"

Now Deven was sure Debra was out of it. It was Deven that craved the gummy candy. Kennedy was the chocolate fanatic.

But rather than remind her, she figured they could just placate her for now.

"Yes, Ma'am," Kennedy answered, apparently with the same idea.

Debra rose then and grabbed her cane hanging from the back of her chair. "DeeDee sweetie, do you mind walking me back to my room? I'm getting a little tired."

Deven tried to stifle a groan. She was there to visit her mom, not Ms. Debra. "You want me to just get your nurse?" she asked.

"They're busy. And my room is right here on the first floor so not far, I promise."

Deven started to object again but stopped short when Kennedy's hand squeezed her forearm. "Sis, if you don't mind," she said with a lowered voice. "I did want to chat with Mommy for a second. It's been a minute."

Deven would've preferred to stay behind but it seemed to be three against one. Even her mom's eyes were twinkling with a silent plea. And because she didn't want to look like a complete bitch, Deven nodded and climbed to her feet.

She took Ms. Debra's arm and guided her to the doorway. Though she could feel the old woman's weight leaning into her, she still felt light. And she walked with a slight limp that threw off her gait.

Debra waited until they were in the hall alone before she spoke up. "I really do appreciate this, DeeDee."

"It's no problem." A lie, but a believable one. It damn sure was a problem she was out here playing escort instead of enjoying quality time with her mother. She wondered what the hell she and Kennedy were talking about.

"You girls mean everything to your mother," Debra was saying as they walked. "She really would be lost without you."

"Yes, I know."

"But it's so good to see her happy again. I think that new gentleman friend of hers is definitely helping."

The words had Deven nearly tripping over her feet. "What gentleman friend?"

"Some man she's been gushing about."

Deven started to respond, but then remembered Ms. Debra was a little *touched*, as her mother used to say. She couldn't take the woman's word as Gospel. "You mean a new friend that resides here?" she asked instead. "What's his name?"

"No, he doesn't live in the home. I'm not sure of his name but she's told me he's called a couple times. I know whoever he is has her acting like a little schoolgirl again." Her chuckling stopped when she noticed Deven's contemplative frown. "Oh, sweetie, I'm so sorry. I didn't mean to upset you. I thought you knew."

They walked on in silence, their footsteps interchanging with the quiet *thud* of Debra's cane. Then she spoke up again, her tone quiet as if she were afraid of even mentioning what had been marinating on her mind. "Can I ask you, why did Kennedy leave? I don't think your mom was the same after that."

Deven stopped in mid-stride, suddenly angry at the intrusive question. So that was why the old woman had asked to be escorted back to her room. To be nosey. And for what? For their family business to be the highlight of nursing home gossip? And here she was thinking this lady was her mother's friend.

"Look Ms. Debra," Deven said through clenched teeth. "That is really nobody's business but ours. Not trying to be disrespectful."

Debra's eyes widened in shock. "Oh no dear, I didn't mean anything by it," she insisted. Her tone wavered then, a feeble attempt to triage the situation. "It's just that, well nobody thought we would see Kennedy again. And well, here she is, you know. It's just, I don't understand—"

"What is there to understand? That's my sister and my mom's

youngest daughter. They are rebuilding their relationship. There's nothing for anybody to rationalize, or worry about, but us." Seething, Deven made an absent gesture down the hall that stretched in front of them. "I think you can find your room from here. Nice to see you again, Ms. Debra." Sure, it was a lie. It was absolutely *not* nice to see the nosey neighbor again. But it was the best she could do to lessen the sting of her abrupt exit.

Deven turned then and headed back in the opposite direction. Back towards her family, back to safety. Ms. Debra's probing had pissed her off, but she didn't know which was worse, her questions or her insinuation.

Back in the activity room, Deven saw her mom and sister had moved to a nearby couch. Both of their heads were bent together as Kennedy's lips moved near Iris's ear as if she were sharing a secret. Deven didn't know why the sight intensified her agitation. No doubt, thanks to Ms. Debra.

As soon as she got close, the women leaned back from each other, and Kennedy rested a hand on Iris's knee. She looked up with an innocence that, for the briefest of moments, reminded Deven of the sneaky little sister she recalled growing up. And then, just as quickly, that look was gone.

Because they were sitting so close, Deven resorted to leaning on the arm of the couch next to her mom. "Everything okay?" she asked.

Iris smiled. "Of course. Why wouldn't it be?" She paused blinking through phases of confusion. "What's your name again, sweetie?"

Deven's spirits fell though she tried to keep her inflection light. "It's me, Mommy. Deven."

Iris nodded though her face remained impassive. "Do you know my daughter, Kennedy?"

Deven sighed and looked to her sister. "It's like a light switch sometimes," she murmured.

"Yeah, I really hate that for her."

Deven paused a beat, then asked the question that had been weighing thick like a blanket. "Hey, why did she ask about your dad?"

Kennedy shrugged. "I don't know. I thought that was kind of weird too."

"Yeah, pretty weird." Deven agreed with a frown. It crossed her mind to ask her what the two of them had been discussing before she walked up. But she had a feeling the answer would be just as elusive.

# Chapter Eighteen

"She robbed me!"

Deven steered with one hand and used the other to pull the phone from her face. No way was she talking to who she thought she was talking to. Not with that attitude. But sure enough, Paul's name was shown on her screen, along with the timer indicating his impromptu call only twenty-three seconds prior. And even more puzzling was the fact that he was referencing Kennedy.

"Paul, wait a minute. What are you talking about? What did she steal?"

"I knew it was too damn good to be true," he continued with his rant. "Things were going too perfect."

"Paul, please calm down. And start from the beginning."

"I need to show you some stuff I found," he said. "Where are you?"

Deven took the off-ramp of the expressway, her eyes dancing between the signs and the GPS map displayed on her navigation system. Twelve minutes away. "I'm headed to that address you gave me," she admitted. "Amber's address."

"I told you the last time I checked the place was for rent."

"I know. I figured I could talk to the landlord or some neighbors or something."

Paul was quiet as he considered the alternatives. "I'll meet you over there," he said quickly. "On my way." And he hung up.

Deven placed her phone in her cup holder. Whatever Paul was about to show her, she had already surmised was about to be some real implicating facts. She turned her attention to the road ahead and focused on her journey.

It had been a pure whim to get up that morning and make a trip to the address Paul had given her for Amber. After leaving the police station the previous day, Deven had toyed with the idea. It felt like a shot in the dark. And what did she expect to find anyway? Kennedy would waltz out the front door and admit to all her wrongdoings? *Hey Sis, yeah, it's me. I'm not really dead and oh yeah, I gave Paul a fake name so I could rob him. Oops.* That would be an answer that solved absolutely nothing.

Burlington County, New Jersey certainly wasn't a side of town Deven frequented. Not that she avoided it, she just never really had a reason to stop during the rare times she passed through. And judging by the living quarters and mini marts fringed along the main roads, the area had an established reputation of equal parts hood and country, and the label had become a staple of the community. It definitely didn't seem like the type of lifestyle Kennedy would pick as a residence. *Maybe that was the whole point*, Deven thought with skepticism. On the surface, this would be the last place someone would look for her. How idyllic if her goal was to disappear.

"Turn right," the robotic voice prompted and on cue, Deven pulled up to a cluster of detached townhomes that had seen better days. In the entryway, a dilapidated sign poked through the weeds that read, Sienna Courts, and Deven knew she had reached her destination.

She turned into the neighborhood, rolling past shabby brick buildings that lined both sides. Screen doors and broken blinds barely sufficed as barriers against the destitution while trash and toys littered the driveways. The street was unpaved, another sign of the community's neglect, and Deven had to ease around potholes as her tires bit the gravel. A few of the inhabitants looked her way as she drove by, their annoyed expressions seeming to mirror each other. They weren't used to visitors, nor were they happy about the intrusion.

Building F was one of four in a cul-de-sac, nestled further back with a steep, pebbled driveway. It looked like two townhomes per building with a wide porch and two doors asymmetrical in the center. Sure enough, a *For Rent* sign was tacked to the door on the left. Deven parked against the curb near the mailboxes and sent a quick text to Paul to let him know she had arrived. Then, not bothering to wait, she turned off the engine and got out.

A breeze tickled the air, carrying with it an earthy musk that reeked off urine. Deven made her way up the path, swallowing her disgust at the living conditions. Even the dogs looked neglected, she noticed as one trotted by. He was scraggly with malnutrition and dander flakes caked in his fur. He didn't even look up as Deven passed, clearly too consumed with sniffing in the nearby patch of grass. No, this was certainly not the sister she knew. Not living here.

The screen door was slightly off the hinges and pulled open easily with a loud creak. Up closer now, Deven could see the *For Rent* sign was merely scribbled on computer paper with the name Marez and a phone number at the bottom. She looked at the door frame, not seeing the doorbell, and balled her fist to bang her knuckles on the wood.

"Kennedy?" she called. "Amber? You in there?" She knocked again, this time a little more forceful.

Then she heard it. Soft first, then a little louder. Footsteps shuffled inside. Deven blinked in surprise and this time, used the side of her fist to pound harder. "Kennedy, open this door!" she yelled, jiggling the locked knob as if it would succumb to her efforts.

Something moved in the window, a shadow maybe? A person? Deven leaned across the porch and cupped her hands around her eyes in makeshift goggles to peer through. The curtain was dark, offering very little in the way of a view with the exception of a sliver of light from somewhere in the room. Otherwise, nothing. *Oh God, what if something was wrong?*

Panic replaced anger as Deven pounded again, her voice now pleading. "Kennedy, please. Open up." A thought popped into her head and Deven had to wonder why she hadn't considered it sooner. The police! She needed to get Officer McKinney down there ASAP.

A rattling sound perked her ears and Deven spun around as a lock clicked out of place. Then slowly, the door pulled open just enough for someone to peek through. The Hispanic woman poked her head out, making sure to keep the door nearly closed. Fear had the woman's eyes bouncing around and Deven took a surprised step in retreat. No, not Kennedy. She was an idiot to even expect her.

"I'm sorry," Deven sputtered, lifting her hands in mock surrender. "I didn't mean to bang on your door. I'm looking for my sister."

The woman blinked once, then twice, her eyes still wide as she shook her head. "Lo siento," she murmured in a thick accent. "No hablo inglés."

*Dammit.* Deven flipped through the handful of Spanish words she could remember, nothing coming close to being able to communicate what she needed to. "Um . . ." She licked her lips and tried again, speaking slower this time as if it would curb the language barrier. "Do you know my sister, Kennedy? Or Amber?"

Still confused, the woman pointed to the sign on her door, indicating the phone number listed. "Marez," she said. "El habla inglés. Lo siento."

Thinking fast, Deven pulled out her cell phone and quickly scrolled to the picture of Kennedy, the one she had used that Paul recognized. She shoved the phone in the woman's face. "Do you know her?" she asked, her voice desperate. "Have you seen this woman?"

The lady glanced at the picture before shrugging. "Yo no sé," she said. "Lo siento." And with that, she closed the door.

Deven glanced around in defeat. She didn't know what the woman had said, but it was clear by her reaction that she had no idea who Kennedy was. She watched the door for a moment longer before deciding to give the landlord a try. Maybe this Marez person knew his prior tenants. But the call immediately went to voicemail and Deven left a half-hearted message that she was doubtful would be returned.

The floorboards of the porch squeaked under her weight as Deven turned back towards the driveway. Apparently, the idea to come out here had been a terrible one. Not only was it a waste but the dead ends were frustrating, not to mention discouraging. What was she doing chasing ghosts?

Deven glanced up as a familiar car pulled to a stop behind hers. The door opened and Paul's head popped into view over the roof. "Hey, what are you doing?" he said, jogging across the grass. "You should've waited for me."

Deven met him in the yard and jerked a thumb behind her towards the apartment. "I thought I could try and see if someone was there."

"And?"

"Nothing. Someone else lives there now but she doesn't know anything." She hugged herself as another rancid breeze wafted through. "Why didn't you tell me Kennedy stayed in this place?"

"I had no idea myself until I came looking for her," Paul said, shoving his hands in his pockets. "Amber—well *Kennedy*, I mean—gave me this address when we first started seeing each other. But we usually met up or she would come to my place. But then again, there's a lot I didn't know about her apparently."

"You and me both." The acceptance tasted bitter. She didn't want to admit her sister was a stranger. "What did she steal from you?"

Paul opened his mouth to answer, stopping short with the slam of a screen door. His eyes traveled behind Deven and she, too, looked back to the building, half-expecting to see the Hispanic woman once more. Instead, a man from the adjacent apartment stepped onto the porch with no shirt and the neck of a beer bottle in his pudgy fingers. Deven tried to ignore the sordid image of the man's plump tummy as he took a lazy sip of his drink. "You need some help?" he asked, leaning on a nearby railing.

Paul spoke up first. "No—"

"Yes!" Deven quickly corrected. She was already pulling out her phone as she hurried back to the porch. It was a long shot, but desperate times . . . She heard Paul right on her heels. "Do you know the lady who lived here before?"

"Sweetie, I know all the ladies." The man grinned and licked his chapped lips. "Who you looking for?"

"Kennedy. Or maybe she went by Amber."

The man frowned. "Nah, I don't believe I've heard those names before."

"She used to live over there," Paul added indicating the apartment next door. "A few months ago."

"Oh nah," the man chuckled lightly. "Ain't no woman by that name lived over there. I've been here for over ten years." He sounded so damn proud of that statement that Deven had to wonder if he'd had one beer too many. Living there was most definitely not something to brag about.

"Come on, let's go," Paul whispered and gave Deven's arm a light tug.

But still, she wasn't quite ready to give up. She held up her cell phone, extending her arm so the man could see her screen where she wouldn't have to move too much closer. "Do you recognize this woman?" she asked, just like she'd done before.

The man squinted at the picture. Even leaned off the railing to get a better look. He nodded and Deven took an appreciative breath as her hope inflated.

"Yeah, I've seen her around," he affirmed. "A few times. I don't think she lives over here though."

Now it was Paul's tone that reflected urgency. He chanced moving closer and stood beside Deven. "When was the last time you saw her?"

"Yesterday or day before."

Deven's jaw dropped as she looked to Paul. She knew they were thinking the same thing. The neighbor sounded completely positive, but she was sure they had misheard.

"You saw this woman—" she pointed to Kennedy's face on her screen—"sometime this week?"

"Yeah. She was next door visiting her boyfriend." He nodded to Building G. "I don't know which apartment though. They were standing outside arguing for a while."

Deven's heart quickened at the new information. Kennedy was alive and well. She didn't know whether to be relieved or pissed. She looked to the building, separated from them by a strip of weeds and bare patches. She didn't see anyone, and the only sign of occupancy was a sleek black Ford F150 sitting in the accompanying driveway. Whoever he was obviously took more pride in his ride than his residence. But her sister could be in there this very minute.

"What were they arguing about?" Paul pushed.

The man polished off his remaining drink and tossed the bottle carelessly in the yard. It rolled to join the others that had collected in a ditch like decoration. "Hell if I know," he admitted. "When you live around here you tend to tune that kind of shit out."

"Thank you so much," Deven said quickly. Taking Paul's arm, she guided him back up the driveway, as far out of earshot as she could because she knew the nosey man was still watching and listening.

Once at her car, she faced Paul, but her mind was already working in overdrive. "Can you believe this?"

"No, not really." Paul gave the man a backwards glance. Sure enough, he was still there, not even being discreet about his attempt to overhear their conversation. "I don't know if I trust that guy."

"Why not? Why does he have a reason to lie?"

"Wait, wait, I didn't say he was lying. I'm just saying he could be mistaken. You see all the beer bottles in the grass."

She had but hadn't wanted to acknowledge his inebriated state. Not when he was saying the things she was so desperate to hear.

"He said he saw Kennedy," she reminded him. "He recognized her from the picture. Said she was here a few days ago. How could he mistake that?"

"Shit, I don't know, Deven." Paul blew a breath and dragged his hand over his face. He was visibly flustered; his normally tanned skin tinted a pinkish hue. "I just know something isn't right and this girl just up and disappeared. You say they tell you she's dead, the neighbor says she's alive. I don't know what the hell to believe."

"Well, there's maybe someone who knows and has some answers for us," she said, taking another look at Building G. She couldn't be sure, but she thought she saw the blinds shift. And what followed was that overwhelmingly eerie feeling like she was being watched. Their nosey informant had apparently gotten bored and retreated back to his apartment. They were alone now, or Deven thought they were. She really didn't know anymore. "I think we need to go over there," she decided.

Paul looked at her like she had lost her mind. "And do what? Demand to see her?"

"If that's what it takes."

"Deven, come on now. That's crazy. You don't know who lives over there. Just like I wish you had waited before you went barging to Amber's apartment."

"Well, what do you suggest, Paul?" She hadn't meant to yell. But dammit the man's logic was aggravating. If she had known he was going to be this much of a hindrance, she would've never allowed him to come.

Paul sighed and placed gentle hands on Deven's shoulders. The gesture was meant to calm her down, but he was surprised to feel the slight tremble underneath his palms. The tension was like a pendulum shifting between them and it was more than obvious Deven was beginning to crack underneath the pressure.

"Okay, we'll go," he relented. "But let's just be careful. And," he added. "If anything looks off, even a little bit, we get the hell out of there and call the police. Deal?"

"Deal." Deven's heart galloped into overdrive with the agreement. Then the fear trickled in, only heightening as Paul moved to lead the way next door. She needed answers, but now she didn't know what she would do when she got them. No amount of time could prepare for seeing a sister everyone said was dead.

This time, Deven stood at the base of the porch while Paul

went up to knock on one of the doors. She held her breath as they waited. He knocked again, then a third time before pivoting to glance at Deven.

"Try the other one," she suggested though the little bit of hope she had was beginning to dissipate. What would they do if no one was home? Come back? Stake out the apartment?

Obediently, Paul knocked on the opposite door, and they waited again. Deven eyed the truck, sure she didn't recognize the vehicle. Maybe Paul had a point, and the neighbor had been drunk or confused. Maybe it was easier to accept that concrete rationale than to sustain belief that maybe, just maybe he had been right. Because then she would have no choice but to face the ugly truth. Yes, that Kennedy was alive. But that she was also a liar and a thief. She didn't know if she was ready to accept that part.

"Let's just go," she called to Paul's back after a moment. "Don't worry about it."

"No, wait a minute. I think someone is coming." Paul leaned his ear closer to the door to listen. "Yeah, someone is coming."

Deven all but ran onto the porch. She, too, clearly heard the heavy footsteps approaching. Then, a baritone, "Who is it?"

She cleared her throat and looked to Paul with a worried glance. "Um, hi. I'm looking for someone and I was wondering if you could help." Silence. Then a lock clicked, and the door swung open wide.

At first, Deven wasn't sure if he was an illusion brought on by stress and desperation. But then, the man smirked, and she knew he was too real. And too much of a coincidence. "Hey Deven," he greeted like they were old friends, though Deven had never spoken to the man a day in her life. But still, she recognized him, and the memory had a breath catching in her throat.

The man pulled a rubber band from his wrist and used both hands to pull his locs back from his face. The same face she remembered from the mall. The same cocky stance as he watched her across the aisle at the kiosk, then again in the food court. The same man she'd figured was stalking her sister, and now he was here in Building G. And he knew her name, said with prepared acquaintance like they had history. *What the hell was going on?*

# Chapter Nineteen

The man looked like trouble, muscles poking from underneath a tight-fitting tee and black jeans slung low on his hips. He had that masculine, rugged thing going on which only added to his intrigue. He leaned against the door frame, lifting his arm above his head to expose an *Only God can judge me* tattoo on his inner bicep.

Paul's eyes shifted between them. "You two know each other?" he asked, clearly stunned by the connection.

Mr. Mystery Man looked Deven up and down and she shuddered under the scrutiny, suddenly feeling soiled. He looked smug, too damn smug. Like he was sitting on some G13 classified FBI secret and it was eating him up not to share it. He didn't answer Paul's question, instead wiggling his eyebrows like he expected Deven to.

"I don't know him," she responded with a helpless shrug.

"Well, he obviously knows you."

The man chuckled and pulled out a pack of cigarettes from the back pocket of his jeans. "I wouldn't say that," he said.

Paul's eyes narrowed. "What's your name?"

"You can call me Deuce."

*Deuce?* Deven rolled the name around in her head willing it to jog her memory. It didn't ring a bell, though she honestly wished he'd given her a real name.

"We're looking for Kennedy," Paul said, taking the reins. "The man next door said you know her."

Deuce took his time putting the cigarette to his lips. "Nah," he said simply, pulling a lighter from his pocket.

Deven waited while he flicked it open, the flame licking the air as he cupped it close to his face to light the tip of his stick. "Well, you know Amber then." It came out more of an accusation than a question.

"Nope."

Paul was fed up and he spun on his heel. "Let's go," he huffed. "He doesn't know anything."

"No, wait." Damn the niceties. Deven strolled closer and stabbed a bold finger in the man's chest. "How the hell do you know me?"

Deuce was unfazed. "We have some mutual friends."

"My sister."

"Nah, I never met your sister."

"Bullshit!" His apathy was infuriating, and Deven would've liked nothing more than to slap the shit out of him. He was toying with her, and he knew it. It was more than obvious by his leer and that little twinkle in his eye. "Where is my sister?"

"I heard she was dead."

"No! You fucking liar!" Deven was being pulled backwards but she struggled, determined to beat the shit out of Deuce. He knew something. No, damn that, he had *done* something to Kennedy. "You muthafucka, I'm bringing the police back and they're going to lock your ass up!"

Paul half-pulled, half-dragged Deven's body from the porch, taking care to dodge her flailing arms. Through the raging sheath of red that clouded her vision, Deven watched Deuce blow smoke into the air, then pucker his lips in a kiss, before leaning back and slamming the door.

She stopped fighting and snatched from Paul's grasp. "I got it, damn," she snapped, stomping to her car. She was fuming, but even more so embarrassed at how she had behaved. And Paul certainly hadn't helped the situation pulling at her like some controlling boyfriend. The gesture, albeit thoughtful and perhaps a little protective, had only served as provocation.

Deven slid into the driver's seat and slammed the door. She was about to drive off when Paul climbed in next to her and she sat back against the leather. "That bastard is lying," she mumbled, almost to herself.

Paul sighed. "Yeah, I know," he agreed. "But what were you going to do? Beat the truth out of him?"

He was right, and as much as she wanted to, her reaction would've done nothing but embarrass her further. Not to mention garner a possible assault charge. It was the adrenaline hyping her up. Deuce looked like he could've taken some punches, and probably thrown a few of his own.

They sat in silence and Deven felt herself calming down. She shut her eyes, willing the frustrated tears not to come. Satisfied she was back in control, Deven chanced a sideways look at Paul. "Do you think we need to bring the police back?"

"I don't think it will help."

"He *knows* something, Paul."

"Yeah, but what can the police do?" Paul countered with a frown. "He's not guilty of anything. Hell, he's not even suspected of anything. We're going on the word of some drunk that lives next door to an address Kennedy gave me but there's not even a record of her being there. You tell the cops that, they'll probably laugh in your face." His eyes flicked out the window and narrowed on something. Then he pulled out his phone and began typing.

Deven watched his fingers. "What is it?"

"License plate," he said, his attention preoccupied with his text. "I may have someone who can look it up for me. It may be nothing but . . ."

"What do we have to lose?" Deven let him finish the message before she spoke again. "I think he was stalking us," she revealed. Paul gave her a look, vying for her to elaborate so she did, relaying how she'd observed Deuce following her and Kennedy at the mall months ago. "I didn't think anything of it," she explained. "But then, not too long after, Kennedy had someone try to grab her in the parking lot of her apartment. Then she mentioned something about an ex she had to get a restraining order on . . ."

"You think it's him," Paul finished, trying to digest her words.

Deven lifted a shoulder in a helpless shrug. "It makes sense, right? Maybe . . ." She paused as she reflected on her thoughts. "Maybe she went into hiding. To get away from Deuce." It was a reach, but not too far outside of the realm of possibility. And it made sense.

Paul's forehead creased in consideration. "But she was here," he said. "Remember the neighbor said she was out here arguing with him. Why would she be over here if she had a restraining order on him?"

"Who knows? Maybe they were trying to work it out and he got abusive again. Maybe he threatened her. That would explain how he knows me. But either way, it's obvious he's lying."

"Yeah . . ." Paul's face was twisted in a way where it was obvious something was still troubling him. Something else entirely.

"What is it?" Deven prompted.

"This just doesn't make sense."

"I know. That's why I'll tell the police to investigate Deuce—"

"No, no not that." Paul started fiddling with his phone again; keying, swiping, and scrolling as he continued. "Yeah, I see what you're saying about Kennedy and Deuce, but how the hell did I get into the picture?" He shoved his phone in Deven's hands and she eyed the screen. A snapshot of Paul's bank statement was captured, pinched to zoom into numerous withdrawals ranging in the thousands. "I was looking over some stuff to see if there was anything else I could share with you about Amber," he went on. "I found three credit cards in my name that I've never applied for. Completely maxed out. So, I did some digging, called my bank, and found out there had been multiple transactions siphoning money out of my accounts for months. The withdrawals and purchases weren't large enough for me to notice, nor frequent enough to raise red flags with the bank. But collectively, it's a lot."

Deven's eyes remained glued to the screen. She didn't want to believe what he was saying but she was looking at the evidence clear as day. ATM withdrawals, purchases at luxury stores, meals at elaborate restaurants . . . it was all there.

"Did you give her your bank card or something?" she asked, dumbfounded.

"No—I mean, yeah once," he corrected. "To buy some baby stuff before I left for work. I saw she purchased a crib and some onesies an hour later and that was it. The card was waiting on my dresser when I got home with no issues, so I didn't think anything of it."

"Paul, I'm so sorry." Deven didn't even know what she was apologizing for, but guilt pierced her like a knife. Kennedy was *her* sister, so, to some degree, she felt responsible. "Listen, we're going to get to the bottom of this," she said with forced conviction. "We will get your money back." Maybe if she said it enough, she would start to believe it.

<hr />

At first, Deven hadn't wanted Paul to follow her home, even at his insistence. But she had to admit, she was comforted knowing that he was there in eyesight, escorting her back to safety. Because if she was honest with herself, a part of her was terrified Deuce knew where she lived and would come looking for her. At this point, she couldn't be sure exactly what he knew. Only that he was dangerous.

The first few streaks of dust were settling in by the time they arrived back to her place. Deven was surprised when she noticed Paul parking in one of the visitor spaces. She had assumed he would pull off once he confirmed she'd gone into her building. Part of her figured he was probably in a rush to get away from her and all her baggage. She had put him through enough trauma for today. Still, Deven didn't object when he waited for her at the entryway and wordlessly, followed her upstairs.

As soon as they were inside, Paul made it his business to check around the apartment, opening doors and peeking through anything that looked remotely like a hiding place. It was obvious they had been contemplating the same thoughts about Deuce, though he would probably never admit it out loud. Deven kicked out of her shoes and crossed into the kitchen to pour them a drink. She would let him do his thing. In fact, she was grateful for it right now. The entire ordeal had put her on edge.

"All clear," Paul announced entering the kitchen. Deven nodded her appreciation and opened the refrigerator to peer inside. The contents were scant at best, but it wasn't it like she had an appetite. She just needed something to do with her hands. "You hungry?" she asked. "I can probably order us some food or something."

"No, you don't have to do all that."

Fair enough. But that drink, on the other hand, was not optional. Deven pulled the Sangria bottle from the door and held it up for Paul to see. "You're not working tomorrow, are you?"

"Nope."

"Me neither." Thankfully. She reached for two glasses from the dishwasher and poured them each a generous portion. She turned then and handed one of the glasses to Paul.

He accepted the drink. "We should toast," he said out-of-the-blue.

"To what?"

Without hesitation, he clinked his glass against hers. "To Kennedy," he said. "The woman who ruined both of our lives."

It wasn't supposed to be funny. But the irony had a laugh erupting. Paul was just as amused, and he chuckled at his own comment.

"It's really a shame," Deven mused.

"What's that?"

"How one woman can do so much damage."

Lost in thought, she swirled her cup to cause the burgundy liquid to stir. Both of them watched the mini tornado take shape in the bowl of the glass.

"How was she as a kid?"

"Well, she wasn't robbing banks and going by aliases, if that's what you mean," she teased.

"That's not what I meant." Paul crossed the room to lean a narrow hip against the bar. "Like did you two get along. Were you close?"

Deven took a considering sip of the sweet liquid. She welcomed the sting of alcohol in her throat. "We were sisters," she said, finally. "We got along okay, I guess. I'm the oldest and she was just an annoying brat like all little sisters."

"Hmm, yeah, I got an older and younger brother. So, I get that. But as you get older, I guess it's not so bad."

Deven shrugged and took another sip of her wine. "I guess. She moved out when she was twelve," she admitted.

"Moved out?"

"She went to live with her dad. We didn't reconnect until she was about seventeen. The move really affected her relationship with our mom."

"Oh wow. That was a big decision for a little girl."

Deven didn't respond and turned back to the Sangria to pour

another cup. Weren't twelve-year-olds old enough to make those types of decisions? She sure had been.

"Well, how did she say it was living with her dad?"

"Rough," Deven murmured. "She said going to live with him was the biggest mistake of her life but she never said why, and she doesn't talk about it too much. Mama said it had to be because he was in and out of jail for petty shit. Fraud, burglary, selling drugs . . ." she trailed off, her comment like alarms in her ears.

"Now we see where she gets it from." Paul's words echoed her thoughts. "I wonder if she still talks to him."

"Mama told me he died," Deven informed him. "Years ago. I don't think even Kennedy knew. They had lost touch, I believe, as she got older."

"Oh wow. That's rough."

She nodded in agreement, her mind whirring with possibilities. "I was thinking earlier I needed to go back to her apartment," she said. "I feel like it's something I'm missing there. Not sure why. I just feel it."

"Do you think you could talk to your mom, too?" Paul offered. "Maybe she remembers something that could help."

Deven shrugged but her expression reflected her doubt. "I can try. But you never know with her."

Satisfied, Paul finished the rest of his wine before placing the glass in the sink. "Well, maybe I should get going," he started. "I'll let you know if Deuce's license plate turns up something."

"Sounds good." And because she felt she owed it to him, Deven touched Paul's arm. "And hey, thank you. For everything. I'm sorry you're tied up in all this."

Paul's gaze never faltered and Deven felt her face warm under his intensity. It was suddenly stuffy in the kitchen; their contact shooting bolts of electricity racing up her arm. As if on cue, her body purred to life. What the hell was she doing?

Flushed, Deven dropped her arm and took a step backwards, nearly colliding into the breakfast table. "Um, do you need me to walk you out?" she fumbled, dragging a hand over the back of her neck.

"No, I got it." Yet still, he didn't make a move. Deven couldn't even be sure she wanted him to. "It's interesting," he went on, his voice thick with arousal. "I never really realized how much you two favor . . ."

"Well, we are sisters."

"Yeah, but I meant in other ways." Paul's eyes were taking a slow, methodical survey of Deven's face now, then hair, and finally trailing down her body. "I have to ask myself, was I so attracted to her because she reminded me of you."

Deven released a staggering exhale and braced against the passion that threatened to drown her like a tidal wave. Don't do this, she silently begged, but she didn't know if the plea was for him. Or her. They couldn't indulge. It would be wrong, so very wrong.

Paul lifted his hand to graze her neck, gently coaxing her to him. She melted against his body, her lips searching for his. The kiss was slow, sensual, and staggering as both took their time savoring each other's essence. Deven didn't bother thinking anymore, only feeling. And oh, did she feel this man in every fiber. The ache left her body quivering.

He moved his lips to her neck as he pulled her coat off and then her shirt, pausing only briefly to pull the garment over her head. Then his hands were everywhere, soft like satin and tender with a doctor's precision. He was taking his time, his movements like a tease that caused her skin to ignite in the echoes of his strokes. When he picked her up to put her on the counter, Deven wrapped around his frame, his name like a melody on her lips. Damn, she needed this. She hadn't realized how much.

Paul lowered his head between her thighs, his tongue conducting a symphony on her core. She moaned and grinded against his lips, imploding as he drank her ecstasy. Then, while her body pulsed with the aftershocks of euphoria, he stood up to enter her, inch by glorious inch. "I've been waiting for this," he said, releasing a restrained breath. And again, her body fused with his, slick with sweat as they moved in a rhythmic dance all their own. Deven felt herself climbing and clenched against the budding orgasm. "Deven, I've always loved you." His whisper was poetic and that was all it took. Deven choked on a scream and was sent tumbling into their interwoven rhapsodies of paradise.

# Chapter Twenty
## Before

She was already regretting her decision.

Deven drove slowly, hoping to prolong the unavoidable as much as possible. It was her first therapy session, so she'd grossly misjudged the distance, arriving much earlier than she'd intended. Now, she was pulling on to the street of the office building with thirty minutes to spare. It would look either really desperate or really pathetic. Neither of which were ideal for first impressions.

The card Paul had given her was in the cupholder. Dr. Felicia Bradshaw. She had sounded nice on the phone (Deven was surprised that she answered as opposed to an assistant or receptionist). She didn't know why the idea of seeing a therapist was so demeaning. Logically, she knew she had nothing to be ashamed of. But in the same breath, it seemed to solidify that Deven had lost control; that she felt like a stranger in her own mind. And how weak she was, that she needed someone else, a complete stranger, to tell her how to fix her broken self?

But that morning, something was different. Deven got dressed, went for a walk, and stopped at the front of the complex, watching cars zoom by with enough velocity to have gusts of wind leaving her breathless. It wasn't just the temporary suffocation that allured her. It was the fact that, for thirty seconds, she wanted to—no, *craved* to—walk out into the onslaught of traffic and find solace with her babies and her dad. And because the temptation was so strong, Deven knew she had to call someone. Kennedy was completely ghost, as she usually was when Benji was in town. Of course, her mother wasn't much help, Justin still had a chip on his shoulder, and as much as it still hurt, her friendship with Paul was now nonexistent since the humiliated run-in with her boyfriend. So, it wasn't like she had too many options.

The business card had been sitting on her dresser like a lifeline. Plus, it seemed the safest and least judgmental. Beggars couldn't be choosers, and unfortunately, Deven really wasn't in a position to turn down assistance. She just didn't expect that assistance to come only two hours later. Even over the phone, as last minute as it was, Dr. Felicia Bradshaw detected the emergency and insisted on a same day appointment. But it was clear she was good at her job. And Deven didn't know if she appreciated or despised that attentiveness.

The office building sat on a private lot in the heart of downtown. It was discreet, that's for sure, because as much as Deven had come downtown for one reason or another, she had assumed the building was a residential home. Just one level, it had a wheelchair ramp alongside a small staircase leading up a large door with *Dr. Felicia Bradshaw* on the glass, and two bay windows with decals: one was a quote by Brené Brown that read, *Let go of who you think you're supposed to be; embrace who you are.* On the other window was a quote from Robert Frost, *The best way out is always through.* The affirmations were comforting.

Though she was early, Deven figured it was best to go ahead inside. Any longer, and she was afraid she would talk herself out of it. So, she turned off her phone and walked up the pavement with the assurance she didn't feel.

The waiting room was intimate with a bench and four chairs, plus a corner table with chips and granola bars neatly fanned in labeled baskets. Underneath the table was a minifridge with a clear door to display the rows of water. There were two closed doors, one with a restroom sign across the wood, and an arrangement of more inspirational quotes inscribed on canvases decorating the pastel walls.

Deven wasn't sure if she was supposed to take a snack and have a seat, knock on the door, or call to relay she had arrived early. As if on cue, the door slid open and a petite, brown-skinned woman with glasses and a bun stepped into the lobby. She looked entirely too young to be a therapist. *Probably her daughter or assistant,* Deven assumed with a polite smile.

The woman extended her hand for a shake. "Good afternoon," she greeted. "Did you have any trouble finding the place?"

"Yes. I appreciate Dr. Bradshaw being able to squeeze me in on such short notice."

"Oh, it's no problem at all." Her grip was surprisingly firm for a woman of her small stature. "And please call me Felicia." Deven's eyes widened, which prompted Felicia's knowing chuckle. "I get that reaction a lot," she continued. "And before you ask, I am thirty-two, I have my doctorate, and I've had my own practice for over three years."

"You just look so young," Deven clarified with a sheepish grin. In reality, she wasn't sure how she felt telling her problems to a woman about her same age. Weren't therapists supposed to be older white ladies with knee-highs and glasses? Well, Felicia did have the glasses part, but everything else didn't seem to fit the narrative.

"If it helps," Felicia went on as she led the way into her office.

"I do have recommendations. Even some awards and a few by-lines in *Psychology Today*."

Deven didn't know if the woman was teasing, but she shook her head anyway. "That's not necessary." She looked at the desk, then the two couches positioned to face each other. A black coffee table sat between the seating areas with a box of Kleenex, and two unopened bottled waters. Felicia immediately stepped out of her heels. "Sit anywhere you like," she invited.

Deven picked one of the couches and she watched the therapist sit opposite her with a clipboard and pen on her lap. "Thank you for calling me," Felicia started with that compassionate smile of hers firmly in place.

Deven nodded, unsure how to respond. Was she supposed to say, 'you're welcome?' "I . . . just needed someone to talk to," she said with a helpless shrug.

"Of course. Talk to me. What's going on?"

Deven took her time, her fingers fidgeting with the holes in her distressed jeans. She had purposefully not said too much during their earlier phone conversation, indecisive if she was even going to follow-through with a session. And frankly, she didn't feel completely comfortable with the very young and very unfamiliar Dr. Felicia Bradshaw.

"I'm dealing with some losses," Deven proceeded with care as she picked over her words. "And I guess I'm just letting it get the best of me."

"Completely understandable. Loss is a traumatic thing. You have to allow yourself time to grieve."

Felicia's response was genuine and Deven found that encouraging. No pushing, no intrusive questions. Not yet anyway. Deven felt the tension in her muscles unclench a little. "I'm trying," she admitted. "I guess, I just don't know how to grieve."

"There's not necessarily a right or wrong way. Everyone handles death differently, so you have to come to terms with the weight of this burden and figure out how to carry it."

Her words were resonating, and they'd only touched minute two of a forty-five-minute session. *Damn.* Deven released a sigh and sat back in the cushions, allowing the hurt to breathe. "I guess I've never tried to do that," she said, lowering her eyes to the floor. "I try to block it out or get rid of it. Not carry it. Like, with my dad. I knew it was coming, but you're never really prepared for death. So, when it happened, I just poured everything into trying to see about my mom so I wouldn't have to deal with it. Now with my babies, I don't know how to cope with this."

"Because you never had to do it with your dad," Felicia finished with an understanding nod.

Deven sighed at the epiphany. Was that why she was spiraling downward? "Maybe."

"Your dad must have been a very special man."

A wistful smile touched Deven's lips. She looked towards the window and almost like a mirage, she saw a reflection of her hero; full and animated with his pre-cancerous charisma. "He was," she said. "I mean, he wasn't perfect, of course. But he was perfect to me. He loved me and my mom very much. And my sister. All he wanted was his family. And it hurt him more than anything when he realized he was going to have to leave us."

"I'm sure," Felicia paused to jot something down on her clipboard. "And your mom. How has she been dealing with all of this?"

"Thankfully, she doesn't have to." Deven's retort was laced with a hint of resentment, and she winced at her insensitivity. "My mom has dementia," she explained. "So, a lot of times, she doesn't even remember my dad." She thought it best to leave out how Iris never seemed to forget Kennedy's dad though. "I guess part of me feels that's a good thing sometimes, not having to remember the pain."

"If you don't remember the pain, then you don't remember him," Felicia countered. "It's not better to live in the unknown. That would mean forgetting about the person entirely, which is even more excruciating. Because there is someone who had an effect on your life, and you can't even remember them or how much they loved you. Would you want to forget your dad and the wonderful man he is if you could do that?"

She was right, and Deven surely didn't want to do that. "No. I guess, I just thought that my mom is able to live better."

"You can live, too, Deven. You *are* living. Remember I said earlier, the grief is a burden you have to carry." Felicia put her clipboard to the side and reached beside the couch for a large tote bag. She sat the bag on the table and held the strap in Deven's direction. "Try to lift the bag," she instructed. Obediently, Deven took the strap and rose, slinging the tote easily over her shoulder. Felicia nodded in approval. "How is it, carrying the bag?"

"Easy. It's light," Deven answered, not quite following where she was going.

Again, Felicia nodded, and she stood to cross to the bookcase behind her desk. She pulled some books down in varying sizes and widths and brought them back to the table with her. Then, one-by-one, she began placing the books in the bag. The strap began to bite into Deven's shoulder as she struggled to hold it up and eventually, she pulled it off and let it drop to the ground. "Now, pick up the bag," Felicia demanded, resting her hands on her hips.

Deven grunted under the added weight, finally managing to hoist the bag back onto her shoulder. She grimaced with the pain.

"Now, how is it?"

"Heavy."

"Exactly." Felicia relieved her by taking the bag from her hands. "So, you see, it's the same bag, the same grief. Some days, you'll be able to carry the load a little easier. Other days, you may fall under the weight. And you know what? All of that is okay." Felicia seemed pleased with her exercise as she motioned for Deven to sit down once more. She passed a sheet of paper across the table where she'd drawn a single line through the middle to separate the paper into two halves. "I want you to do something for me," she said. "Take a few minutes and write down a memory that comes to mind with your dad. Don't think, just write. I'll tell you when time's up."

Deven accepted the pen Felicia handed her, took a breath, and started writing. She allowed the words to flow through the ink and as the sentences took shape, so did the memory. All of the emotions came flooding back, the despair, the passion, the desperation . . . she loved her dad and it crushed her to hear his pain. By the time Felicia called *time* Deven hadn't finished, and she felt just as incomplete as her dad had all those years ago. Out of all the memories, she felt bad that this was the one that was most prominent.

"Would you like to share the memory?" Felicia asked.

Deven stared at the ink, the slight smudge on the last word where her pinky had accidently dragged on the paper. "I heard my parent's arguing one night," she read, blinking back tears. "And it scared me because I had never heard my dad cry. They didn't know I was listening, and I didn't hear everything. But what I did hear was about my sister. He mentioned he wished she was never born because she was messing up the family since she didn't belong to him. And my mom cursed him out and told him she never wanted to see him again. He apologized and said he didn't mean it. That he was just upset. And I hated how my mom was being so selfish because my dad didn't deserve that. He was a good man and he loved all of us very much. But he left and I was scared I would never see him again. But thank God I did. Maybe that's how I try to ease the pain now. Thinking maybe, just maybe, I will see him again like before. That is why it's so hard to let him go. I just wish there was something that I could do this time to bring him back," she finished, looking up. Felicia didn't comment, but Deven could tell it wasn't exactly the core memory she was expecting.

# Chapter Twenty-one

She felt like shit.

Deven lay quiet in the bed, listening to Paul's heavy breathing as he slept in the peaceful bliss of his orgasm. She didn't even know when or how they'd even made it to the bedroom. Or how many times she had climaxed from the kitchen and the hall. All she knew was that her body was pulsing, whether from the wild sex or the guilt, she couldn't say which.

Her cell phone rang, loud and distant from somewhere in the house. It could've been Justin. Deven shut her eyes against the harsh reality and tried to quell another bout of rising remorse. What was she supposed to tell him? How could she face him? And poor Paul. What did that mean for their friendship now? Complications, she surmised with a frown. None of which she had time to deal with. What was she thinking? Of course, she hadn't been. Not with her head anyway.

Paul stirred next to her and Deven shifted to watch him. He looked adorable when he slept, those pink lips of his partly ajar and turned up at the corners as if he were smiling in his solace.

He'd fallen asleep immediately after round three (or was it four?) so he lay naked with the covers tangled in his legs.

Deven sighed and pulled the sheets to her breasts, tucking them tight under her arms. The whole ordeal had her acting on impulse, completely uncharacteristic of her. From the visit to the mystery apartment, the near-fight with Deuce, now sleeping with her friend slash dad's doctor slash missing sister's boyfriend? It was like something out of a reality show.

A hand grazed her shoulder and she flinched, bolting up in the bed.

"Hey, you okay?" Paul was awake now, the last fragments of slumber drooping his eyes.

"Sorry."

"For what?"

*Sleeping with you. Cheating on my boyfriend. Liking it.* "For waking you," she decided, keeping the linens tight against her frame.

Paul stifled a yawn and sat up, shimmying closer to her until they sat hip-to-hip. "Hey, don't worry about it," he said, placing a kiss on her shoulder. "I've been waiting for the chance to wake up next to you." Another kiss, this time his tongue danced across her skin. She trembled under the gesture, willing her body not to react. His words came tumbling back like a sack of bricks. He had said he loved her. Damn, what had she done?

"Paul . . ." It came out much weaker than she intended and Deven had to scold herself at the plea in her voice.

"Do you know how much I've wanted you, Deven?" Paul's forehead rested against hers and she closed her eyes, warming under the intimacy.

Her cell phone rang again, not enough to startle her but enough to snap her out of her daze. "Paul, we can't," she whispered.

"I want you again"—he kissed her neck—"and again"—a kiss

on her cheek—"and again." He was making his way to her lips and almost instinctively, Deven's lips parted to receive him. Another ring and she snatched back as if she'd been electrocuted.

"No." As if to prove her point, Deven swung her legs over the side of the bed and stood, dragging the covers with her to wrap around her body like a mummy. "Paul, please. I'm sorry but this—"

"What, Deven? What was this? Don't say 'a mistake.'"

His questions were laced with anger, but the pain in his eyes was even more unbearable. She had no words so all she could do was shrug helplessly. "I'm sorry."

"I don't get you, Deven. I've made my feelings clear to you from the beginning. Don't act like this was just a fling in the heat of the moment."

"I'm not! I—"

"What? You don't have feelings for me?"

It sounded rhetorical, but Paul looked to be waiting for an answer. Flustered, Deven rubbed the back of her neck and tried again. "It's not like that, Paul," she said with care. "I do like you."

That calmed him down and he pulled himself from the bed. Deven had to look away to keep from staring at his chiseled body. He placed his hands on her arms to massage them. "So, what is it, Deven, honestly?" He paused. "Is it because I'm white?"

"No, of course not!" But the retort made it more than obvious that wasn't completely far from the truth. Shame colored her cheeks, and she averted her eyes. "It's not just that," she clarified. "I'm in a relationship. You just got out of a relationship. With my sister—"

"You know it's not like that."

"Technically it is." His fingers were fogging her rationality, so she stepped back to put some distance between them. "There is just too much going on right now, Paul. You know that. Do we really have time to worry about dating and sex?"

Paul curled his lips in a mock frown. "Technically, we already handled the sex part so it's really just dating now."

Deven rolled her eyes, refusing to be amused with his joke. "I'm serious."

"I am, too." He took a step closer, raising his hands up to show he had no intention of touching her again. "I want you, Deven. All of you. But not if you have reservations. So, if you say this was a mistake, it shouldn't have happened, and never will again, I can respect that. I mean, shit will hurt like hell, but it is what it is."

Deven chewed on her bottom lip and watched him. He was completely sincere, she knew that. She just wasn't sure if she was completely ready to give Paul up. He was a great friend, the sex had been amazing, but would it be fair to tell him what he wanted to hear for her own selfish reasons? "May I think about it?" she asked, her voice frail.

"Of course."

She paused, using her eyes to reference Paul's nudity. "May I think about it with clothes on?"

It was only after he smirked and strolled past her that Deven risked letting loose the breath she had been holding. Now what was she going to do?

By the time, she showered and put on some lounge clothes, Paul had made himself comfortable in the living room. As requested, he had re-dressed and had even made them each a cup of coffee. Deven entered the living room, snatching her cell phone from the kitchen counter as she walked through.

"Someone has been looking for you," Paul announced, passing her a mug.

Deven sat down across from him on the chaise and took a sip of the steaming drink. It kept her from saying what she didn't want to admit; that she was dreading looking at her call log. Just her luck it was Justin. She couldn't speak to him right now, not with her guilty conscience.

"Thank you for the coffee," she said instead. It was bitter and needed way more milk and sugar, but it was an excuse to change the subject. "Anything from your friend about Deuce?"

"No, nothing yet. He's working on it and if he finds something, he's going to let me know as soon as possible."

Deven took another sip, straining in the awkward length of silence that followed. She could tell Paul was itching to say something but was refraining from doing so. The respect thing. She had to admire his chivalry.

Deven gathered her courage and risked looking at her phone. Four missed calls, two text messages, and two voicemails. Paul was right. Someone was definitely trying to hunt her down. She opened the phone and scrolled to the call log. Sure enough, Justin was the top contender with three of the calls. She started to check the messages, already figuring they were also from Justin, when the last missed call number caught her eye.

"What is it?" Paul asked, obviously sensing her anxiety.

Deven's fingers fumbled over the keys as she punched in the number and extension. "Police department," she relayed. "I asked Officer McKinney to look into some stuff about Amber Wright. I think she found something."

Paul waited, just as eager, while Deven listened through the various prompts before the officer's voice came through the receiver.

"McKinney," she greeted with a professional urgency.

"Hi, Officer McKinney. It's Deven." Deven flicked fearful eyes at Paul as he crossed to sit next to her. "I saw I missed your call."

"Yes, Ms. Reynolds. I told you I would let you know when I found something."

"Yes?"

"I did get a hit on that the Amber Wright name and information you gave me." She paused and cleared her throat. "Ms. Reynolds, I think you better come down to the station and see for yourself."

"I'm on my way." Deven hung up, already jumping to her feet. "I have to go."

Paul rose with a nod. "I know. I'm coming with you."

"Paul, no. I need to—"

"Not argue with me so damn much." He grinned as he cupped her face, his thumbs caressing her cheeks. "You're not doing this alone, okay?" He moved closer and Deven's eyes closed, expecting the kiss. She felt his lips graze her forehead and she had to swallow the disappointment. Complications, she had to remind herself. As if the cop's call wasn't proof of that. She would go down to the precinct and see about the new development. Her feelings for Paul would have to take a backseat.

⟶•⟵

Officer McKinney was waiting in the lobby when they arrived and immediately waved them on back. Instead of her office, this time she headed to an interrogation room that felt stiff with its gray walls and ceiling. A single metal table sat in the middle, edged with four matching chairs that only enhanced the uncomfortable atmosphere.

Officer McKinney gestured for them to have a seat. "Can I get you two a water or anything?"

Deven wouldn't be able to hold down anything if she wanted to. The worry coupled with Paul's coffee from earlier was already doing a number on her stomach. "I think we're okay," she said, and Paul agreed. Now left alone, she began to pace, unsure of what to expect. McKinney still hadn't explained anything, and even Paul had been clueless.

"Do you think they found Kennedy?" she asked, her eyes cutting to the two-way mirror dominating one wall.

"No, they probably would've told you that over the phone."

Deven swallowed. Yeah, that did make sense.

"Why don't you sit down, Deven?"

"I can't."

"Listen, I know this is troubling, but whatever happens we're going to handle this. Okay?" His smile was comforting which broke Deven's heart even more. Why had she slept with him and threatened their entire friendship?

The door creaked open, and they both turned with bated breaths. Officer McKinney entered again and stepped to the side to allow someone else to pass first. The woman strutted through, hands on hips and a scowl etched on her face. She looked to be in her thirties, with mocha-brown skin and hair slicked into a high ponytail that bounced with her stride. She reeked of luxury and entitlement, from her Dior heeled boots to the Birkin purse dangling from her manicured fingertips. Not to mention the jewelry winking from her neck, ears, and wrists like she'd just stepped off a runway.

Right behind the woman was her mini-twin, a girl looking to be in her late-teens, maybe high-school or college. She, too, was dressed fashionable and expensive, but she didn't carry that same attitude as her companion. She peered from behind designer-framed glasses, her baby face nearly hidden in the mane of curly hair.

Deven looked between them before tossing a concerned glance to Paul. It just kept getting messier and messier.

"Ms. Reynolds," Officer McKinney spoke, closing the door for privacy. "This is Ms. Wright."

"Amber Wright?" Deven glanced at the woman, ignoring the roll of eyes at her apparent ignorance.

"Yolanda Wright," she corrected with a raised brow. "As in, wife of Benjamin Wright of the Wright Hotels." Yolanda pulled the young girl closer, the gesture protective as much as it was controlling. "*This* is our daughter, Amber. The one whose identity your thieving sister stole." Amber lowered her eyes in apparent humiliation. Deven could only feel sorry for her.

"Listen—"

Yolanda held up a stiff finger. "No, bitch, you listen," she snapped, continuing her rant. "Amber here is graduating in a few months, early might I add, with a full scholarship to Stanford. She is a young, beautiful, educated, black woman and her dad and I worked *very* hard to make sure she was equipped with everything she needed to succeed. And then, gutter rats like you all, who probably can't afford anything besides a Four-For-Four at Wendys, come trapezing in and stealing what others have earned." She spun to McKinney, that damn ponytail swinging over her shoulder. "I want them arrested."

"What?" Deven didn't know which part of this three-ring circus was more shocking. "Arrested for what?"

"Hold on a second." Paul extended an arm across Deven's chest, probably hoping she didn't try to fight the abrasive woman.

Yolanda cut her eyes at him. "And who are you? Her lawyer?"

"Now, wait a minute," Officer McKinney snapped, stepping between the brewing tension. "Everyone, sit down and shut the hell up with the nonsense. Right now."

Like stubborn children, everyone shuffled to take their seats, Paul and Deven across from Yolanda and her daughter. Glares darted across the table sharp enough to pierce metal, but judging by McKinney's outburst, everyone knew better than to object or try to speak.

"Now, let's start this over." McKinney leaned a hip on the edge of the table and crossed her arms over her breasts. "Ms. Reynolds asked me to look into an Amber Wright name, as she indicated there may be some connection with the death of her sister—"

"Are you fucking kidding me?" Yolanda was on her feet again. "My daughter is a victim here and you're trying to bring up crazy allegations?"

"Mrs. Wright, if you don't get control of yourself, I *will* escort you out of this precinct," Officer McKinney said, her tone firm. "Now sit. Down!"

Yolanda obviously didn't like being told what to do but she knew she had no choice. She glowered at Deven while lowering herself back to the chair.

"Now, let's start from the beginning." McKinney nodded to Deven for her to speak. The thing was, now that Deven had permission, she really wasn't sure what to say. With everything she and Paul had discovered, all fingers pointed to exactly what Yolanda Wright was alleging. That Kennedy was a stone-cold identity thief. How the hell could she admit that?

"I was mistaken," she said, looking directly at the cop to keep from meeting Paul's questioning frown. "About the Amber Wright thing. I thought the person may have had something to do with Kennedy, but I was wrong. I guess I was so desperate for answers, I was grasping at stuff to try and make sense of it."

McKinney was visibly agitated. "Where did you get the name and information for Amber Wright, Ms. Reynolds?" she asked. "And how did you figure it was some kind of connection?"

Deven looked to Paul, searching for help.

"Deven showed me a picture of a girl's night out," he jumped in. "Kennedy was in the picture and their mutual friend, Amber. But Amber got married and moved away years ago. Deven just never really liked the friend much."

It was a weak excuse, but it was the best they could do. Deven was grateful for Paul. Her mind was too convoluted to think of anything remotely rational at the moment.

"I apologize for wasting your time," she said standing.

"Hold up, that's some bullshit!" Yolanda stood again as well. "My daughter had some fraud on her credit a few months ago. Credit cards and shit opened in her name. A bank account her father and I set up when she was four, has been completely depleted. That's over three hundred thousand. Gone!" She spat each word with venom as she narrowed her eyes at Deven. "Now these people claim there is some connection with some girl named Kennedy. They know something!"

"Mrs. Wright—"

"I want them investigated," Yolanda yelled. "They stole my daughter's money. Or they sure as hell know who did."

McKinney cast wary eyes at Deven. "Ms. Reynolds, do you know anything about this fraud and stolen money Mrs. Wright is alleging?"

Deven pursed her lips and shook her head. "No, I don't," she lied.

"Ms. Reynolds, I really hope you're not lying to me. Because if I find out otherwise . . ." The officer let the warning hang suspended between them.

"Oh, you don't have to worry, Officer." Yolanda was already headed to the door with Amber scurrying to catch up. "They know something. And my husband and I will make sure that they *and their sister*, are thrown in jail."

<hr/>

"Why would you tell them about Amber?" Paul hadn't even driven out of the parking lot before he started firing off questions.

Deven held her fingers to her temples to stave off the beginnings of a headache. "I don't know," she confessed. "I guess after we spoke the first time, I just thought . . . I don't know."

Paul's hand found hers across the middle console and as much as she knew it was best, she couldn't bring herself to let it go. "I get it," he said. "You figured it would still be her using that name."

"Yeah, and maybe we would have a few more answers. I didn't know it was just a random rich girl." Deven shook her head struggling to digest the recent news. "She took that girl's college savings, Paul. How heartless can she be?"

"She is an heiress to the Wright Hotel chain. I seriously doubt she's going to go hungry because that money was taken."

Deven shook her head. As true as it was, it didn't make it any better. Nor did it justify Kennedy's actions. *Who was this person?* "I just can't believe I never saw this," she murmured to herself. "I mean, I know my sister likes to shop and spend money. I know she likes plastic surgery and getting her hair done and all that. But stealing, Paul? Hell, did she ever even have a real job?"

Paul's cell phone buzzed, and he pulled it from his pocket, easily driving with one hand. He used his thumb to swipe while his eyes toggled from the screen to the road. "I think we may have some answers soon," he said with a slight smile. "I got some information from my law enforcement friend on that license plate number for Deuce. He's going to email me in a minute."

"Good. I could use some good news instead of hearing about how I'm going to go to jail for some stolen money I had nothing to do with."

"No, you're not. No one is going to jail. Except maybe your sister."

The thought was unsettling and had queasiness ascending from Deven's belly. "See, that's the thing," she sputtered. "I don't *want* my sister to go to jail. I don't *want* her to get in any trouble."

"Even if it's proven that she stole money? She stole from me, too, Deven," he added at her hesitation.

She sighed. "I know that's what you say, Paul—"

"But what? You think I'm lying? You think the Wrights are lying?"

He was getting upset. He had even moved his hand to break their touch. Deven didn't want him mad at her. She wanted him to be there for her like he'd been all this time. But dammit she wasn't ready to give up on Kennedy. Not yet. Not again.

"I just want to hear her side first," she said carefully. "I'm not saying anyone is lying. I'm just saying we don't have all the facts and I'm not just going to condemn my sister without answers. That's not fair to anyone."

Paul was clearly dissatisfied with her response, but thankfully, he didn't push the conversation anymore. They lapsed into strained silence the rest of the ride home and Deven was okay with that. She needed the silence. It was better than having to listen to more animosity.

It was still early by the time they pulled back into the apartment complex. Deven didn't wait around for Paul, instead hiking through the parking lot without caring if he followed. She heard him running to catch up, then the hand on her forearm to stop her in her tracks.

"Deven, I'm sorry," he said stepping in front to block her path. "I am. I wasn't trying to be insensitive."

Deven felt her attitude slowly beginning to dissolve, her body liquefying under the exhaustion. "I know," she said, simply. She really was too weak to argue any further. The police department visit had not gone as expected. Really nothing had gone as expected. And here she was struggling to hold onto the shreds of sanity she had left.

She followed Paul up the stairs, already looking forward to her bed, when his hand shot out against her chest.

"Wait," he whispered.

His body was blocking her view so obediently, she stopped and held her breath. "What is it?"

That's when he shifted, ever so slightly, and she caught sight of her front door, swaying open back and forth in the afternoon breeze.

"Did you leave the door unlocked?" Paul asked, already knowing the answer.

"No." Fear iced her voice as Deven grabbed his arm. "Let's go back to the car and call the police."

"One second. If someone is still in there, we need to catch them before they leave."

It was crazy, but he was already moving towards the door, his arm still stretched in Deven's direction to make sure she stayed put. Then he disappeared inside. Deven snatched her cell phone from her purse and dialed Officer McKinney's number. It went right to voicemail. "Officer McKinney, it's Deven," she spoke in an urgent whisper. "I'm sorry to bother you, but please come to my apartment. I think someone broke in." She hung up and took a tentative step closer to the door. From her vantage point, nothing seemed out of order. The couch, TV, and everything in the living room looked the same. Who would want to break in? And what the hell were they trying to steal?

She released the breath she had been holding when Paul appeared in the doorway. "No one's inside," he confirmed, motioning for her to enter.

"Did they take anything?"

"I don't think so," he said with caution. "But he did leave this." Paul held out a single sheet of paper in Deven's direction. The message had been written in red marker, the threat piercing through the five words like a knife: *Stay out of it – Deuce.*

# Chapter Twenty-two

Deven watched McKinney look around for the second time, poking her head in doors and focusing in on her technological wares. She knew the officer was thinking exactly what she and Paul had deduced. If it was indeed a normal robbery, why had nothing been taken? Deven's fingers curled around the note in her pocket, the paper digging into her palm.

"Are you sure you didn't leave the door open by mistake?" McKinney asked. Her insinuation was evident as she used a finger to lift the lid on a jewelry box and peer inside.

Deven nodded her insistence. "Yes, I'm sure," she said. "I always lock my door." Her hand tightened and the note crinkled. Deuce had made his presence clear. But now Deven wasn't so sure if she should share those facts. Because if she did, McKinney would want to know about who he was and what the hell they had been doing over there. The story would sound as crazy as it was, that's for sure.

Deven tossed a look to Paul who stood watching in the bedroom doorway. They hadn't really discussed a plan while they waited for the police to arrive. McKinney was already suspicious in her own right, apparent at the station and now as she searched the apartment. Calling her had been complete impulse, fueled by fear at the break-in, but now Deven was starting to regret it. Things weren't adding up and McKinney was far from stupid. But now everything had changed. Her life was possibly in jeopardy.

On sight, Deven pulled the note from her pocket and held it out for the officer to see. "We know who did this," she admitted.

McKinney frowned, took the paper, and unfolded it. Her eyes scanned the message and she looked up with a questioning gaze. "Who is Deuce?"

"My sister's boyfriend," Deven said. She had decided she was going to straddle the fence between the truth and lying by omission. Telling everything now about Kennedy's connection to Amber Wright would only make her look like an accessory.

McKinney pulled a pen and notepad from her back pocket. "Her boyfriend, you say?" she echoed as she jotted in the pad. "Why would this Deuce character break into your home? What does 'stay out of it' mean? Stay out of what?"

"I've been looking into my sister's disappearance."

"Ms. Reynolds, we confirmed the body in the morgue belongs to Kennedy, remember?"

"Yes, I know. And I'm not saying you're lying, but that makes absolutely no sense because that woman is not my sister."

McKinney had stopped writing and she was now staring at Deven with an incredulous look. "Ms. Reynolds . . ." Her lips moved to say something else, but at that point, no other sound came out.

Frantic, Deven rushed on. "You know how when you're in the Witness Protection Program you go into hiding with a new identity? I think that's what happened."

"Ms. Reynolds, if your sister was in the Witness Protection Program, I assure you, we would know about it."

Deven shook her head and tried again. "I don't mean literally," she clarified. "I just think she went into hiding to escape this guy, Deuce. I believe he's abusive."

McKinney lifted an eyebrow, her face unreadable. "Have you witnessed some abuse or violent disputes between them?"

"I haven't personally, no. But the neighbor has. And I've met him," Deven added as an afterthought. "He is definitely hiding something. So, I'm not sure if he tried to hurt her and she escaped and went into hiding. He may be hiding her. I don't know but, it's something."

Silence. Deven suddenly felt ridiculous, and she wished Paul would say something. Anything to make her sound less like an idiot in denial of her sister's suicide.

McKinney flipped the cover down on the pad and looked to the note again. "And does any of this have anything to do with Amber Wright?" she asked, her face hardening.

"I-I . . . don't know." Deven lifted her hands feebly before letting them fall at her sides. "It may. Deuce may have stolen the money."

Another pause. "Deuce." It was said more like a statement, then a question. Like *are you sure you're saying the right person* kind of inflection.

Deven shifted uncomfortably under her intense stare. "I don't know. He's into that kind of stuff so it's not far-fetched." In actuality, she didn't know what kind of stuff Deuce was into. She and Paul were too preoccupied to discuss the email from his friend about his discovery. But after their chance meeting with the man, Deven stood firm on that belief. He was into some shit. And whether her sister was his accomplice, his pawn, or his hostage, Deven knew he was pulling the strings in their whole operation, whatever that was. This break-in and the note he left behind proved that more than anything.

"These are some pretty strong accusations," McKinney said, finally. "But in light of this"—she held up the note between her index and middle finger—"I'm going to have to look into this Deuce person. Do you have a real name?"

Deven looked to Paul, surprised when he shook his head. "No," he said. "We don't." She started to object, but something told her to keep quiet.

McKinney held his gaze for an extra few minutes before she brushed past him and headed to the front door. "I'll look into it," she said. "In the meantime, do you feel safe here? Is there somewhere you can go until we find this man?"

"I'll be fine," Deven said, though she didn't know how true that was. She would probably have to do like her sister did and call Benji to install some cameras.

McKinney nodded. "You two take care," she said. "We'll be in touch." And with that, she was gone.

Deven closed the door behind her and looked to the window, satisfied when she saw the officer's silhouette disappear down the stairs. She turned to Paul. "Why didn't you tell her the information you found out about Deuce?"

"My friend obtained this information as a favor," he reminded her. "If it gets out, he was using his position to pull records and release this information to me, we all could get in trouble. Mainly him."

Deven sucked in a sharp breath. She certainly hadn't thought about that.

"But the cop is right, I don't feel comfortable with you here," he said.

"It's not like I have anywhere else to go." Shit, she hadn't meant to say that. Now it sounded like she was throwing hints for Paul to ask her to stay with him. And she could tell by the sudden glint in his eye he had caught the subtext of her comment, and liked the idea, so she quickly rushed on. "So, we never got to discuss what your friend emailed you about him." Deven turned her back on Paul to move into the living room. "We need to see how dangerous this man is." She felt his eyes on her back and she prayed he wouldn't circle back to the uncomfortable conversation.

Thankfully, he didn't as he joined her on the couch and pulled out his phone. "Let me check the email."

Deven tucked her legs under her as she watched him scroll, then read the message aloud. "His real name is Dion Morris," he started. "Age twenty-eight, alias is Deuce. Apparently, he's in the system so Officer McKinney will have no problems finding him. Look." He scooted closer and held out his phone for Deven to see the screen. "Incarcerated multiple times for drug possession, assault, robbery, parole violations . . . He did six years in Wilcox State Prison."

Deven scanned the email message that corroborated his exact words. Damn, what was Kennedy doing dating this criminal?

"It seems he's real smart, a tech guy," Paul read on. "Builds computers, hacking, stuff like that. So now people hire him as a Tracker."

Deven's eyebrows drew together. "A Tracker? Like tracking people or something?"

"Looks that way."

She sat back in thought. "So, do you think he uses his tech skills to track people down and then robs them? Like Amber?"

"I don't know, it just doesn't make sense," Paul shook his head. "So, he tracked me down? And Kennedy dated me to distract me?"

He was right. It still didn't make sense.

"We need to go to Kennedy's apartment," she decided. "There

must be something there. Something I overlooked. After I found that picture of you, I wasn't even thinking about anything else." Her mind flipped to Benji. He was sneaking something while they were there. And he had called trying to get back in the apartment for some reason. Of course, he knew something too. Why hadn't she reconsidered that part?

Deven jumped up and headed for the bedroom to get her cell.

"What's going on?" Paul followed, watching as she snatched her phone from the nightstand.

"I'm going to call Kennedy's friend Benji," she said as her fingers flew over the keys to type a message. "Have him meet me at her apartment so I can dig around and see what the hell he's up to."

Paul grabbed her wrists, tight enough to stop her movements but tender enough to have electric currents heating her skin in response. "Hey, that's enough for today," he coaxed, pulling her device from her now limp fingers and tossing it on the bed behind her. "Why don't we relax for a bit? I can run you a bubble bath, order some food . . ." His hands had moved to caress her arms and Deven's body quivered with the ache. She knew it was risky having him here. But dammit, she was ready to risk it all.

Her lids fluttered closed, and she felt his face a taste away from hers, his rich, musky scent like an intoxicating spice that tantalized every sense at once. Her mouth tingled to feel his, even felt his cool breath stroking her lips and they parted with the invitation. Maybe she could—

"What the fuck is going on?"

The voice had Deven snatching back and nearly stumbling in her haste. Her eyes flew to the door, widening at the source of the interruption.

Justin stood in the doorway of the bedroom, slightly tousled from his flight and a rolling bag at his feet. Shock, anger, and jealousy cloaked his face as he shot eyes of pure hatred at Deven, then Paul. She didn't even have time to react. Justin was across the room in two strides and threw Paul a punch to the face. The crack of knuckle on bone had Deven wincing, and she threw herself in front of him, her arms outstretched to keep her boyfriend at bay.

"Justin, stop!"

The gesture had Justin in a frenzy, and he looked at Deven with a deranged look she had never seen before.

"You really going to cheat on me with this dude and have the nerve to defend him?"

"Please, it's not like that!"

"The fuck is it like, Deven?" He snatched away when she attempted to reach for his arm. "Nah, don't fucking touch me!"

Calmly, Paul walked to the door without so much as a comment.

"Paul!" Deven cried.

He turned then, his eyes brimming with hope. But what could she say then? *Don't leave me? Please be my friend. I need you,* all words that were caught in her throat. She didn't know she was crying until the tears blurred her vision. But still through the haze she saw Paul's figure disappear out of sight. Then the slam of the front door resonated like the exclamation point of his finality.

Deven reached up to drag her hands over her wet face, then her hair. Justin was waiting, his seething inflaming the air between them until it was nearly suffocating. She owed him an explanation. That was the least she could do. She took a breath and sank to the mattress. "Paul has been helping me," she said, keeping her voice, and eyes low, as she spoke. "I've been doing some digging into my sister's case."

"What case? She's dead, Deven. And what the hell does that have to do with you and him fucking?"

She flinched at his piercing words. No use denying it. "My sister isn't dead," was all she could mumble.

"You know what? Fuck you, you crazy, lying, cheating bitch!" Justin swung his arm, sending the bedside lamp flying across the room. The shatter of the wall plaster startled a choked scream from Deven. He stalked to the door, snatching up his bag along the way. Then, for the second time, another loud slam shook the walls as Deven was left to cry alone.

# Chapter Twenty-three

**Excerpt from the diary of Kennedy (Age 11)**

*Daddy wants me to come live with him. He said that him and Ms. Erika with a k have been looking on the internet and that when I turn twelve, I can decide who I want to live with. I don't know how I feel about that yet. I mean I think it would be fun to live with my daddy and even Ms. Erika with a k and her little girl but it would feel so weird not being around my mom and Deven all the time. And then what about my friends at school? And my teachers? Daddy says I can come visit any time I want. He says it'll be like it is now, just flipped so I would live with him and see Mommy on the weekends. Which I guess is not so bad. I don't know. It will probably be cool with her. I'm sure she would want me to go. And Daddy seems so excited to have me around all the time because he says he misses me when I'm gone. And I miss him too. He said we could maybe move into a bigger house, and I could have my own room and my own space. Plus, a new* school. A better school. Then he told me all the things we would do together like cooking and movies and skating. He even said if I was really good, he would let me have a dog which is what I really, really want! But I don't know, it's such a hard decision. How could they let almost twelve-year-olds make this kind of choice? I'm going back home this weekend and I'm going to make sure to talk to Deven and see what she says about it. And I trust her, so I know she'll tell me the truth whether it's a good or bad idea. I just don't want to stay and wished I had moved. And I don't want to move and wish I had stayed.

# Chapter Twenty-four

*Where was he?*

Deven hung up the phone for the fourth time and stared at Benji's name on the screen. She figured he would've answered, or at the very least, called her back by now. She had left a message for him last night and sent a text that morning letting him know that she planned on returning to Kennedy's apartment if he wanted to meet her there. Now, she sat outside the building watching the pedestrians while she waited for him to reach out.

She scrolled on her phone for a bit, her finger hesitating for the briefest of moments over Paul's phone number. He wouldn't answer. She knew that. She had hurt him too bad. And Justin, well she had woken up to a three-minute slew of cuss words and empty threats on her voicemail that she had deleted. And one check of her social media disclosed he had blocked her on every platform. There was really nothing she could say to repair that damage, and she wasn't even sure she wanted to. Maybe it was best to just let both of them go. She had too much on her plate right now anyway.

Deciding there was no point in waiting any longer, Deven climbed from the car and headed to the apartment. It felt different this time, coming back alone to Kennedy's residence. The last visit, she had Benji there to assuage her discomfort. But now, making the journey up those familiar steps was unnerving. As if on cue, a chill ran up her spine and Deven spun in place, expecting to see someone following her. But there was no one, at least no one she could see. She picked up the pace, fumbling with the keys and rushing inside, slamming the door behind her.

Everything still looked the same, as if the apartment had been frozen in happier times. Cold bit her face as she blew warmth into her freezing hands and Deven wandered to the thermostat. Sixty-eight degrees. She pressed the touchpad to turn on the heat, listening for the hum of the heater. She would have to make a point to call the power, well all of Kennedy's utilities, to make sure they were turned off. She'd been so focused on everything else that it hadn't even crossed her mind until now to take care of her sister's affairs. The thought brought on a feeling of déjà vu, and Deven remembered having to conduct this same business when her father passed. Her mother just wasn't prepared with the knowledge, nor the mental capacity, to handle it. And here she was again, in the same boat. Unless she found something that said otherwise, Deven had to assume the worst. Which made her even more determined during this second search of Kennedy's apartment. There had to be something here. It just had to be.

More focused, Deven peeled out of her jacket and marched to Kennedy's bedroom. Since she found the picture of Paul here last time, she would start where she left off. Deven pulled open the nightstand drawer, shuffling through its contents. Nothing else suspicious, thankfully. Selfies of Kennedy and Benji, a few pictures of couples Deven assumed were friends, and some old holiday greeting cards. She nudged the drawer closed and tried the other nightstand, just to be sure she hadn't missed anything.

Then she crossed back into Kennedy's second bedroom. It looked a little scarce this time, Deven immediately noticed. There weren't as many clothes scattered around and she wondered who had taken them. Benji, maybe? But why?

She stepped over a few discarded shoes with no mates, some more papers, and walked into the closet of the bedroom. The built-ins carried into here as well, though smaller to accommodate the tight space. A few loose hangers hung on the rack while more trash littered the floor. Bench seating with drawers underneath formed a U-shape, and Deven absently pulled and closed the drawers, nothing of too much importance grabbing her attention. A shelf lined the top with shoe boxes, and she reached above, pulling one down. Red bottoms, she noted, eyeing the expensive shoes nestled in the tissue paper. And the crisp leather was indicative they had never been worn. Boxes two and three appeared to be the same, snakeskin boots and six-inch heeled sandals, respectively. Deven had just about given up as she leaned up to place the boxes back in their original positions. She fell short, the boxes tumbling from her hand and scattering around her like confetti. Damn. She stooped to pick them up, noting that one box had touched a corner of the U-shaped seating, pushing it inward to reveal the removable bench. Deven frowned, curious why she hadn't noticed it before. She lifted the wood and peered inside, her eyes rounding like saucers.

More shoeboxes, but this time they weren't filled with shoes. But what they were filled with was even more disturbing. The first thing Deven noticed was the stacks of money, neatly bundled with currency sleeves and arranged in ascending order by bill denominations. Just eyeballing it, Deven figured it was over $50,000. She touched the bills, crisp like they were straight from the printer, but real as real can be. Deven sat back on her heels, her mouth agape.

Her eyes caught the passport books and driver's licenses next, organized just as neatly next to the bills. Deven picked up the IDs and flipped through them. Lisa Turner. Maya Watson. Rochelle Holmes. Vanessa Kirk. All different names, addresses, and identifying information. But the pictures were all Kennedy. Sure, she had various hair sizes and colors, braids, blonds, and wigs, and even the facial features had slight variations with makeup or surgeries, but the woman in the picture was clearly the same. "Oh my God," she whispered, looking at the grinning picture of Kennedy on Melissa Trainor's ID. She ignored the passports, already knowing they were going to serve as affirmation.

Deven recognized one of the other shoe boxes as the one she'd seen with the gun in it. Though the piece was gone now, the paperwork was no less incriminating. Envelopes of bills, notices, receipts, and statements cluttered the box, the jarring red *Overdue* stamp bold and brazen on the aged paper. Again, not one of them had Kennedy's name, but a myriad of other names that Deven didn't recognize. Yolanda's threat came back to echo in her head. Stolen identities. And tons of them, dating back several years.

Movement had Deven's ears perking, and her head whipped towards the doorway. Sure enough, the footsteps were slow and muffled against the carpet moving in her direction. She held her breath and crawled towards the back of the closet. Oh God, Deuce had found her. Her heartbeat hurtled against her chest so hard it felt like each thump was cracking her ribs.

The footsteps stopped at the door to the bedroom. Deven's breath hitched, and she bit her tongue to keep from screaming out loud. Would the neighbors even hear her? The graphic image of a single gunshot ripping through her flesh had her straining against sobs. The footsteps entered. Then stopped. Then another step. Deven saw the person's shadow spill across the floor. They were right outside of the door now, their breathing amazingly calm. And heavy. It was him. He'd told her to stay out of it and here she was still digging up shit she couldn't handle. Now he'd come to—

A scream exploded from her throat as the figure rounded the corner.

"Deven, what the hell is wrong with you?"

Not Deuce's voice. Benji's. Thank God. Deven didn't realize terror had prompted her to shut her eyes against the unknown assailant. She lifted her lids now and relaxed as she stared into Benji's face, creased in confusion.

"I didn't know it was you," she heaved, struggling to calm down. She'd been holding her breath so long her chest was burning.

Benji took a step closer, his eyes skimming the closet. "Who did you think I was?" he asked.

"Someone else,' Deven answered, simply. She watched his gaze land on the hidden compartment in the bench before lifting to meet her stony stare. When he didn't say anything, she stood up, keeping her eyes level with his. "What's going on, Benji? And don't lie to me," she added when he started to open his mouth. "I'm so serious right now. What the hell is my sister into?"

Benji's jaw tightened, and she watched the inner conflict tugging in his eyes. She knew he was loyal to Kennedy, but he already knew he wouldn't be able to lie his way out of this. Not when all kind of evidence was scattered between them.

"We steal identities," he said as if that was explanation enough.

Deven blinked, waiting for the reality to hit. It should have shocked her. Why wasn't she shocked? Maybe because deep down she already figured that was what made the most sense. As much as it hurt to admit. "How long?"

Benji shrugged. "Since we were teenagers."

Deven picked up some of the papers, crumbled and carelessly tossed in the box. "So, you do all this to steal from other people." Amber Wright, Paul, so many other nameless, faceless people who had been used as mere pawns in their twisted thievery.

"It's not as bad as it sounds," Benji said. "Most of the people are well off and won't even miss a few thousands."

"Oh, don't give me that Robin Hood bullshit," she snapped, enraged at his apathy. "You hardly steal from the rich and give to the poor. You both are just a bunch of con artists." He didn't deny it and Deven had to laugh at his utter audacity. They may as well have been talking about the weather or a basketball game as opposed to their illegal activities. "You know what, it doesn't even matter." As if to prove her point, Deven threw all the papers back in the box and slammed the bench seat back in place. "I don't even care about this shit because you and Kennedy will both get your karma with scamming people. All I want to know, is where is my sister?"

Benji's lips curved in amusement. "I don't know," he said.

"You're lying."

"Okay."

"Dammit, Benji stop this shit!" Her hands balled into fists as she gestured wildly to the secret stash. "You act like I can't just call the police and have your ass thrown in jail."

That wiped the smirk off his face. Good. Now he saw she was serious. Benji's eyes narrowed to slits as he took one menacing step forward. He looked dangerous and as much as Deven wanted to cower under his presence, she fixed her stance and crossed her arms.

"You seriously need to think about what you say to me," he warned.

She wasn't just scared, she was terrified, but she still managed to take a step closer to him until their faces were a kiss apart. "Where the fuck is my sister?"

His pause was meant to be intimidating, and under normal circumstances it would've been, though she never would've admitted it to him. Benji finally relaxed and he took a step backward, holding his palms up. "Look, I'm not trying to go there with you," he said, his tone light. "For real. I don't know where Kennedy is. But I highly doubt she's dead like the police are saying."

"Yeah, I get that now. But that still leaves me with a whole bunch of questions and no answers." Frustration had Deven plopping down to the bench. "Whatever this is you both are tied up in is coming back to me. And her boyfriend is breaking into my home, threatening me—"

"Wait, who?" Benji frowned. "Whose boyfriend?"

"Kennedy's."

"Nah, she doesn't have a boyfriend. Not a real one anyway."

Deven wanted to ask how he could be so sure, but she just shrugged. "The neighbors said she was arguing with the man and now she's gone, and Deuce is leaving me threatening messages. Plus, the cops are talking about jail for an identity that was stolen."

Benji shook his head. "Wait, wait. Hold up. You're talking about Deuce?"

"Yeah. The neighbor said that was Kennedy's boyfriend."

Now, Benji did laugh as he too, sat down on the bench. "Nah, sweetheart you got it all wrong," he said. "Deuce was doing some work for Kennedy."

"What kind of work? Or do I want to know?" Deven tossed a pointed look at the bench indicating the scams they were running.

"Hey, judge all you want. But our shit is a legit business and we know what we're doing." Benji winked, obviously proud. Deven's stomach turned. "But Deuce, on the other hand, I can't say all his shit is on the up-and-up. He's a tracker, and let's just say he pulls out all the stops to get the job done."

Deven's head clouded over with confusion. "So, Kennedy hired him to look for someone?"

"Yeah, that's what she told me."

"But who?"

"Hell, if I know. Ken doesn't tell me everything. He's somebody her dad referred."

The mention of Kennedy's father had Deven's head jutting up. "Hold on. I thought her dad was dead," she said. "He died years ago in prison. Kennedy said she lost touch with him a long time ago."

"Well, he is in prison," Benji commented. "But no, he's very much alive, and Kennedy still talks to him. What difference does it make?"

It made all the difference. Deven could feel her blood beginning to boil. Because not only did it mean Kennedy had lied, but it also meant her mother had been just as deceptive. She jumped to her feet and stormed to the door. Good day or bad day, she didn't give a damn anymore. Her mother had lied to her face. What other truths had she withheld? And why?

# Chapter Twenty-five

"Deven!" Jan opened the door with a bright smile. "I didn't think . . ." She trailed off, her face immediately flickering to reflect her concern. "Oh my. What's wrong?" She quickly stepped to the side and ushered Deven into the room.

Deven sniffed. She knew she looked a mess. One look in her mother's hallway mirror confirmed that. Her eyes were swollen, her cheeks streaked with dried tears. And she felt even worse. She and her mother had always been so close, and Deven had taken pride in that relationship. She had never used her mother's dementia as a crutch for their distance, instead relishing the good times as if they were still a reality. But now, she felt completely betrayed. They never had secrets. Apparently, she was the only one who had honored their mother/daughter bond. Sure, she was angry. But the hurt was feeding on her like a parasite, leaving her weak and exhausted. And it was written all over her face, body, and attitude.

"I'm okay," Deven lied with a smile that wasn't very convincing. "Is my mother busy?"

"For you? Never."

There was a time when Deven believed that. Now she really couldn't say. "Can you give us a little moment?" she asked. "I'm not taking her out of the room."

"Of course." Jan paused, then added, "Deven, if you need anything, I'm here. I know you have your mother, but I think of you like my own."

Deven nodded her appreciation. Though she really doubted the kind nurse would understand. So, no, she couldn't discuss this with her. There was a conversation meant solely for Iris. She used those few precious minutes after Jan left to muster her strength. Then she turned and walked into the line of fire.

Even though it was late afternoon, her mother was in bed, burrowed under the covers with scenes from a game show on the TV illuminating her face. Deven paused in the doorway and studied Iris's profile, noting the trace of merriment playing in her eyes. For a moment, she actually looked like the old Iris. The Iris that wasn't encumbered by dementia and grief. Deven saw a ghost of the mother she'd known, instead of a shell of the woman she'd become.

A commercial appeared on the thirty-two-inch screen, and Deven entered with a forced smile. Iris turned at the intrusion and her eyes fluttered in surprise. It was clear she hadn't been tuned into the TV at all, but gazing into some glorious memory in the recesses of her mind. "Oh, Deven. I didn't see you there." She remained in the bed but lifted her arms for a hug. "How are you sweetheart? I didn't know you were coming."

Deven leaned into allow the embrace, noticing an envelope nearly hidden under the pillow at her mom's back. "I just came to talk to you," she said as she sat down on the bed. "You feeling okay?"

Iris smiled. "I'm wonderful, sweetheart."

She looked it, Deven noted. Joy radiated on her mother's face.

A great mood, which was very rare indeed. What was she so happy about? That's when Ms. Debra's words echoed once more: *"It's so good to see her happy again. I think that new gentleman friend of hers is definitely helping."* Is some unknown mystery man the reason for her change in demeanor?

Iris's hand reached to grasp hers and Deven had to hold the leash tighter on her attitude. Either that or she was likely to explode.

"Mommy, something has happened that's a little concerning for me," Deven began.

Iris's smile fell a few degrees. "Oh? What's going on? Is everything alright?"

"Well, no. Not really. Kennedy's dad . . . is he still alive?"

Now the smile was completely gone, replaced with a look of horror riddled with guilt. "Why are you asking me that?" she whispered.

"Just answer the question, Mama. I need to know."

To her surprise, Iris set her jaw in a frown and inclined her chin. "No, you don't need to know," she countered, with gathered strength. "What difference does it make, Deven? He's not your father."

Deven was taken back by the potency in her voice. "So, you knew. All this time you knew Kennedy's father was alive and you lied to me anyway."

"Well, he's in prison for another three years. What difference does it make?"

"If it doesn't make a difference then what was the point of lying to me about it?"

The question had Iris faltering as she opened and closed her mouth with no response coming out. "Because it was none of your business."

Applause erupted from the TV show, loud and infuriating. Deven jumped up and pushed the power button to encase them in silence. "What's none of my business?" she asked. "What the hell is going on with you two?"

"Nothing—"

"Stop fucking lying to me!"

Deven's outburst shook the room and Iris recoiled under the rage. Her eyes were wide, so the muddle of emotions became more pronounced: shock, anger, hurt, regret. Even her complexion had colored with shame and the hands in her lap were now gripping each other to control the trembling. She was still at a loss for words and her eyes fluttered again, like they usually did when the confusion was settling in. But Deven was not about to be swayed to back down because of her mother's condition. She clearly was of sound mind and body for whatever she'd been doing that was worth lying about.

Iris caved, her shoulders slumping with defeat. Quietly, she reached behind her and pulled a stack of envelopes into view. They were banded by a rubber band, all except one. Her fingers lingered on the envelope, almost as if she were savoring the moment. Then, she carefully pulled a folded piece of paper from the torn flap. "Read it for yourself," she invited and held the letter in Deven's direction.

Deven hesitated, unsure if she was even ready for this secret. She took the paper and lowered her eyes to the ink.

*Hey baby,*

*Thank you for the pictures. I miss you too. You know I've always loved your fine ass. Even when you married that corny asshole. You were always mine. And when I get out of here, I'm going to make that shit official. I'm so glad you agreed to it. You and me against the world like it always should've been. I can't wait to show you just how much I've been thinking about you. Tell me, do you still taste the same? You make sure you dream about me. I love you.*

*All my love always,*

*Your husband, Keith*

Deven had to blink to make sure she had read correctly. Stunned, she looked up at Iris who had suddenly found renewed interest in the seams on her comforter. "Your husband?" she asked holding the paper in the air like it was filthy.

"He's not. That's just something we say." A ghost of a smile played on Iris's lips. "Wishful thinking, I suppose."

"How long has this been going on?"

Her mom touched the stack of battered envelopes. "Long enough," she murmured, her voice yearning. "I've always loved that man."

Deven shook her head. "No, you loved my dad."

Tears glistened on the corner of Iris's eyelids as she beckoned to her daughter. "Come sit down, Deven."

"No." The thought of being near her mother and listening to more lies was unbearable.

Iris patted the mattress. "Please, sweetie. Just let me explain. I owe you that, don't I?"

She had a point. Deven sank to the edge of the bed, adamant on keeping a fair distance between them.

"Your father and I started having some problems shortly after I had you," she explained. "I was dealing with post-partum depression, and I think that started driving us apart. So, when I met Keith that day at the gas station, he just . . . I don't know there was something about him . . ." She gave a sigh that sent pain charring through Deven's body. The passion for this man was literally oozing from Iris's pores and she was glimpsing what her dad must've felt. How much his heart must've broken to know he loved this woman only for her to be in love with another man.

"I didn't mean to fall for Keith," Iris went on. "I loved your father too, but Keith just came at a time when we were drifting apart, and he was there for me when I needed someone. I needed to feel loved and beautiful again and Keith did that."

"So, you cheated on Daddy." Deven said with disdain. She didn't give a damn if her words were hurting her mother.

"I . . . made a mistake," Iris murmured. "Jamie and I were on a break and Keith called, one thing led to another . . ."

Deven grimaced. She had never heard the complete story, but this certainly put a different perspective on her entire childhood.

"Your dad, of course he was upset when I got pregnant because I didn't know if he was the father. But he was there throughout the entire pregnancy and by the time I had the baby, he and I had decided to make it work. He loved me so much and he took care of us and—"

"But you loved Keith," Deven spat. "You just thought you should stay with my Daddy because he had money and took care of his family instead of a bum ass dope boy."

"It wasn't like that." Iris's voice cracked as she spoke, signaling that it was exactly like that. "I did love your father. He was sweet, and kind, and gentle. But I loved Kennedy's father, too. It was a different kind of love, sweetie." She swiped away more tears. "I loved them both in equal but different ways. I didn't plan to, but it happened."

Deven had never taken her mother for a gold digger. All this time, she idolized her parents because of what they perpetuated. They made it seem like they were the perfect, loving, couple that had achieved the American dream and overcame adversity. But now, Iris was telling her otherwise. She loved her husband, but more so for what he could do for her. She loved the image and what being with him represented. But Keith, he was the one that always had her heart. Deven wondered if her father died hurting in the truth or comforted by the lies.

Iris sighed, closing her eyes. "Kennedy was born, we did the DNA testing and confirmed Keith was the father. I didn't even know if I wanted to tell him. We hadn't talked in nine months because I promised your father that I would cut it off completely.

But when I talked to him, all of those feelings came rushing back. He wanted to be part of Kennedy's life. So, we had to make it work."

Deven remembered the argument she heard between her parents. She'd always known her sister was a source of contention in her family. But she had no idea how much. Nor why. Now that she did, it certainly made everything worse as opposed to better.

Deven looked to the window to watch the clouds hanging in the sky. Anything where she didn't have to face her mother. "Why did you tell me he was dead?" she asked.

"I thought he was for the longest," Iris admitted. "You know after Kennedy moved with him, I lost touch with both of them. Even after she returned, I only heard about him through her because it wasn't like he and I spoke. I knew he was still in the streets, in and out of jail, and it was only a matter of time. Then he wrote me out of the blue one day. Said Kennedy had given him the address and it was like, all that love came back again. Then one visit when Kennedy came with you, we were talking about him, and she said that he wanted my number to talk on the phone and I said yes."

Deven's frown deepened at that, remembering one of the only times Kennedy visited their mother at the assisted living home, the hushed whispers between them when they didn't realize she was looking. She looked again at the letter, the words intense and agonizing. *You were always mine. And when I get out of here, I'm going to make that shit official. I'm so glad you agreed to it.* "What did you agree to, Mommy?" she asked, cutting her eyes back up at the woman.

Iris pinched her lips together, obviously not wanting to speak the words aloud. "I . . . we . . . are going to be together when he gets out," she said, her voice low. "Kennedy mentioned that he wants me to have my will changed to include him. And I'm going to do it."

Deven bolted up like the sheets were on fire. No way her mother could be saying this. "Are you kidding me?" She didn't care if she was yelling. "You're changing your will to include Kennedy's dad? To give him money Daddy left you? What the hell are you thinking?"

"Deven! How can you talk to me that way?"

"How can you be so damn gullible, Mama?" She was pacing so hard it was a wonder she hadn't burned a hole in the floor. Her whole body convulsed as rage spewed like lava. "I can't believe this shit! I will never let you do this."

"I love him," Iris' voice was surprisingly calm. "I can do what I want to do. Your father left me that money to be happy and I am going to be happy. With Keith."

The pressure in Deven's chest felt like she was smothering, and she took a few breaths to release the tension. Either that or she would combust. When she was sure she had calmed down, Deven turned again to face Iris, seeing the woman for the first time.

She felt her mother's hand on hers and she hadn't realized Iris had inched closer. "I know I've made some mistakes," she was saying with a watery smile. "I know I wasn't perfect. But your dad loved me anyway. Kennedy loved me anyway. I just pray that you can do the same."

She wouldn't lose control. And she couldn't even fault her mother. She could, however, fault the man who was playing on her mother's weakness. Deven eased her hand away from her mother to break the contact. "I need to talk to him," she said. "Keith. I think he may know . . ." Deven had to stop herself from revealing more. She hadn't told her mom about Kennedy. She didn't even know if she planned to, yet. With everything else, how was Iris going to handle knowing the ugly truth about her youngest daughter, which could, or could not, have come from the influence of Keith, this man Iris had been in love with for so long? "Where is he?" Deven reiterated.

Iris dried her face before picking up the envelopes. She looked at the stack and pushed it her way. Deven read the address, frowning when the name of the prison glared back. Wilcox State. Paul had mentioned that was where Deuce spent some time. Benji had also mentioned because of Kennedy, her father had put her in touch with Deuce to find someone. Maybe it was time to pay a visit to the man that had ripped her family apart for over twenty-five years.

# Chapter Twenty-six

Deven had never been to a prison so she sure as hell didn't know what to expect after making the two-hour drive. The building was surrounded by farmland on the outskirts of town and looked as intimidating as any building that housed the nation's convicted murderers, robbers, and rapists. The two-story sandstone stood erect with its looming towers, all enclosed by a chain-link fence that extended skyward, like razors jutting up from the pits of Hell.

She was nervous as she pulled up to the only entrance and she knew exactly why. Holding her breath, Deven flashed the ID and waited while the security guard in the booth keyed in something on the computer. The nod and wave motioning for her to proceed had her releasing a breath. She'd gotten clever and taken a page out of her sister's book for this visit. Deven eyed the driver's license, well Kennedy's driver's license, that she had found at the apartment. She already knew she wouldn't be on any kind of approved visitation list to see Keith. But of course, his daughter was. Kennedy wasn't the only one who had tricks up her sleeve.

Deven parked in the designated visitor's lot and readjusted the wig she wore; a quick twenty-dollar find that looked the Great Value version of something Kennedy spent thousands on. It would have to do. It wasn't like she was trying to fool Keith, just the security personnel. She exited her car and tried to walk casually—or as casually as one could going into a prison.

The lobby smelled like a soiled locker room and looked just as bleak with its metal floors and walls. A few women who looked like they knew the routine well were a few steps ahead. Deven fell into line behind them. They approached another guard that held out his hand for their IDs once more before ushering them further through the metal detector and then the conveyer belt for their purses and bags. Deven noticed that no one spoke, and she wondered if that was some kind of prison etiquette that everyone was expected to know. The girls in front certainly did, so Deven just tagged along and tried her best to hide her anxiety. Not only was she sneaking around and committing, what she assumed was, a felony by using Kennedy's ID to get in the prison, but she was about to face her mom's long-time lover. And her dad's nemesis. And if that was the case, didn't that make him a man she loathed as well, even if he hadn't technically done anything but steal her mother's heart and was attempting to steal her money?

Finally, after verifying they weren't sneaking in weapons, or other contraband, they were escorted into a large, cafeteria-style room with metal picnic tables and benches. Deven watched the other visitors pick random tables and sit down to wait. She hesitated. Wasn't there supposed to be some kind of partition with phones for them to talk on? They were actually about to sit across from criminals? In touching distance? There had to be a rule against that.

"Ma'am, have a seat," a short female security guard said, her face slack with boredom. "The prisoners will be out in a second."

Deven nodded and chose an empty table in one of the corners with a prime view of the prison courtyard surrounded by an electric fence. The whole aura looked depressing and Deven wondered how anyone could live in these conditions and keep their sanity.

A buzzer sounded, startling her and she caught one of the far doors open. Prisoners were herded into the room in a single-file line, punctuated by officers on either end. They all wore matching navy jumpsuits with white block numbers embossed on their backs and handcuffs binding their wrists to a chain around their waists. The clanks and shuffling feet almost moved in unison, but other than that, silence. Maybe they weren't supposed to speak unless the guards gave them permission to.

As the prisoners entered, they fell out of line to their separate tables with loved ones greeting them with smiles or tears, or both. Deven waited, eyeing each pair of hardened faces. Shit, she hadn't thought this completely through. Would she even recognize the man when she saw him?

Thankfully, she didn't have to. Deven felt eyes drilling into her and she turned her head to locate the source. The first thing she noticed was that the man was a stark contrast to her father. She had to curse herself for comparing but she couldn't help but scrutinize everything that could intrigue her mom. He was tall, a good five inches taller than her dad. And broader as well, though it was hard to discern if his muscles were there before or a product of his most recent prison bid. He had a bald head and thick goatee which made his dark complexion even more pronounced. Not to mention the tapestry of tattoos riddled up and down his arms and neck which added a certain visual appeal to his chiseled frame. Deven had to admit, she was sorely disappointed because the man didn't look half-bad. Not that it justified her mother's affair by any means. But dammit he did have a hypnotic sex appeal.

Which made it all the more entertaining now because he was staring at Deven like he'd seen the ghost of Christmas past. Despite his noticeable disbelief, Keith still walked towards her with the aura of a man in charge that was used to the world parting to make room for him. *Cocky bastard.*

"I take it you know who I am," Deven said as soon as Keith had taken his seat across from her.

His cuffs rattled as he rested his hands on the table. "Of course, I do," he confirmed. "But what I don't know is why you're here. Where is Kennedy?"

"That's what I want to know."

Keith's lips curled up into what looked like a sneer. "And why the hell would I know that, Deven?" He looked around as if to remind her about his limiting circumstances. "And how did you find out I was here anyway?"

"My mom."

At the mention of Iris, Keith's face softened, and a swell of love flooded his eyes. If Deven wasn't so pissed at him, his reaction would've been romantic. "How is she?" he asked, all edge erased from his tone. "Your mother. How is she?"

His Achilles heel, Deven noted. And he didn't even bother trying to hide his vulnerability. Not when it came to her mother. Had her father ever talked about Iris that way?

"Fine," she said.

"Did she tell you to come see me?"

"No, I told her I needed to talk to you."

"Why?"

Deven leaned forward and lowered her voice, though she seriously doubted anyone was paying attention to them. "Kennedy is . . ." she paused, then decided, "missing. It seems like she's running a few scams and I'm not sure if she is in danger."

"Danger? Did she contact Deuce like I told her?"

Deven's ears perked. "Why would you tell her to contact Deuce? What was going on?"

"She came by and told me she had a little stalker situation," he revealed. "Apparently the person attacked her at home."

Deven nodded, remembering the incident the night she came home from the hospital because of her miscarriage. "Did she say who it was?" she asked. "Male, female, ex-boyfriend?"

"No. All she said was that she thought she knew who the person was, but she didn't give me any details. My old cellmate, Deuce, I knew was into some shit where he could find the person, so I put them in contact with each other."

"I think he found whoever she was looking for," Deven said. "But the thing is, no one seems to know where she is now. Not Deuce, not Benji. And the police think something may have happened."

Keith's frown was so deep it was a wonder his face didn't fold over in the creases. "You think she's in trouble?"

"I don't know. That's why I'm worried. I'm not sure if she's missing because something happened to her, or she's afraid, or she's hiding because she's done something illegal . . . so I have no idea. I just want some answers."

"I don't have any answers for you," Keith retorted with a shrug.

"Well, why don't you tell me what the fuck has been going on these past few months with Kennedy. I know she's been talking to you and I'm sure she mentioned whatever was going on with her."

Keith chuckled as he twirled some of the hair in his beard. "And where do you come off telling me what I need to do, Deven?" he asked.

"That's the least you can do."

"I don't owe you shit."

Of course, he wouldn't think so. "Everything that happened is because of you," Deven chided. "You stole my mom, my family. They had all these problems in their relationship because of you. That shit is foul, Keith."

"You don't think I know that?" he hissed through clenched teeth. "I've done a lot of fucked up shit that I never thought twice about. But I swear to you, nothing in this world has hurt me like knowing how much damage I did to your mom." He used his fingers to massage his closed eyes and took a staggering breath. "I was young and stupid," he said. "When I met your mother, I was even more stupid and stubborn and hotheaded. Couldn't nobody tell me shit. So yes, I played around and no, I didn't give a damn who I hurt because they had hurt me."

"How did my mom hurt you?"

"She didn't choose me, dammit." His fists tightened with the admission and anywhere else, Deven knew he probably would've punched a wall. "She chose Jamie. That shit hurt like hell because I loved that woman. I was willing to give her everything and then some, but none of it was enough because I didn't have the money or the status." He sighed before continuing. "When she called me and told me she'd had a baby and she thought it was mine, I got excited. I thought maybe this was our chance. But then she told me she and Jamie had settled on being together regardless of the DNA outcome and shit infuriated me all over again."

Deven listened, trying not to feel sorry for him. But still he was tugging on her heart. Then man sounded so utterly exhausted. And broken.

"It was my girlfriend's idea to fight for custody," Keith said with shame in his voice. "Looking back on it, I'm sure she thought it was a good idea so we could get more government assistance; food stamps, welfare, all that. She was already living on benefits for one child, and another meant more benefits coming into the house. But hell, I didn't care. I just thought it was a good way to get back at Iris and Jamie. I figured they would hurt like I was hurting, and Iris would see how good of a father I was. But when Kennedy came to stay, it was rougher on all of us. More mouths to feed so I had to hustle more, my girl was pissed trying to take care of her kid and Kennedy because I was always gone doing what the fuck I wanted and getting into more trouble. Shit was hard and the kids . . . the shit they were exposed to, I'm ashamed to even repeat honestly. I wasn't ready to give up my lifestyle for no kid. I think that's what your mother saw in me before I even knew it, so that's why she knew I wasn't ready for no damn family, and she chose your dad. But God has a way of humbling you even when you're not ready." He looked around again, now lapsed into deep thought.

"Mama lost contact with you," Deven said as she remembered. "Why didn't you just let Kennedy come home? Why did she have to wait until she was eighteen before we could talk to her again? That wasn't fair to her, or us."

"I know," Keith murmured, his eyes downcast. "I wasn't trying to be fair. I was being selfish. My girl and I were doing a lot of illegal shit and we stayed moving around trying to keep under police radar. Guess it finally caught up to me. Look, I'm not proud of any of the shit I did," he added. "In fact, I'm embarrassed as hell. I can be man enough to admit that. That's why I'm trying to have a better relationship with your mother now. And Kennedy. I can't change what happened, but I can try to repair my relationships."

"If that's the case, then why the fuck are you trying to steal my mom's money?"

Keith's face furrowed at the question. "The hell are you talking about? I'm not trying to steal her money."

"I read one of your letters. You were saying you were glad

she agreed to *it* and she said she was changing her will to include you."

"Whoa, whoa, hold up. I ain't know nothing about that and I would never ask your mom to do some shit like that." Keith's eyes were earnest as he shook his head. "I know I told her I was glad she agreed to accept my phone calls and us maybe pursuing something, even if it's only a friendship. Look, I may not have liked your father and maybe in the past that would have been some shit I would've done. But I don't give a damn about her money. I just want to be with *her*, if she'll have me."

"But . . ." Deven pinched the bridge of her nose, Iris' comments coming back to play in her mind as her confusion started to clear, little-by-little. *Kennedy mentioned that he wants me to have my will changed to include him. And I'm going to do it.* Trying to scam their own mother? There had to be something else. Some-*one* else.

"I need to know where Kennedy is," Deven insisted. "I found a bunch of different scams that she's been running. Using other people's driver's licenses, passports, taking lots of money from a lot of people. She could be hurt. Or worse, she could've scammed the wrong type of people and gotten tangled up in something she can't get out of. Do you know anything about any of this?"

Keith's eyebrows drew together. "No, not Kennedy. She wouldn't do anything like that."

"That's what I thought. But I guess she picked up a lot more from you than you realized," Deven said pointedly, her eyes accusatory as they bore into his.

The realization of his influence had shame coloring his face and he lowered his gaze to the handcuffs on his wrists. "I . . . didn't know," he said shaking his head. "I always told her—I tried not to expose her to the stuff I did because I knew she would just end up in a place like this. And I didn't want that for my baby."

"Well, she's out there. And she's following in your footsteps. I know she's not really dead. So where would she be?"

"Dead?" Keith seemed genuinely alarmed by Deven's words. "What the hell are you talking about?"

Deven opened her mouth to speak, but the buzzer sounded once more, drowning her out. Everyone started rising to give their final goodbyes as officers motioned the prisoners to a door.

"Let's go, let's go," one of them yelled.

Keith stood too but he kept his eyes trained on Deven. "What do you mean dead?" he asked again.

Deven stood as more and more people began cluttering the walkway. She couldn't very well explain what she meant now. "Can you call me?" she asked, shifting through people. She didn't even know if the man had her number. But it was clear they had more discuss. Keith didn't speak, only stared as if he were trying to solve a complicated math problem. He trudged into the line with the rest of the prisoners and was ushered out of the room.

It felt like she could breathe again as soon as Deven emerged from the building. She took a greedy gulp of air, refreshed by the first few sprinkles of dew. As soon as she made it back to her car, she snatched off the itchy wig and ran her fingers through her short crop of hair. Today had been eventful, but not quite as productive as she would've liked. Keith's words continued to echo in her mind and again, she felt a pull of sorrow at the lifestyle that Kennedy had been adopted into after she'd left their mother.

Back at home, the first thing Deven did was check all her rooms and closets. The door had been secured with the new double locks thanks to the locksmith, but still, she couldn't be too sure. Though the more she found out about Deuce, the more she wondered if he wasn't trying to threaten her at all.

Maybe warn her. Staying out of it, like his note read, may have been more for precaution because she wouldn't like what she would find. That last part had certainly proven more true than anything.

Confirming that everything was still as it should've been, nothing out of place, no more ambiguous notes or dead bodies or bloody weapons or any of that other stuff that predators left behind to tease their prey, Deven ran herself a bath and poured herself a glass of wine. She needed to wash the stench of prison off her. Iris had asked that she call after the visit, though Deven was sure it was more so to hear all about Keith as opposed to what she needed to talk to him about. So that, too, could wait.

Deven downed her drink, poured herself a second glass, and knocked that back just as quickly. Anything to take the edge off. It didn't take long for the alcoholic buzz to intoxicate her senses and without realizing it, Deven was dialing Paul's number, desperate to hear his voice. The call went straight to voicemail. Had he done that on purpose maybe? She was babbling into the receiver before she could stop herself.

"Paul, I'm so sorry." She sniffed back tears. "I messed up. I know I did, but I'm so sorry I hurt you. Please just call me so we can talk. I need you. I love—" She clamped her mouth shut so hard her teeth chattered together. What the hell was she saying? "I love having you in my life and I'm so sorry if I haven't shown you the appreciation you deserve. You were there for my father, my babies, and now my sister, and I just—I don't know, I just miss having you around because you made it all better and I can't deal with this right now and it's just too much. I went to the prison today and Keith told me a whole bunch of stuff I didn't know about my mom and the happy childhood I thought I had." She ran out of breath, completely exhausted from her rant. "Please just call me. I can't do this without you." Deven hung up and heaved a sigh. The message sounded selfish, and she could've kicked herself for it. Paul was hurting over his feelings for her and here she was, thinking of her own family issues. It would probably be a cold day in Hell before he called her back.

Deven didn't realize just how tense she was until she submerged her body in the scalding hot water and every muscle began to scream in glorious anguish. She eased down until only her head was visible and let her tears dribble into the bathwater.

Part of her didn't want to believe Keith. Part of her still wanted to live in the joyous bliss of her ignorance, where her childhood was happy, and her parents were in love, and her sister was happy with the family she craved. But Deven had seen the look in Keith's eyes as he spoke. It was all true. Every last bit of it. The reality was like alcohol on an open wound. The agonizing pain had now left her bleeding and raw.

The distant ring of her cell had Deven lifting up, goosebumps immediately speckling her skin from the touch of chill in the air. A flicker of hope had a smile blooming. Paul. She hoped he had forgiven her. Maybe he could come over and they could sort all of this mess out.

Deven wrapped herself in a towel and jogged to her bedroom. Her phone lay on the nightstand where she'd placed it, the caller long gone. She frowned at the missed call, not recognizing the number on the display. Then the notification icon prompted her to dial into her voicemail. No, not Paul. Keith. His message was short, but his urgency was more than clear even in its brevity. "You need to find my ex, Erika Garrett. I don't know where Kennedy is, but she sure does."

That was it. Deven listened to the message again then hung up. Erika Garrett? She immediately recognized the name from one of the prescription bottles she had found in Kennedy's bathroom. Whoever this mystery woman was, what the hell did she have to do with her sister? Deven pressed the first few digits to call Officer McKinney, then stopped. No, this wasn't really the time for the police. She needed someone else to track down this Erika woman. And she knew just the person. But the million-dollar question was, would he be willing to help? Because at this point, Deuce was her only hope.

# Chapter Twenty-seven

She probably should've been afraid. But thankfully she wasn't. Deven had resolved that if Deuce wanted to do something to her, he would've done it already. He had the means, he knew where she lived, and he couldn't deny that he knew exactly what she was up to. So, he wasn't trying to hurt her. Scare her maybe (which he had already succeeded in that aspect). But at this point, the chances of him trying something were probably pretty slim. At least that's what Deven told herself as she made the drive back to his place. She prayed her assumption was right.

Unlike before, there was a new car parked in Deuce's driveway, an ice blue Tesla that looked like he drove it straight out of the showroom. Again, Deven parked on the curb and walked up to his porch trying not to admire his fancy new ride. Or the financial means it took to get one. It was clear whatever he did, he was good at it. She knocked and waited.

When he didn't readily come to the door, she knocked again, struggling to calm her rapid heartbeat. Unless the car belonged to his neighbor, which she doubted, then he was definitely home.

Deven wondered if Deuce was sitting just inside the door, amused at her impromptu visit. So far, she'd shown her natural black ass with him, so to ask for help, or even show her face around here had been a bold risk on her part.

Deven had just about given up when she heard the locks slide out of place and the door opened on its squeaky hinges. He'd gotten his locs freshly twisted, she immediately noticed but she wasn't sure why. Perhaps because it added to his mystery, now hanging loose to frame his angular face. Once again, he was smoking, and Deven fanned the air to waft the stench in the opposite direction. His expression was unreadable as he waited, and she knew that was her cue to justify her presence. But at least he looked calm, which was a good sign.

"Hey Deuce. Can I come in?"

He used his thumb and index finger to remove the cigarette from his lips. "Nah," he said. "What you need?" He didn't move from the door, and she caught the sound of a TV playing somewhere in the background.

Deven shifted, the discomfort beginning to settle in. "I need your help," she admitted.

Deuce's face lit with amusement as his eyes flicked behind her, then back again. "Who sent you?"

"No one sent me. I need your help to find somebody."

Deuce let out a disinterested grunt. "Go to the police."

"I can't." And because he didn't seem impressed by the request, Deven rushed on. "Keith said I need to find somebody so you were the person I knew could do it."

He paused, the mention of Keith obviously piquing his interest. Then his eyes narrowed.

"What do you need?" be asked, taking another drag of his nicotine.

"An address for an Erika Garrett." If the name sounded familiar, Deuce didn't let on. He leaned a shoulder against the threshold of his doorway.

"I don't do shit for free."

She had figured as much. Since it was clear he wasn't going to let her in or proceed without an incentive, Deven yanked open the straps of her purse and pulled out a small stack of hundreds. She held it out, the bills crispy in her fingers. Thank God she'd had the good sense to stop at the bank on the drive over.

Deuce glanced at the money and to her surprise, laughed out loud. "The hell is that? Gas money?"

"It's $1000," she said, certain that was more than enough.

"Sweetie, $1000 will get you the zip code to her last place of employment. You want me to lock her down, you need to come off a lot more than that." He started to close the door and Deven quickly stuffed her toe between the door and the jamb to keep it open.

"Okay, I can go get some more," she agreed. "I'll go to the bank. But can you just please hear me out first and let me know if you can do this?" She didn't care if it sounded like she was begging. She was desperate. Deuce didn't attempt to open or close the door any further, so Deven took it as permission and rushed on. "This woman, Erika Garrett, apparently has information on the whereabouts of my sister. I need an address of where she is staying. Can you find her in a few days?"

Even in the sliver of darkness from Deuce's living room, Deven caught his smirk. "Sweetie, I can find her in a few hours. $5000. And I'm giving you a deal only because you are cool with Keith and it's his daughter."

Deven winced but gave a nod at the steep price. It was necessary, she supposed. And if he could do the job, then it was well worth it. She thought for a minute, then asked, "Deuce, are you able to tell me who Kennedy hired you to track down?"

Another pause. "Look, I'm not trying to get in the middle of that shit," he said. "She told me the girl was a friend of hers and that's it."

"But you know the friend's name. And why she was looking for her."

"You want me to track Erika, or not?" His voice was laced with agitation.

Deven sighed. He was being somewhat helpful. She had to appreciate the little effort he did provide. "Well then can you just tell me why you were in my apartment?" she asked. "Why do you want me to stay out of it? What do you know?"

"You're giving me way too much credit. I don't know what you think. And I wasn't in your apartment. Never was. $5,000. Cash." He gave the door a nudge, prompting Deven to slide her foot out of the way so it didn't get smashed. Then he closed it in her face, leaving her standing on the porch alone in confusion.

———⟶•⟶———

Deuce had promised a few hours and Deven hadn't pressed for a more accurate estimate. Did he mean 'few' like two, or a 'few' like nine? It was hard to say, and he was so damn vague that she couldn't tell one way or the other. So, after she'd pulled the additional funds from her savings and ignored the guilt at that being some of the money from her dad's life insurance, she dropped it back off at Deuce's place and headed home. With the sun starting to set and the nighttime creeping in, she seriously doubted she would be doing any more investigating tonight. Exhausted, not to mention hungry. Hell, when was the last time she'd actually had substance in her stomach? Probably was the reason she felt so mentally, emotionally, and physically drained.

It had been only two weeks since that life-altering knock on her door. Two weeks that felt like two lifetimes. And all the while Deven had felt like she'd been gripping a crumbling wall with only her fingertips, not able to pull herself up from the peril, and too afraid to plummet below at what she might find. So, though Deuce wasn't the most likeable guy in all his greedy, selfish splendor, Deven prayed he would prove to be as good as he alleged. Her psyche couldn't handle any more of the unpredictable. *Speaking of unpredictable . . .*

The sight of Paul's car had Deven's heart skipping a beat. He was standing outside of the driver's side door, bundled in a coat and hat against the brisk evening air. The red scarf around his neck danced in the breezing as if it were flagging her down. But she didn't want to get her hopes up, so Deven pulled into the parking space next to his and took an uneasy breath.

He was watching her closely as she climbed from the car and for a second. They both just stood there in awkward silence, the wind slapping color into their cheeks as his scarf continued to billow. Finally, she spoke up first to break the tension. "You want to come inside?"

Deven watched his face relax a little, a little reminder of this man's beautiful heart. She had hurt him, but here he was, nervous as if he had done something wrong. She wanted to hold him tight to crack their icy dispositions. She led him upstairs and into the warmth of her apartment.

As customary, Deven peeled out of her coat and went about checking around. She knew she was stalling. She had just talked to Deuce, and he had made it clear he hadn't been in her place at all. And though she wasn't certain who the culprit was, Deven still moseyed about her bedroom and then her bathroom while she thought about how to broach a conversation with Paul.

By the time she re-entered the kitchen, he had shrugged out of his own outer layers and sat at the breakfast table in his sweater and jeans. Two steaming mugs were on the table while the smell of mint chocolate singed the air. His eyes were on her as she entered and, not knowing what else to do, she took a seat at the table, their knees bumping against each other.

"Great minds," she said, using her fingernail to tap the side of the cup. "I needed something soothing."

"Same here." But neither one moved to take a drink. Deven's stomach did a somersault as he searched her face for something. She cleared her throat. "Are you hungry?"

"Yeah. You want to go somewhere and get something to eat?"

"I would rather order in, if that's cool with you." They were like two high-school kids filling their first-date jitters with idle chatter.

The tiptoeing had Deven's anxiety mounting, and she braved taking a swig of the blistering liquid, if only to give herself something to ease her apprehension. She sucked on her tongue a little to ease the heat, then realized how sensual the gesture could seem and she quickly recovered. "I'm glad you came by," she said at Paul's continued silence. "I've been wanting to apologize."

"I know. I heard a good bit of it on my voicemail."

The joke had Deven's muscles loosening. Leave it to Paul to make her feel better. "Well, I felt horrible," she admitted. "And humiliated. But mostly horrible because I hurt you. And I lost a very good . . ." Deven clamped her lips shut, not wanting to mortify him even more by referencing him as something so menial as a *friend*. Not when he meant so much more and she knew he considered her just as esteemed. "What I mean is," she tried again. "I lost someone that means a lot to me." Her eyes searched his, silently begging for him to tell her otherwise. She really didn't want her assumption to be true.

Her heart swelled when Paul's hand reached across the table and stroked her wrist. The sensation was encouraging as much as it was erotic. Deven had to tighten her thighs to keep from being distracted by the sudden pulsing. *Easy girl.*

"You haven't lost me." His voice was sincere, his eyes just as compassionate. "It was embarrassing as hell, but I can't blame Justin honestly. I'm sorry for putting us in that position. But my feelings were—*are* still very real, Deven. I can't pretend they're not there or they'll just go away because we don't talk to each other for a few days."

"I know." And she did know. But did she really want them to go away? Hers certainly hadn't. "Well, we're not—he's not . . . in the picture anymore."

She waited, already anticipating his next questions about her thoughts on their prior discussion. To her surprise, he gave her arm one final squeeze before leaning back to pull out his phone.

"I'll order that pizza," he said punching in a number. He wouldn't push. That respectful gentleman was just as sexy as the man who had kissed her breathless. She half-listened to him ordering the food while she continued sipping her hot chocolate, grateful it had chilled to a more tolerable temperature. She would not, under any circumstances, sleep with this man. It would be wrong on so many levels. Especially now that he had made it plain. The sexual gratification wasn't worth the distress. Not this time.

"Pizza will be here in an hour," he announced hanging up his phone. He sat it on the table and laced his fingers together like he was preparing to listen to a lecture. "So, what else have you found out about your sister? I know it's something because you're too hellbent on solving this yourself like you're on *First 48*."

Deven giggled. "Well, since you asked . . ." and she dove in without even realizing she had needed to. The weight of it all felt like a boulder on her back so she talked and talked, grateful for the release. She told him everything, what she found at Kennedy's apartment, the information she found out from Benji and her mom, the will, even visiting Kennedy's dad in jail. She could tell the way the frown engraved on Paul's face that he wasn't too pleased with that last part, but just as interested in what the man had to say.

". . . then he told me that his ex, Erika Garrett, is who I need to talk to," Deven explained. "But he didn't know how to get in touch with her. So, I went back to Deuce."

"You did what?" A mix of shock and anger marred Paul's face

as he just stared wide-eyed. "Deven why would you do that? That's dangerous. You should've called Officer McKinney."

Deven shook her head. "No, I can't do that. With everything that we found out, you already know it's a lot of illegal shit that's going to look even worse. Especially after what happened when she brought in Amber Wright."

Paul's frown remained in place, but she could see that he knew she had a point. "I still don't like you going over there," he said, finally. "And definitely not alone. What did he say?"

"He said he would find her."

"Just like that?"

"Hm mmm." Since he was already on edge, Deven thought it best to leave out the $5000 part. That would just add salt to the wound. "I don't know exactly how long, but he did say he could do it in a few hours."

"And then what?"

Deven half-shrugged. She wasn't sure. She hadn't gotten that far yet. She certainly couldn't just bust in the woman's place wielding fists and demanding information. "I'm going to go check her out," she decided, the ideas running as she spoke. "Nothing crazy. Maybe go see where she lives and when the time is right, try to talk to her."

"I don't really like that." Paul's frown had deepened. "We don't know this lady. How do you know Keith even knows what the hell he's talking about?"

"I . . ." she didn't know. "Don't really have a choice now," she finished. "I mean, what do you think?"

"Well, I get what you're saying about not calling the police. I don't like it," he added. "But I understand it. So, just promise me you won't do anything without me. I mean, as soon as Deuce sends you the information, you let me know, and we can look into it together. Okay?"

Deven nodded, not wanting to verbalize the lie. Truth was, she couldn't put Paul through any more than she already had. He'd already done more than enough by just being there. And having him tag along would do more harm than good. Especially if this Erika woman was as dangerous as he was insinuating.

Like a sign, Deven's phone buzzed with the incoming text notification as soon as Paul had risen to greet the pizza delivery man. She snuck a look at the message, eyeing the address that Deuce had sent. Well, he certainly had earned his money. Deven put her phone back down as Paul re-entered the kitchen with pizza boxes in tow.

"Ready?" he asked spreading everything on the table.

Deven had to grin at the double entendre, her mind already on the events that were sure to unfold the next day. "So ready."

# Chapter Twenty-eight

She should've been exhausted. Deven watched the early morning sun streams spill through the blinds. Even as she teetered on the edges of delirium, she was more wide-eyed and alert than insomnia should've allowed. It was the nerves, she knew. They had her adrenaline at an all-time high. Deven would rather make that attribution than the other underlying culprit: Paul was asleep on the couch in the living room. It had taken all of her restraint to keep from running in there, ass-naked, and throwing herself on his lap for a midnight snack.

It had been his idea to stay over. She'd insisted otherwise, adamant on re-establishing those boundaries they'd crossed before. But they had talked until well past midnight, and he'd had several glasses of wine. Not enough to completely inebriate him, they both knew, but what was the point in taking the risk?

So, he had accepted some pillows and bedspreads from her room and crashed for the night. And it had certainly been quite the temptation.

Deven tossed the covers back and instantly shivered at the

burst of cold air that tickled her legs. As much as she wanted to, she couldn't really afford to be distracted by Paul. Not today. What she did need to focus on was trying to get rid of him as quickly, and as unsuspectingly as possible. She needed to get to this address Deuce had provided and figure out what the hell Erika Garrett was up to. Paul had been right to inquire because Deven didn't have any kind of plan for when she arrived. What if the address wasn't even good anymore? What if she was out of town or had a fake address on whatever files Deuce referenced? Well then, she would have to go to the police, Deven resolved with a dejected frown. Of course, she didn't want it to come to that. But what else was she supposed to do?

She crept into the living room, treading carefully so as not to wake Paul. She was surprised to find him sitting up in her recliner, his cell phone propped to his ear. He glanced up when she entered and waved her over as he continued his conversation.

"Yes, Ma'am I get it. It's going to be okay, I promise." He placed his hand over the receiver and mouthed *your mom* and Deven's eyebrows shot to her forehead.

"My mom?" she mouthed back. "At this hour?"

Paul gave a sheepish grin before directing his attention back to the phone. "Yes, I know Ms. Iris. I will be sure to tell Deven to call you, okay?" Pause. "Your daughter." Another pause. "No, that's Kennedy. Your other daughter, Deven."

Deven tried not to let his words bother her as she sank to the sofa to wait for him to finish. Finally, he hung up and sat back with a lazy smile. He seemed a little disoriented, so it was obvious Iris had woken him up out of a dead slumber.

"Paul, I'm so sorry. I didn't even know my mom had your number."

"Yeah, we talked a few times after your father passed. I believe he may have given it to her in the event she had questions or just needed support. That was the first time I've spoken to her in a while."

Deven nodded. It made sense. "What did she say?"

"It wasn't a good day but she asked her nurse to call me so she could talk."

"About Dad?"

Paul frowned. "I don't think she remembered that's where she knew me from. She just talked a lot about herself actually. Regrets, mistakes, wishing she could've given her girls a better life."

Deven didn't want to verbalize how she felt the exact same way.

"Did you tell her?" Paul asked then. "About your sister?"

"I can't do that to her. Kennedy was her baby, her favorite. That would crush her." It pained her to think about putting her mom through that anguish. Eventually it would come to that. But she preferred to delay the inevitable as long as possible.

"Take things slow," Paul said. "But don't avoid it. So, what's your thoughts on the will situation? Since you said Keith denied knowing about it."

Deven reflected on the thoughts that had been swirling in her mind all night and morning. No matter how much she had looked at it from all different angles, she had settled on the only conclusion that made sense. "I think someone is using Kennedy," she said. "I think I was right when I said that she's in too deep with this scam shit. Maybe even trying to get some money from my mom to pay off whatever debts she has incurred. Deuce said she hired him to find a *friend* and whoever this person is, may be roping my sister into doing some illegal shit. Not sure why, maybe the person has some dirt on Kennedy, maybe it is an abuse situation like I assumed with Deuce. Now, I just think it's someone else. And I think Erika may know this mystery person, which is why Keith is sending me to talk to her." At Paul's continued silence, Deven could only shake her head. "I know it's wild," she said.

"Very," he agreed. "But hell, this whole thing is wild." He then stood up to stretch and Deven noticed he'd opted to sleep shirtless, the bends and angles of his abs catching little streaks of dawn. His skin seemed to glisten like porcelain and Deven wanted nothing more than to feel him underneath her.

"What's your plans for the day?" His question had her snapping out of her fantasy and the lie dribbled from her tongue like water.

"I have to work. Probably going to go in pretty soon. What about you?"

"Okay, I didn't know if you needed me to stay with you."

Deven couldn't help but warm at his empathy. And she felt bad for lying to his face. It was for his protection, she had to remind herself. "I'll be okay. But," she added to diffuse the rejection. "You can maybe come by later if you want. To talk."

She caught the gleam in his eyes before his smile spread, slow and hopeful. "You sure you're ready for that conversation?"

She wasn't. But she owed it to him. "I think it's time," she stated. If there was one thing this meeting with Erika was about to teach her, it was to face everything head on. She had way too many regrets already. She wouldn't make the same mistakes with Paul.

---

Two hours later, Deven still didn't have a plan. But she couldn't let that deter her. So, she got dressed and drove towards the outskirts of the city before she lost her nerve. Keith hadn't attempted to call her again, nor had Deuce, though she knew it was ambitious to even expect more contact from either man. Kennedy was her sister, and this was her "problem" and hers alone. She would have to handle it, as such.

The GPS guided her to a historic side of town. A labyrinth of quaint streets with Victorian-style homes in majestic architecture flanked both sides, elevating the Old Town character. Sweeping branches of tulip trees reached up and over the roads, almost like archways in the neighborhood, large enough for only the sunlight to infiltrate and cascade silhouettes to dance across the pavement. It was definitely a New Jersey hidden gem that spoke of old money and generational wealth. It reminded Deven of the type of place her parents would've eventually retired to welcome grand-babies. Yet something else that would never happen.

Slowing her car to a crawl, Deven's eyes glazed over the residential numbers inscribed on the mailboxes. 1426 was positioned on a corner lot with a wrought-iron fence and painted in various monochromatic shades of blue to embellish its architectural detail. A pearl white Mercedes was parked in the driveway with a KBABY3 license plate.

Deven was tempted to pull into the driveway right alongside KBABY3, but at the last minute, she drove on by, her eyes staying fixed on the house. There was nothing out of the ordinary, nothing too suspicious, nothing to otherwise suggest this was the humble abode of a drug dealer's ex-girlfriend, that had apparently, gotten her life together since he went to prison. So far, Erika Garrett was seeming like yet another dead end. Which made it all the more suspicious that Keith would insist otherwise.

Deven wheeled through a cul-de-sac and back around to the house to park on the opposite side of the road. Again, she surveyed the home with its manicured lawn and gabled roof, not really sure what she was looking for.

Before she had made a decision on what to do, the front door opened and a woman, who Deven could only assume was Erika, stepped out onto the wraparound porch. Even from this distance, Deven could see she was petite and wore braids in a bun coiled at the top of her head. She was dressed casually in some jeans and a long coat that swept her calves as she twisted, first to lock the door, then to trot down the three steps onto the walkway that wound towards her car. A large Louis Vuitton purse swayed from the crook of her elbow and when she looked up, most of her face was hidden from view due to the oversized aviator sunglasses perched on her nose.

Deven watched her climb into her car and peel out of the driveway. She had to make a split-second decision. Either stay behind and wait, maybe even try to take a look around the house while she was gone. Or follow and see where she was headed. Deven glanced back at the house before pulling away from the curb to dart out behind the Mercedes. It seemed like the safer of the two options.

At first, Erika drove with no sense of urgency and Deven had to struggle to maintain an acceptable distance. It wasn't like she had experience with this sort of thing. What was considered too close without making it obvious she was tailing? Two cars between? Three cars between? This probably would've been something she should have consulted the experts about, like Benji, or Deuce, or Keith. Deven had to laugh at her own thoughts. The idea that she'd been so casually surrounded by criminals here lately, much more than she'd ever been in her life, shouldn't have been so pedestrian. But the fact that she was now tailing some random woman in hopes of finding out what happened to her missing-maybe-dead sister shouldn't have been either. And yet here she was, picking up speed as they broke onto the expressway.

When the Mercedes took the very next on-ramp, only to double back, Deven figured she must have forgotten something at the house. But Erika kept driving past the community and kept straight into the downtown district, with its cobblestone walkways and concentration of historic brick buildings with steeples and towers gracing the skyline. Most of the streets were one-way with metered parallel parking strips skirting the curbs. Signage adorned the various windows and entryways to entice residents for shopping, eating, and other pursuits.

When Erika pulled into a parking space, Deven didn't have any other choice but to pull behind her. She didn't want to risk circling back through the one-way streets only to find she was gone. Deven held her breath as she waited for Erika to exit, praying like hell she wouldn't notice her sitting there staring. Thankfully, Erika got out only to spare her an absent glance as she hiked onto the curb to pop change into the meter. Then she crossed the street to a credit union and disappeared inside. Deven sighed and rested her head on the headrest. Still nothing overtly suspicious, if she didn't count the twenty-minute drive only to turn around. But even that wasn't too bad. Erika may have just changed her mind with where she wanted to go. Completely normal. But so far, the little trip to the bank hadn't been worth her time or apprehension.

Deven counted seventeen minutes before Erika emerged and walked next door to the adjoining boutique. Then another eleven minutes before she was back on the sidewalk, only to stroll into the neighboring bookstore. Deven had to swallow her swells of impatience. Just her luck to pick a day to follow Erika when she just peddling away in town. But what did she expect? The woman to burst from the bank in a ski mask with a pillowcase full of stolen cash? She had to confess, part of her did.

After another thirty minutes, Deven climbed out of her car, dropped a few quarters in the meter, and hiked to the bookstore. It was best to confront Erika instead of waiting around for a bunch of nothing to happen. As Deven scissored her way across the street, the vibration of her cell phone had her stopping just outside of the door beside a sidewalk sign displaying new titles and book specials. She pulled her phone from her jacket pocket, anxiety having her body aching as she read the number. Paul. *Shit.* She debated answering it only briefly before declining the call. Trying to explain her whereabouts and what she was doing would've been too much of a hassle, especially because he would more than likely deduce she was up to no good. As soon as she swiped to reject his incoming call, the text notification popped up, part of his message peeking previewed on the top of the screen: *hey, call me. I looked into . . .* and that was all she could see without opening the entire message. Deven put her phone on silent and stuffed it back into her pocket and breezed inside.

The bookstore smelled of coffee and chocolate, the sweet musky fragrance greeting Deven as soon as she pushed through the door. A bell chimed to signal her arrival and the cashier, a young sprightly woman with blond hair and a bright smile, flicked a gaze in her direction. "Hi, welcome to Books and Brew. Can I help you find anything?"

Deven smiled politely as she whipped her head around the intimate space. "I'm okay thank you."

"Okay please let me know if you need anything." And the cashier turned back to the glossy magazine flipped open on her counter.

From Deven's vantage point, she could pretty much see around the entire store, with the exception of a few reading nooks and crannies. Heads were bent over the tops of shelves immersed in the literature, but Deven didn't see Erika's high braid bun and glasses. She gave the store one last look around before approaching the cashier.

"Excuse me, is there another way out of this store?" she asked. "I saw a woman come in here and now I don't see her."

"There's a café next door. You can get to it from here, but it does have its own separate entrance." The cashier pointed towards the back of the store where there was an archway with an arrowed sign *Brew this way* fixed to the doorframe.

Deven thanked the woman and followed the direction, passing a set of bathrooms before crossing into the adjacent coffee shop. The whir of a blender bellowed, releasing an even stronger smell of coffee grinds and chocolate throughout the room. A male barista with a dusty crop of brown hair and an apron with the name *Sam* embroidered across the front, lifted a hand in greeting as Deven looked around at the sparse patrons. *Where was she?*

"Can I get you something?" Sam asked as Deven walked up to the pastry display case.

"Yes. Did a woman with braids come through here?"

"Yeah, just walked out," he said nodding to the frosted glass door.

Deven thanked him and hurried out. Damn, she was quick. If she didn't know any better, the woman was trying to—

"Bitch what the fuck are you doing following me?"

Startled, Deven tumbled backwards into another sidewalk sign. Sure enough, Erika was waiting just outside the door, eyebrows pointed downward to disappear behind those oversized frames. Even through the tinted shades, Deven could see her eyes narrowed in a menacing glower. She took a step towards her and Deven threw up her hand in panic.

"Listen, I'm sorry," her words were coming out in a jumbled mess. "I wasn't trying to follow you. I thought you could help me. I'm looking for Erika Garrett."

Erika lifted her chin, her jaw tightening. "Don't know her," she snapped. "Now get the hell away from me." She was lying. That much was clear.

Deven's voice was pleading. "Erika, I need to talk about my sister, Kennedy. Keith said you would know her." The shades were too dark so Deven couldn't tell if Erika reacted to the comments. Nor did she give any outward display that the names meant something.

"I don't know," she said, this time, not quite as sinister.

"Keith said you—"

"I don't give a fuck what Keith told you," Erika snapped. "That girl emancipated herself and left when she was sixteen after her dad got in trouble again. Last time we saw her, she was cracked out somewhere in front of a homeless shelter. How the hell should I know where she is?"

It wasn't just the words that had Deven disintegrating, but also the malice with which she spoke them. Pure and utter hatred reverberated through each syllable. *Emancipated at 16? Cracked out? Homeless shelter?* She couldn't tell if Erika was spewing her poison just for animosity's sake or if there was really some truth to any of it. Did Kennedy *used* to have a drug problem before she turned her life around? Kennedy was doing well for herself. Erika's interpretation couldn't be accurate.

"Erika, please," she tried again. "I think my sister is in danger."

To her surprise, Erika's head snapped back and she let out a cackle. "Danger? Little girl, your sister is dead."

Her words, as piercing as they were, only served to confuse Deven even more. "What? You said you haven't seen her," she reminded her pointedly. "So have you not seen her, or do you know she is dead?"

Erika shook her head. "You are so damn stupid," she said with a snarl, her voice oozing with acid. "You and your stupid ass mama. I'm not going to tell you again. Get the hell away from me." She took care to space out each word like six, isolated, threats that sent a chill down Deven's spine. Rather than object, she closed her mouth and just watched Erika power walk back to her Mercedes. She probably should've been deterred by Erika's warning, but the woman's defiance had only heightened her determination. And what did she mean by her and Iris being dumb? Where the hell did that come from?

Deven waited until Erika's car had completely disappeared before she rushed back to her own. She didn't need to follow her this time. She had the address. And dammit she was going to get to the bottom of this once and for all.

# Chapter Twenty-nine

Just as she hoped, Erika's Mercedes was nowhere to be found when Deven pulled back up to the house ten minutes later. But she didn't know how long that would last. If her suspicions were true, Erika may have been keeping Kennedy in the house. The attitude, blatant lying, saying she didn't know where Kennedy was then saying she was dead, were all telltale signs that she was clearly hiding something. So, if she wasn't holding Kennedy, Erika damn sure knew where she was. Of that much, Deven was certain.

Instead of pulling close to the house, Deven parked a little way down at the curb of a home that looked (and that she hoped was) empty. Then cut back through the backyards until she came to the wrought-iron fence.

Erika had put some money into the landscaping. A peer through the vertical pickets in the fence's wall panels showed a large deck overlooking a scenic view of the backyard garden. The centerpiece was a gorgeous cascading tiered fountain that had the ambient sound of pouring water like a soothing hum. Off to one corner of the lot was a shed and Deven figured that was where she would start.

The fence was a little tough to climb, especially having to wade through the bushes that bordered the bottom. But Deven was able to hoist herself up and over. She ended up losing her footing on the landing, sending a ricochet of shooting pain through her body as she landed hard on the ground. Her arm was throbbing, and her cheek burned but Deven picked herself up and stooped into a low run towards the shed. She braced against the pain as she pulled open the door to the shed.

Dust immediately seized her throat and stung her eyes. She coughed and squinted through the cloud. There was the faint odor of something musty and, with the exception of a rusty lawn mower in the corner, the shed was empty.

Deven closed the door and winced at the squeak of the hinges. Her head whipped back to the house as she held her breath. A dog barked in the distance and the pouring fountain water continued, uninterrupted. Otherwise, silence. Not even the curtains stirred. Deven knew she had to hurry. Erika probably had only a few more errands before she returned and Deven sure as hell didn't want to be caught in there when she did. She crouched again and made a dash for the deck, weaving between the outdoor sectional and tables, to the back door.

She jiggled the locked knob, then spotted the rock flower bed and snatched up one of the polished pebbles. Holding her breath, she slammed the rock into the glass, nearest to the doorknob. It shattered with ease and, again, Deven froze to listen. No alarm. No movement. Nothing. She eased her hand carefully through glass shards, wincing only once as a piece nicked her hand. The cut burned but she still managed to grip the doorknob from the inside and fumble the locks out of place. It opened without so much as a squeak.

Deven entered the kitchen and breakfast area, immediately noticing its pristine condition. Not a dish in the sink, not a bowl of fruit on the tempered glass counter, or even a picture hanging on the walls. Where there should've been a table were two moving boxes and Deven opened the flap on one to see it was empty.

Next, she moved into the living room keeping her ears perked for any noise other than her roaring breathing. There was a recliner in here with a rug and a mounted flat screen TV. Overall, the furniture was just as sparse here as the rest of the bottom floor. A brand-new luggage set had been shoved against one wall.

Deven peeked out of the front bay window as she passed, relieved when she still didn't see the Mercedes. A chandelier dripped from above the foyer illuminating an ornate curved staircase that led up to the second floor. Again, Deven listened and was met with silence. "Kennedy?" She half-whispered and then proceeded to ascend the wooden steps. On the top landing, a narrow hallway gave way to numerous doors, each surprisingly empty with the exception of a few more moving boxes. *Did Erika even live here?* More closets and a couple of tiny bathrooms, and Deven pushed on, the flood of discouragement being to seep in.

At the end of the hall was the largest bedroom with a dresser and a few more boxes resting on a floral accent rug. The headboard and footboard of a disassembled bed were stacked against a wall, along with the accompanying mattress. Deven crossed into the room and kneeled down by one of the boxes. Her arm was killing her and the tiny cut from the glass had a nagging tingling sensation searing her hand. Plus, she'd wasted a lot of time. No Kennedy, no clues. She needed to just get out of there because there was no telling where Erika was.

Deven peered absently into the box, not expecting much of anything but some last-minute junk from an apparent move. The pictures caught her eye first, a bunch of different candids of a much younger Erika and Keith on vacations. Deven shifted those to the side and picked up one of a family opening presents on Christmas Day. This time, it was Erika and Kennedy and another girl who Deven didn't recognize. But seeing Kennedy's face had a gasp escaping her lips. She looked to be twelve, so Deven wondered if this was their first Christmas together after she moved in. All three of them wore matching holiday pajamas with Santa hats, each holding up a wrapped present. A skimpy tree had been squeezed in the background.

Deven pushed through more pictures of Kennedy and her new family, though none of the subsequent images were as lively as that Christmas photo. Kennedy's eyes had begun to look sad and haunting and as the pictures picked up her aging, so had it picked up her decrease in weight and joy. She looked downright miserable with her sunken features and baggy clothes. In fact, the other girl too, whoever she was, with her glasses and short hair that had been snatched back into a gel ponytail. Erika, on the other hand, was always fashionably dressed and smiling like she had won the lottery.

A peak of lilac purple had Deven's eyes rounding, and she stuck her hand in the bottom of the box to pull the diary into view. Kennedy's diary. Her fingers trembled over the cover and the broken heart-shaped lock. She had been right. Erika knew what was going on. Otherwise, why would she have her sister's diary?

Deven opened the book to a random page and sat down with legs crossed to read, her sister's words chilling her to the bone.

*I am so miserable and I want to go home. I wish I had never come here. It's not fun and my dad is always gone. Ms. Erika with a k says he goes to jail because he gets in trouble a lot, so I always have to stay here with her and April. We move all the time, and I don't have any friends and they won't let me call my mom. Please God, I just want to go home. I can't be here anymore!*

Deven blinked back tears as she thumbed forward a few more pages, her sister's words painting ugly, rancid pictures of abuse and drugs and neglect and negative influences and mingling with the wrong type of crowd. She felt the little girl's pain leaping from the page and clutching her heart like a vise grip, desperate and longing. Why didn't anyone help her? She read another passage:

*I'll be 16 tomorrow and April is taking me down to the Juvenile Court so I can fill out my emancipation paperwork. I'll be so glad when all this is done so I can get my life started. We're in Charlotte now, far away from my mom and sister because I'm pretty sure they're still in New Jersey. As soon as I can, I'm getting the hell out of here and going back to my mom's. Fuck Keith and Erika. I'm done with this shit.*

That was the last entry Kennedy wrote while at her dad's. Her next entry was a year later, apparently her first night after moving back in with Deven and her parents. So, Erika had been right. Kennedy was emancipated at sixteen and moved out. She had used drugs and been homeless for a little bit. The Kennedy now was completely different from the horrors that were described in her childhood, and Deven could only attribute that to Kennedy turning her life around after they connected on social media. But that still didn't answer the question. Where was her sister now?

Thinking fast, Deven pulled out her phone, ignoring the numerous missed calls and text messages. She snapped pictures as quickly as she could, first of the diary, then a few of the photos of Erika and Kennedy. Just as swiftly, she opened a message and scrolled through the texts Paul had sent. He was urging her to call him. *I found out who Erika Garrett is*, the last message read. Deven's fingers flew over the keys. *Me too. Look! She knows Kennedy and she knows where she is. Tell Officer McKinney.* Then she attached the pictures.

A creak in the hallway had Deven freezing afraid to turn around. Oh shit, she hadn't even heard Erika return. She stayed still, hovering over the open box. Her back was to the door. Any minute now, Erika would catch her, and she would have to figure out how the hell she was going to get out of this mess. Another step, and then another. The person was moving slow and meticulous, her boots thudding against the polished hall hardwood. Deven placed the diary on top and rose, debating if she had time to dive into the closet. That's when the shadow entered the room. Deven's eyes lifted to the woman. She blinked and let out a strangled breath at the sight of the gun. But more than that, who the gun was attached to from across the room. Her legs went limp, and she struggled to speak but no words came out.

"Hey Sis," Kennedy greeted with a wink. "I see it's time to have a little chat."

# Chapter Thirty

"Oh don't stop on my account," Kennedy invited, using the gun to gesture to the open box. "Erika told me you had been following her, so I knew it was only a matter of time before you got bold enough to come snooping for yourself."

Deven moved slow, her eyes frozen on the gun in Kennedy's hand. She watched the finger on the trigger for any kind of subtle movement. Hell, she was afraid if she even breathed too hard it would set the gun off.

Kennedy noticed her stare and chuckled to herself. "Oh, don't worry, Sis. This is just for protection. I'm not going to shoot you." As if to prove her point, she waved the gun in the air like it was a flag before putting it in the waist of the back of her jeans. "See?" She held up her hands, palms out to display their emptiness. "No gun. Now will you relax?"

Her putting away the gun didn't make Deven feel any better. But it was her fear of disobeying that had her easing back to the floor to take a seat at Kennedy's insistence. At this point, she didn't know what she was capable of.

Kennedy sat across from her and crossed her legs as if she were making casual conversation. "So, I heard you've been looking for me," she started with a gloat in her eyes. "I'm flattered. I told you once, you were a fixer, didn't I? And look at you. Just had to fix this too, instead of leaving well enough alone."

Really? Was that all she had to say? Deven had to bite her tongue to hold her anger at bay. "Kennedy, what the hell is going on?"

She shrugged. "You tell me. You're the one that's been doing all the digging. What have you found out?"

She really expected Deven to spell it out? Fine. She could entertain her. "First off, there's a woman in the morgue they're saying is you. And then you're missing for weeks, and I find out about all your little scams, so I see you're on the run."

That had a chuckle escaping Kennedy's lips and she covered her mouth in a mock apology.

"You robbed Paul and a whole bunch of other people and now you're just acting like all this shit is okay."

Kennedy's eyes lit in amusement. "Oh wow. I see you've been busy," she teased.

"How can you just sit there and pretend like you're not a con artist?"

"Oh, I'm not pretending anything. I am most definitely a con artist. And damn good at it too."

Deven was stunned silent. Part of her expected this to be some kind of twisted joke. But the only one who seemed to find humor in this mess was Kennedy. It was appalling and infuriating all at once. "I can't believe you," Deven said shaking her head. "Why Kennedy? Robbing people? Stealing identities? All this illegal shit? This isn't you."

Kennedy rolled her eyes and glanced away. "You don't even know me," she mumbled.

"What are you talking about? You're my sister. I love you."

"You have no idea what we went through at Keith's house," she snapped. "No fucking idea. Because no, you were too busy trying to be an only child that you didn't give a damn what happened to your sister."

Deven opened her mouth, wanted so badly to refute that belief, but she couldn't bring herself to say it. "I love you," she insisted again instead. "I've always wanted what's best for you."

"No, you've always wanted what's best for YOU, Deven." Tears clogged Kennedy's throat, but her voice remained clear and firm with assurance. "But it's okay. It took a while, but you've been forgiven."

Something was off. Something Deven couldn't quite place. Maybe it was the look in her eyes or her hands, folded steady in her lap. "Keith wasn't a bad dad at first," she started, her gaze now in a faraway place. "I actually loved him. No, the real problem was Iris. She wanted to have her cake and eat it too. Shit was unfair." She seemed to be rambling now, though about what, Deven couldn't be sure. But she did know better than to interrupt. "So, you went to see Keith, huh? Did he give you the answers you were looking for?"

"No, he told me to find Erika and she would have the answers."

Kennedy turned up her lips. "Ah, I see. So, he found another way to defer his mess onto someone else instead of addressing it. You know, for a big strong criminal, he can sure be a bitch."

Abruptly, Kennedy rose and left the room. Deven heard clattering around downstairs for a minute before she returned, surprised when she brought with her two glasses of wine. The red liquid sloshed against the side of the glass as she held it out. "Are you thirsty?" she asked. The question was so earnest that Deven had to wonder if her sister was bipolar. The hospitality was in direct contradiction to their dialogue, and Kennedy's fluctuations were making her even more nervous. Deven accepted the glass, but didn't drink it, instead clutching it in her lap with trembling fingers.

"I bet he didn't tell you how terrible it was living with him did he?" Kennedy asked sitting down once more and taking a generous sip of her own wine. "You would think he would take responsibility and admit that he was a shitty father figure. The drugs, the constantly moving from place to place, so never having a stable childhood, all the men and women in and out of our house . . ." Her voice cracked, and she took another sip of wine, blinking back more tears.

Deven's heart broke, remembering her sister's diary entry. "I know," she murmured. "I read about it. I'm so sorry, Kennedy. You deserved better."

Kennedy polished off her wine and sat the glass down, running her fingers around the rim that was now stained with her lipstick. "Oh, I see you've been catching up on your little sis," she said with a ghost of a smile. "Well since you know some of the happenings, did you know Keith left cocaine out once? Right on the fucking kitchen table beside the breakfast. I guess he forgot about it or got busy because he was on the phone in the other room." Kennedy paused and lowered her head, her hair covering her face. "I tried it," she mumbled. "I was fucking fourteen, trying drugs because that's all we were around. Damn near died since he didn't want to go to the ER because they would start asking too many questions. Do you know how much that could fuck up a kid?"

Deven listened in horror. No, she couldn't imagine it. A child lying there dying but couldn't even receive medical attention. No, Keith hadn't villainized his daughter, but he sure as hell hadn't been completely transparent about their circumstances. "I'm sorry," Deven croaked, and she meant it. "I—we had no idea. Mom and me. After you asked to go live with him, she said you said that you never wanted to be bothered with us again. And then every time she called, you all had moved somewhere else, until finally you just stopped answering altogether. Like you just disappeared until we connected again on social media."

Something flickered in Kennedy's eyes, sorrow yes. But underneath that was something else. Something malicious that had a tremor of fear itching up Deven's spine. Had she said something wrong?

"Yeah, that was fun," Kennedy mused with a fleeting smile. "Meeting you for the first time after all those years." She intentionally exaggerated the *all*-word to emphasize the extensive time frame as she took her time standing up. The turn of her body had the gun in her waist flicking into temporary view and Deven sucked in a breath. The conversation had her mouth dry like cotton and she yearned to drink the wine that Kennedy had given her. But she couldn't. She needed to be alert for whatever her sister was about to say. Or do.

Kennedy went on, walking casually back and forth as she spoke, almost like she was reflecting on fond memories. Or she was a tigress on the prowl. "You were just like I thought you would be," she said. "Loving, caring, kind-hearted, just like a big sister was supposed to be. It was too bad I knew it was all bull-shit."

Deven's heart quickened. "Wh—what do you mean?"

"But see, the thing was, I saw right through you. I've always seen right through you. That's why it was so fortunate that *I* was now your sister and not Kennedy. The poor girl couldn't see how much you hated and manipulated her."

It was as if the room had been spinning and came to a screeching halt. Deven shook her head, sure her angst had clouded her mind and gotten some of Kennedy's words skewed. She blinked to clear the confusion, but everything remained just as muddled.

"I tried to tell your sister that the relationship was bullshit," said Kennedy—well the woman rather, because now Deven didn't know who the hell she was talking to. "She used to sit up and talk for hours about you. My sister this, and my sister that, and I miss Deven, and I know she's worried about me. But I tried to tell her that I was her sister now, because I was there with her in the trenches, going through all of the pain and suffering with her while you lived on with your rich parents in your fancy house. Why couldn't she see what you had done to her?" The woman turned around with a scowl so deep that it had morphed her face into someone ugly and unrecognizable. Slowly, so slowly like the code to a locked safe, it all started to fall into place.

Kennedy had left at the age of twelve and been off the grid for years with the exception of a few phone calls. Then six years later, Kennedy had reached out to Deven on social media, and . . . someone had returned to their lives. But that someone apparently hadn't been Kennedy. Which meant this woman—this *stranger*— she was talking to had been pretending to be her sister. Deven's mind clicked through the contents of the shoe boxes back at Kennedy's apartment. IDs, money, passports, credit cards, *identities*. Was that what this had been all this time? This con artist using Kennedy's identity?

"Who . . . who are you?" Deven whispered, her whole body quivering now in anticipation of the answer she dreaded to hear.

Now the woman's smile was triumphant as she sat down and extended her hand. "I'm Erika's daughter April," she greeted with phony enthusiasm. "It's a pleasure to finally meet you, Deven."

# Chapter Thirty-one

She couldn't breathe. Everything hurt and it felt like someone had taken lit matches to her lungs as she panted, struggling to gulp in enough air. The edges of her vision darkened like a sordid vignette until all she saw was the devilish glint in this woman's eye. This woman, not Kennedy. Not her sister. Never was. Deven had been propelled into a state of delirium where her truth was ethereal within its own suffering.

April threw up her hands in a presto-type of motion as if she'd just performed the greatest magic trick. "I know it's kind of hard to process," she said beginning to mosey around the room. "And I didn't expect you to ever find out. Hell, it was going good until Kennedy got in the way."

"My—my sister?" Deven heaved, that flame igniting even more. It hurt so bad and all she wanted to do was scream.

"Yeah, that's the one," April nodded, relishing in her anguish. "See, the thing is Deven, none of this was supposed to happen. It started out as a little prank honestly. Just a quick way to get a few dollars out of you and your rich ass daddy. It was my mom's idea to take it a little further." She laughed as if she'd just been told the punchline of the world's funniest joke. "You see, she never really liked your mom because Keith was still so in love with her. That shit was too obvious. And she and I, well, we were already pros at the fraud shit. So, reaching out to you seemed like the perfect opportunity to capitalize on the ultimate scheme. I knew how to contour my makeup just right to even look a little more like her. And well, the rest was too easy! You and Iris just welcomed me in with open arms like you didn't even get rid of that girl. Like everything was supposed to just go back to the way things were. I guess it was the guilt eating at you because it worked so brilliantly. Don't you think?"

April was maniacal as she paced in front of Deven with that sinister laugh of hers. Each confession only ripped her heart once more until it was nothing more than tattered ribbons. How did she never know, not once, that she'd been conned by the ultimate con artist? "Did Keith, know?"

"Nope. Nobody knows. Not even Benji. Just me and Erika. Had all your asses fooled, huh?" April took a mock bow and clapped as if there was a round of applause in her honor. The way she pranced around so damn proud only aggravated the situation. Shit was repulsing and Deven gagged as she did her best to hold down her vomit.

The realization was numbing. Her mother's will, Paul, everything was just scam after strategic scam by a mother/daughter con duo. And everyone else were just puppets while they pulled the strings.

"So . . . my sister, my *real* sister . . ." Deven trailed off, unable to speak the words as the beautiful woman in the morgue, the woman with the sad eyes floated into her thoughts. She couldn't . . . it couldn't be . . .

April steeled; her mood not quite as callous as she spoke. "I didn't kill her, if that's what you mean," she said.

The comment had Deven dissolving into a flurry of fitful sobs. "How could you?" she cried. "Oh my God how could you do that?"

"I didn't do shit," April snapped and Deven, surprisingly caught the quiver in her tone. Was she actually remorseful? "Kennedy and I got very close when she came to stay with us, but she was weak. She couldn't really handle the lifestyle like us. Hell, all of us were using, me too, even though I was only a teenager. But see, she couldn't handle it and got strung out after she was emancipated. But that's not my doing."

Deven crumbled to the floor, rocking and bawling as she pictured her baby sister so young and helpless and vulnerable. She could barely hear April over her own cries. "What happened?" she screamed in agony. "What happened to her?"

April put a hand to her lips and took a steadying breath. "That was not supposed to happen," she reiterated. "Like I said, we lost touch after she left, and we never heard from her again. I came to live with you, Jamie, and Iris, your parents were giving me money and nice things, I was sending it to Erika, we were set. Even afterwards, your daddy still took care of me—"

"Of course, he did!" Deven yelled. "He was a good man and he loved Kennedy like his own daughter."

"I know. So that's why it was a sweet come-up." April paused, her face hardening. "Then Kennedy came back in the picture all of a sudden. I guess she had gotten clean and found out what we were doing. We couldn't let her ruin everything we had worked so hard to build. And Erika, like I said, she was just so fucking thrilled she was conning your mother that she wouldn't let me stop, even if I tried. Then that one night when Kennedy attacked me outside, after your miscarriage, I knew I had to do something to get in front of her. But I didn't know where she was. So, I talked to Keith, and he put me in touch with Deuce to track her down. I had her come over so we could talk . . ." April trailed off, squeezing her eyes shut. "The pills weren't even my idea. That was Erika's."

"You killed her! You murdered Kennedy, you bitch!" Deven felt like she was choking on the words as they singed her throat. *Her poor sister.*

"It was an accident," April reiterated, her voice clipped. "They were just supposed to calm her down and put her to sleep. Erika wanted to get her addicted again so she could go away. So, I laid out some pills. Kennedy was so mentally distraught about what was going on that she took them on her own."

Deven scoffed and that seemed to enrage April. "You don't have to fucking believe me," April yelled. "I was there. Not you! I was ALWAYS there with Kennedy. Never you. So don't act like you were the perfect sister."

Deven looked at the woman through her obscured vision. All she saw was an evil monster. "I loved Kennedy. She's always known that."

"No, you didn't." April stooped to pick up Kennedy's diary from the box and held it up in the air. "I told you she was so weak-minded that she couldn't even see it. But I saw it from the beginning. As soon as she came to live with us, and she told me stuff about you. I wasn't sure until I read it for myself in her diary. You've been gaslighting Kennedy since you were kids."

Fear had Deven's eyes widening, and she shook her head feverishly. "That's not true!"

"It's not?" April snorted. "So, you weren't jealous of her since she was your mom's favorite? When you saw an inkling of maybe, just *maybe* your mom loved Kennedy a tad bit more because she was her only connection to Keith, you didn't make it your mission to ostracize your sister? Telling her your mother didn't like her? Making her feel lonely?"

Deven's blood chilled. "Hell no!"

"And you didn't hear your dad say that it was Kennedy that was standing in the way since your parents kept having so many problems?"

This time, Deven could only listen to her breath roaring in her ears. "I loved Kennedy," she whispered.

April was unfazed. "And you weren't the one that pushed and pushed for Kennedy to agree to move in with her dad so she didn't have to be in the way anymore?"

"That was what she wanted!"

"You can turn off the act now, Deven. I mean damn it has been years, but you don't think I know all the shit you did as a child? Your little 'pretending' like you had your sister's best interest at heart, but it really was just a mind game for your little rivalry?"

Deven was panicked as she shook her head. "No, no, that's not true! I loved . . ." The color drained from her face as April walked to her purse and pulled another book into view. A diary. This time, HER diary. How did she get that?

"I figured you still had yours," April said, waving the diary in the air. "In fact, you told me you did. So, I broke into your apartment and what do you know, I was so right about you. All this time . . ."

The pieces began to click into place. "Wait, it was you? You broke into my apartment and left the note from Deuce?"

"Well, I couldn't very well let you know that it was me," April shrugged and tossed the book on the floor at Deven's feet. "Read it."

Deven shut her eyes against the harsh reality. She didn't need to read it. There was only one entry, and she knew exactly what it said, word-for-agonizing-word. She'd been young and stupid, and she never thought that it would come back to haunt her.

"Please, no," she whispered, her eyes pleading as they looked up to April.

The woman seemed satisfied with the reaction. "Just like I

thought," she said with a sneer. "There's only one person responsible for why Kennedy isn't here. And that is you, Deven."

No, she did not believe it. None of it was true. April was lying again, like she had always done, and this was clearly just another one of her mind games, one of her cons. Deven would be damned if she allowed this woman to warp her childhood anymore.

"Look, I hate this has to end," April said finally with a shrug. "It was a fun ride. I have to catch a flight, so I'll leave you. Don't try to search for me, you won't find me, I promise. And hey, look on the bright side. At least Kennedy is out of your way, and you can be the only child like you've always wanted, right?"

April gave a wink and sauntered out of the room, leaving Deven trembling on the ground. No, she couldn't let her get away with this. She mustered as much strength as she could, crawling to the hall. The front door closed and Deven stumbled to her feet, nearly toppling over herself to make it to the stairs. She was pulling out her cell phone and stabbing at the digits she could barely see through her cloudy vision.

Paul answered immediately. "Deven? Where are—"

"Paul, get to the airport," she cried as she raced through the front door with renewed vigor. "Kennedy it's—she's getting away. Call the police, hurry! They killed her!"

And with that, Deven took off down the street to where she'd parked her car. Neither April nor Erika were anywhere in sight but that didn't matter. Deven just had to get to the airport. They could still catch them. She prayed that Paul and the police would make it there with her.

Deven flipped on her hazard lights and bolted onto the expressway on two wheels. Her duress had been replaced with a determined anger. No, she hadn't been the best sister, but dammit she was going to get the women who had ruined so many lives, including poor Kennedy's.

She got to airport in record time, and she hopped out, leaving the car running as she dashed through the automatic doors. Her head whipped like it was on a swivel as she searched the masses for the familiar face. *Please don't let her get away.* That's when she caught April riding up the escalator with that conniving smirk of hers. And she was looking right at her, taunting, daring. Deven took off towards the escalator, shoving her way through the throng of people, who grunted and moaned at the disturbance.

Deven felt the hand on her arm and nearly snatch her off her feet. She whirled around, peering into the wide face of a guard with the expression of a pit bull. "Ma'am, Ma'am!" The guard tried her best to restrain Deven's flailing arms.

"No, stop listen to me, that woman murdered my sister and stole money," Deven yelled thrashing wildly to point at April. She tugged but the guard's grip was firm as she tried to pull Deven back in the opposite direction. Away from the escalators. Away from April.

"Ma'am, you can't get through this checkpoint without a boarding pass."

"No, you don't understand—"

"Ma'am, we can check the flights and find the person but you're going to have to calm down before I have you arrested."

Deven froze at the guard's threat, and she could only meet April's gaze as she looked on in obvious amusement at the chaos. The guard continued, "That's better. Now, let me escort you to the ticket counter so can find the person. What flight is she on?"

"I don't know!" Deven wailed.

"Okay, who is she? What's her name?"

Deven opened her mouth and could only shut it again as April reached the second-floor landing. And then, blowing her a kiss goodbye, the woman disappeared into the crowd.

# Chapter Thirty-two

*"It's the same bag, the same grief. Some days, you'll be able to carry the load a little easier. Other days, you may fall under the weight. And you know what? All of that is okay."*

Dr. Felicia Bradshaw's words played over and over in Deven's head like a mantra. All of that is okay. All of that is okay. At the time, they had been discussing her grief for her dad and her babies. Today was for someone else entirely. It was interesting how those same reassurances had an elliptic return, almost like a hint or warning. Either way, Deven was grateful for them, especially today. She knew they would need to rely on that comfort to strengthen each other.

Deven's heels sunk into the soil as she treaded carefully across the cemetery. It had rained earlier, so the air was still moist with the lingering remnants of dew and an earthy musk that clung to the early morning breeze.

She wrapped her arms tighter around her mother, making sure to keep her steps slow and steady, as much for her sake as Iris's. They needed this preparation, even if only a few extra seconds of silence.

"Have I ever been here?" Iris spoke in a panicked whisper on the cusp of confusion. "Nothing looks familiar."

"It's okay, Mommy," Deven said. "You're here now and that's what matters. This is important."

That seemed to relax Iris a little, but Deven felt the tears welling and she willed herself to keep her composure. She had hoped for a good day from her mom, but so far that hadn't proven to be the case. Maybe it was a little selfish, but a good day would mean she and her mom could share this weight of grief. It ached having to suffer this alone. Again, Felicia's voice calmed her. *"It's not better to live in the unknown. That would mean forgetting about the person entirely which is even more excruciating. Because there is someone who had an effect on your life, and you can't even remember them or how much they loved you."* She had to swallow her sobs. It was a good thing her mom's nurse, Jan, was waiting patiently in the car. But Deven would handle this one as best she could. They needed this moment.

A hand rested on top of hers and squeezed, tender and encouraging. Deven looked to Paul on the other side of her mom, both of their hands on her back to guide and support. He was smiling at her now which prompted her own appreciative smile in return. "Thank you," Deven mouthed over her mother's head.

She had to admit, she was surprised when Paul offered to accompany them to the cemetery. Things were still up in the air with them and Deven hadn't wanted to give him the wrong idea. Since Justin was out of the picture, she didn't need another boyfriend. She needed a friend. When she relayed that to him, she figured his discontentment would ensure he left, for good this time. But he hadn't. He was here when she, and her mom, needed him most. And that friendship was enough. For now.

They continued weaving through the headstones, three figures adorned in black like shadows. Deven had made the trip so many times alone, so as foreign as it felt, automatic pilot kicked into gear. She knew the plots without looking and her legs propelled her forward to the tree near the fence. Underneath its low-hanging branches were two headstones. One was where her father rested.

They stopped at the grave and Deven kneeled to retrieve the previous flower arrangement she had brought, now wilted from the winter chill. The inscription on the stone seared her angst. *Loving father, husband, brother and friend.* Deven sighed. "Hi Daddy," she greeted. "I've missed you. I brought, Mommy this time. I know you've been asking about her." Deven reached for her mother's hand and Paul helped guide Iris into a kneeling position beside her. She clutched the bouquet of blue Dahlias and white orchids against the base of the headstone, her hand lingering on the flowers. The gesture had Deven glancing over. A single tear streaked down her mom's cheek, glistening against her skin like crystal. She remembered. It had been a good day after all.

"I'm sorry," Iris said, simply. "I love you."

Deven grabbed her mother's hand and held it to her breast. "Mommy, there is someone you need to meet." She rose, lifting Iris up with her, and they turned to the other headstone next to her father. Kennedy Marshall. *On Angels wings, you were taken away. But in our hearts, you'll always stay.* It had been only fitting to bury her sister, her REAL, sister next to the rest of her family.

Iris touched the stone, the tears now flowing freely. "My poor baby," she sobbed, her voice cracking.

Deven knew she needed privacy, so she allowed Paul to take her hand and steer her away. "You're doing great," he commended as soon as they were far enough for Iris to properly mourn her daughter.

Deven released a breath. "It's hard," she admitted. "This whole thing has been an emotional roller coaster."

"You should take some time to yourself. Maybe go away for a few days. Your mental health is just as important."

Deven nodded. "I'm learning that. Maybe I will." She stopped short of inviting Paul to go with her. Too soon. Maybe one day.

They stood in comfortable silence, both lost in their own thoughts. Then Iris padded over to join them, wiping the tears from her damp face. "Thank you," she said, pulling Deven in for a hug. "Now I have both of my daughters again." Deven got lost in the folds of her mother's coat and warmed at the peace that flowed between them.

"Paul, can you take her back to the car? I just need a minute."

"Absolutely. Are you going to be okay?"

Deven nodded and watched them leave. She made her way back to Kennedy's grave and lowered herself to sit Indian-style next to the headstone.

"There is so much I wish I could change," she started. "So many words left unsaid. So much life you were robbed of. I read somewhere that grief is love with nowhere to go, and I'm grieving you hard, baby sister. You never appreciate exactly how much someone means to you until they're gone. I learned that with dad, with my twins, and now with you." Deven's voice shook, and she sniffed, not bothering to stop the flow of tears. "I love you so much. And I am so, so sorry. I'm sorry I couldn't save you. I'm sorry I didn't know. And I'm sorry that I couldn't give you all the love you deserved when you were alive."

Deven caught a glimpse of movement out of the corner of her eye and her head snapped up as Deuce came into view. Dressed in all black with his locs piled into a low ponytail, he stood tall and erect. She relaxed. "Still stalking, I see."

"Working." Deuce corrected.

"Am I a job now?"

"More like a final report."

Deven looked back to Kennedy's headstone as Deuce joined her. His silhouette suffused her kneeling frame, shrouding them both in a thin veil of shade.

"You knew, huh?" She spoke the obvious. "You told me you didn't know Kennedy. That was actually true."

"Yeah. I never met your real sister. Unfortunately, she was just a gig April hired me to do."

"Why didn't you tell me?"

Deuce shrugged, shoving his hands in his pockets. "Wasn't my place to tell. Keith put me in touch with April to help her because she said she had some kind of stalker. He didn't know it was his daughter and I sure as hell didn't know the family connection until I did my research. But like I said, it really wasn't any of my business."

Deven grimaced. The truth was ugly, but it was the truth, nonetheless.

"For what it's worth," Deuce continued. "I hate all of this happened. But I'm glad you got your answers. Hopefully you got that closure you wanted. "

The darkness lifted and Deven heard Deuce walking away. She didn't bother stopping him. No, she didn't have her closure. Not while April and Erika were still alive somewhere, up to their same old deception and thievery. But if and when she was ready to look for them, she knew where Deuce lived.

Alone again, Deven reached in her purse. Her fingers grazed the spirals of a notebook and she pulled Kennedy's diary into view. She used the edge of the book to dig into the damp earth, creating a makeshift hole. Then she placed the diary inside and covered it, leaving only a lilac corner peeking through. "To taking secrets to the grave," Deven murmured, kissing her fingertips and touching the tiny, new mound of earth. Then she rose and started the trek back to the parking lot.

On her way by a trash bin, Deven reached in her purse again for the other item she'd brought along. Her own diary with its single entry. Deven flipping the cover open and ripped the page from its spiral binding. She tossed the book in the trash, then tore the loose-leaf paper again, and again, and again, until it was nothing more than shreds with a jumble of cruel words and even crueler intentions. But like her feelings, she lifted the papers in the sky and released them, letting them billow away to get lost in the clouds.

# Epilogue

## Excerpt from the diary of Deven (Age 13)

My dad got me and my sister this diary and I guess I have to write in it now. This is stupid. But if it'll make him happy, I guess I can do it. Where do I start? Um . . . I'm supposed to be asleep because my sister's 12th birthday is tomorrow and she's having this big party this weekend. I'm really not excited about it. I mean, I like Kennedy and all but sometimes she's just in the way. I overheard my dad mention how it was because of her that my mom wouldn't get back with him. Like, I know she loves Kennedy and all, that's her daughter. But she was honestly a mistake. My parents don't think I know this, but Kennedy is a "break baby." My mom made a mistake while she and my daddy were on a time-out, she got with Kennedy's dad and got pregnant. Now my parents are trying to work it out, but my mom's mistake keeps them arguing. And I know it's because my dad looks at Kennedy and sees her daddy. She doesn't even look like us. I *mean I don't hate her or anything. I just don't like her. And I wish she would just go away. It's funny because she really sits up and cries because she thinks Mommy doesn't love her or something and I just laugh and tell her she's right. Because she's stupid if she thinks Mommy doesn't love her. She's the baby of COURSE Mommy does. So if she wants to believe that, I'll let her. I may have even lied on Mommy a few times so Kennedy would believe it. She's so dumb honestly.*

*She told me weeks ago that her dad asked her to come live with him because she could do that when she was 12, like make a choice on who she wanted to live with. I've been telling her she should go. All the fun she'll have and since Mommy doesn't like her anyway. I heard her last night crying about it, and she came to my bed wanting to talk but I just pretended to be asleep. She doesn't understand if she left, my dad would come home for good, my parents wouldn't fight, I would get my own room, and my own life. And she could have her own family at her dad's house and his new girlfriend and her new sister and all the cool stuff she says she does at his house. It's a win-win. I'm going to keep working on her so she sees why she needs to leave. We don't want her here. I hope she leaves and never comes back. Good fucking riddance.*

**THE END**

If you or someone you know is suicidal or in a crisis, please contact the National Suicide Prevention Lifeline at 1-800-273-TALK (8255). Trained workers are available to talk 24 hours a day, 7 days a week. All calls are confidential.
www.suicidepreventionlifeline.org

To get general information on mental health and locate treatment services in your area, please contact the Substance Abuse and Mental Health Serviced Administration (SAMHSA) at 1-877-726-4727 or visit MentalHealth.gov.

*It's Okay To Not Be Okay.*

# Bonus Material

*Have you ever seen a semicolon tattoo or a semicolon representation? Do you know the significance and how it relates to mental health? Read below for more information!*

What is *Project Semicolon*? *Project Semicolon* is a non-profit movement dedicated to presenting hope to those who are struggling with mental health, suicide, self-injury, and addiction. As the *Project Semicolon* website reads: "A semicolon is used when an author could've chosen to end their sentence but chose not to. The author is you and the sentence is your life." Originally created as a day where people were encouraged to draw a semicolon on their bodies and photograph it, it quickly grew into something greater and more permanent. Today, people all over the world are tattooing the mark as a reminder of their victory, survival, and personal strength to overcome internal struggle. *Project Semicolon*'s purpose is to give permission to discuss personal experience, strength, and hope with others and raise awareness of suicide prevention, depression, addiction, and help stop the mental health stigma.

Amy Bleuel, the Founder and President of *Project Semicolon*, states the project's mission statement is "a global non-profit movement dedicated to presenting hope and love for those who are struggling with mental illness, suicide, addiction, and self-injury. *Project Semicolon* exists to encourage, love, and inspire. Stay strong; love endlessly; change lives." The Vision for *Project Semicolon* is "That together we can achieve lower suicide rates in the U.S. and around the world; That together we can start a conversation about suicide, mental illness, and addiction that can't be stopped; We envision love and hope and we declare that hope is alive; We envision a society that openly addresses the struggle with mental illness, suicide, and addiction; We envision a conversation embraced by churches and addressed with love; We envision a society that sees their value and embraces it; We envision a community that comes together and stands together in support of one another; We envision a world where an escape is not found within drugs or alcohol; We envision a world where self-destruction is no longer an escape to be used; We envision a revolution of LOVE and declare that our stories are not over yet."

Of course, reading about the project and drawing semicolons won't end mental struggles. But it will start the necessary dialogue for assistance. It will give hope via a social cause, allowing more empathy and resources to be widely available to help prevent the second leading cause of death among individuals between the ages of ten and thirty-four in the US (*www.suicidepreventionlife line.org*). As the world pursues efforts to raise awareness for mental illness within families and communities, those who deal with it typically feel less alone and desperate—it helps to make them more inclined to ask for help while feeling safe and unjudged.

No matter how we get there, the end result is what's important: help and support for more people to also be able to say, "I'm still here."

# Discussion Questions

1. What first piqued your interest about the book? The title, the cover, or the synopsis? Why?

2. What was your initial expectation from the book? Did it rise to the occasion?

3. What did you like most about the book?

4. What did you like least about the book?

5. What are some of the overarching themes of the book that you believe were executed well?

6. *Behind Her Lives* toggles between present and past events, while interweaving diary entries. Do you like how the book is structured? Were you able to follow the story effortlessly?

7. Is there any particular instance in the book that really stands out?

8. To which character did you most relate and empathize? Why?

9. Were you able to "guess" the ending? Was it satisfying?

10. If you could be a part of the book, which character would you like to be?

11. What did you think of the twists in the story?

12. What could the author have done to make the story more interesting for you?

13. Did your feelings about the book change from when you started reading it when you finished it? What were the turning points for you?

14. How do you feel the mental illness aspect was handled?

15. What will you remember most about this book in a few months?

Read more about Kennedy's story
in the novella
"Pseudo"
from the collection *Justified*
Available now from
Dafina Books

Visit our website at
**KensingtonBooks.com**
to sign up for our newsletters, read
more from your favorite authors, see
books by series, view reading group
guides, and more!

Become a Part of Our
**Between the Chapters Book Club**
Community and Join the Conversation

**Betweenthechapters.net**

Submit your book review for a chance to win exclusive
Between the Chapters swag you can't get anywhere else!
https://www.kensingtonbooks.com/pages/review/

CPSIA information can be obtained
at www.ICGtesting.com
Printed in the USA
BVHW052112141122
651679BV00019B/104